Ghastly Glass

"A unique look at a Renaissance Faire. This is a colorful, exciting amateur-sleuth mystery filled with quirky characters, who endear themselves to the reader as Joyce and Jim Lavene write a delightful whodunit."
—*Midwest Book Review*

Wicked Weaves

"Offers a vibrant background for the mysterious goings-on and the colorful cast of characters."
—Kaye Morgan, author of *Ghost Sudoku*

"This jolly series debut . . . Serves up medieval murder and mayhem."
—*Publishers Weekly*

"Fast-paced, clever, delightful."
—John Lamb, author of *The Treacherous Teddy*

"A creative, fascinating whodunit, transporting readers to a world of make-believe that entertains and educates."
—*Fresh Fiction*

"[A] new exciting . . . series . . . Part of the fun of this solid whodunit is the vivid description of the Renaissance Village; anyone who has not been to one will want to go . . . Cleverly developed."
—*Midwest Book Review*

"[A] terrific mystery series . . . A feast for the reader . . . Character development in this new series is energetic and eloquent; Jessie is charming and intelligent, with . . . saucy strength."
—MyShelf.com

"I cannot imagine a cozier setting than Renaissance Faire Village, a closed community of rather eccentric—and very interesting—characters, [with] lots of potential . . . A great start to a new series by a veteran duo of mystery authors."
—*Cozy Library*

Berkley Prime Crime titles by Joyce and Jim Lavene

Peggy Lee Garden Mysteries

PRETTY POISON
FRUIT OF THE POISONED TREE
POISONED PETALS
PERFECT POISON
A CORPSE FOR YEW

Renaissance Faire Mysteries

WICKED WEAVES
GHASTLY GLASS
DEADLY DAGGERS
HARROWING HATS
TREACHEROUS TOYS

Missing Pieces Mysteries

A TIMELY VISION
A TOUCH OF GOLD
A SPIRITED GIFT
A HAUNTING DREAM

PRAISE FOR THE MISSING PIECES MYSTERIES

A Spirited Gift

"An engaging mystery . . . Fans know this writing duet can always be banked on for a strong thriller." —*Genre Go Round Reviews*

"Readers will find themselves drawn into the investigation of the death. Throw in a little ghostly activity, the promise of a pirates' treasure and the reader will be hooked." —*Fresh Fiction*

A Touch of Gold

"Paranormal amateur-sleuth fans will enjoy observing Dae use cognitive and ESP mental processes to uncover a murderer . . . Readers will enjoy." —*Midwest Book Review*

"The Lavenes once again take readers into a setting with a remarkable past, filled with legends and history . . . The characters are vivid and fascinating." —*Lesa's Book Critiques*

"Spunky and interesting characters . . . Another great read by the Lavenes!" —*The Romance Readers Connection*

"Will have cozy mystery lovers on the edge of their seats until the very last page . . . Jim and Joyce Lavene are superb storytellers." —*Fresh Fiction*

A Timely Vision

"Grabbed my attention on page one . . . Puzzles are unraveled and secrets spilled in a fast-paced paranormal mystery full of quirky characters you'll want as friends."
—Elizabeth Spann Craig, author of *Quilt of Innocence*

"A delightful yarn . . . Kept me turning pages until it was done."
—Patricia Sprinkle, author of *Friday's Daughter*

continued . . .

"This opening act of a new amateur sleuth is a wonderful mystery . . . The heroine is sassy and spunky . . . Joyce and Jim Lavene have . . . another hit series." —*Midwest Book Review*

"I could almost smell and feel the salty sea air of Duck as I was reading. The authors definitely did a bang-up job with the setting, and I look forward to more of Dae's adventures and the hint of romance with Kevin." —*A Cup of Tea and a Cozy for Me*

"This is a mystery with strong characters, a vivid sense of place, and touches of humor and the paranormal. *A Timely Vision* is one of the best traditional mysteries I've read this year."

—*Lesa's Book Critiques*

PRAISE FOR THE RENAISSANCE FAIRE MYSTERIES

Harrowing Hats

"The reader will have a grand time. This is an entertaining read with a well-crafted plot. Readers of the series will not be disappointed." —*Fresh Fiction*

"The Renaissance Faire Mysteries are always an enjoyable read . . . Joyce and Jim Lavene provide a complex exciting murder mystery that amateur-sleuth fans will appreciate."

—*Midwest Book Review*

Deadly Daggers

"The Lavene duet can always be counted on for an enjoyable whodunit . . . Filled with twists and red herrings, *Deadly Daggers* is a delightful mystery." —*Midwest Book Review*

"Will keep you entertained from the first duel, to the last surprise . . . If you like fun reads that will let you leave this world for a time, this series is for you." —*The Romance Readers Connection*

"Never a dull moment! Filled with interesting characters, a fast-paced story, and plenty of humor, this series never lets its readers down." —*Fresh Fiction*

A Haunting Dream

Joyce and Jim Lavene

BERKLEY PRIME CRIME, NEW YORK

THE BERKLEY PUBLISHING GROUP
Published by the Penguin Group
Penguin Group (USA) Inc.
375 Hudson Street, New York, New York 10014, USA
Penguin Group (Canada), 90 Eglinton Avenue East, Suite 700, Toronto, Ontario M4P 2Y3, Canada (a division of Pearson Penguin Canada Inc.) • Penguin Books Ltd., 80 Strand, London WC2R 0RL, England • Penguin Group Ireland, 25 St. Stephen's Green, Dublin 2, Ireland (a division of Penguin Books Ltd.) • Penguin Group (Australia), 250 Camberwell Road, Camberwell, Victoria 3124, Australia (a division of Pearson Australia Group Pty. Ltd.) • Penguin Books India Pvt. Ltd., 11 Community Centre, Panchsheel Park, New Delhi—110 017, India • Penguin Group (NZ), 67 Apollo Drive, Rosedale, Auckland 0632, New Zealand (a division of Pearson New Zealand Ltd.) • Penguin Books (South Africa) (Pty.) Ltd., 24 Sturdee Avenue, Rosebank, Johannesburg 2196, South Africa

Penguin Books Ltd., Registered Offices: 80 Strand, London WC2R 0RL, England

A HAUNTING DREAM

A Berkley Prime Crime Book / published by arrangement with the authors

PUBLISHING HISTORY
Berkley Prime Crime mass-market edition / December 2012

Cover illustration by Robert Crawford.
Cover design by Annette Fiore Defex.

For information, address: The Berkley Publishing Group,
a division of Penguin Group (USA) Inc.,
375 Hudson Street, New York, New York 10014.

ISBN: 978-0-425-25179-9

BERKLEY® PRIME CRIME
Berkley Prime Crime Books are published by The Berkley Publishing Group,
a division of Penguin Group (USA) Inc.,
375 Hudson Street, New York, New York 10014.
BERKLEY® PRIME CRIME and the PRIME CRIME logo are trademarks of
Penguin Group (USA) Inc.

PRINTED IN THE UNITED STATES OF AMERICA

10 9 8 7 6 5 4 3 2 1

This book is dedicated to the old stories of Duck and the Outer Banks, including "Bring Me Duck" by Suzanne Tate as told by Ruth Tate.

Chapter 1

"Ann? Is that really you?" Kevin Brickman gasped as he stood in the middle of the laughing crowd at the newly dedicated coffee shop. "When did you get here?"

"Just now," Ann Porter, his ex-partner at the FBI, answered. Her pale face was devoid of emotion, though her voice trembled when she spoke. She was a tall, gaunt woman with string-straight, straw-colored hair. "I hope you're happy to see me. I've missed you, Kevin."

"Can I get you something to drink?" he asked, obviously shocked, not sure what to say. He hadn't seen her for years. "They have wonderful lattes here."

She took his hand and kissed it, oblivious to the people around them. "I've come a long way to find you. Can we please go somewhere and talk?"

Kevin's gray-blue eyes found mine, as though asking for understanding.

What could I say?

Ann had not only been Kevin's partner in the FBI, she'd also been his fiancée—until she'd lost it one day when another child they'd been looking for was found dead. There was no way to know if she would ever recover after she was institutionalized.

Kevin and I had known each other a little over a year, since he'd moved to Duck, North Carolina, where I happen to be the mayor and owner of Missing Pieces, a local thrift store. We'd been through so much during that time—with him opening the old Blue Whale Inn, and us working together on various problems that had come up in town—it seemed like longer.

I admit it. I'd come to think of him as mine. I thought I'd finally found the right person for me, without having to leave the Outer Banks. Kevin was one of the few outsiders, people who weren't from Duck, who just seemed to fit right in.

Everyone gathered in the coffee shop seemed to be staring at us. Duck was a small town, barely more than five hundred residents during the winter. Just about all of them knew there was something going on between Kevin and me—one of the bad things about living in a small town—so those gathered around us now could tell Ann's arrival was . . . unexpected. The festive moment we were all celebrating—Phil's deciding to keep the Coffee House and Bookstore open—faded quickly for me. I had to decide what to do.

Of course Kevin and Ann needed time to talk. They'd been planning their wedding when she'd had her breakdown. I knew he never expected to see her again. What could he be going through?

I wanted him to know that I understood. I didn't know what to expect from her, but I wanted him to know that I cared about him. "It's okay," I whispered, smiling at him. "Do what you have to do. We'll talk later."

"Dae, this is Ann Porter, my partner when I was with the FBI. Ann, this is Mayor Dae O'Donnell."

"Hello, Dae." Ann stared at me with ragged anger in her cold blue eyes. "I'm Ann—Kevin's fiancée."

I acted like her words, her arrival were nothing to be troubled by. Like I hadn't specially picked out the blue sweater Kevin was wearing. Like I hadn't just kissed him a few minutes before when everything seemed so wonderful and life was falling into place.

"It's very nice to meet you. Welcome to Duck. If there is anything I can do to make your stay better, please let me know."

"Can we go now?" She tugged on Kevin's arm.

I wished I was telepathic and could just say, *Go*. But my gifts didn't work that way. Instead, I said, "I'm going over there to get a piece of cheesecake. I'll talk to you both later."

I watched them walk outside, then got in the long line for coffee and cheesecake, though my heart wasn't in it.

"Dae, who is that she-zombie Kevin's leaving with?" My friend Shayla Lily stood next to me in the line. "I don't think I've ever seen her before, and from the look on *your* face, I'd say you never want to see her again."

"It's okay," I told her. "She's Kevin's ex-partner."

Shayla sucked in a sharp breath. She knew about Kevin's history before he came to Duck. "No way! You mean the crazy psychic girl who he thought was put away for good?"

"I don't think that's the way he feels about her."

"Dae?" Trudy Devereaux, another friend, stared at the door as she watched Kevin and Ann walk away from the coffee shop. "I think that girl wants your man."

I explained to Trudy about Ann, still smiling. "It's going to be fine. You'll see."

"Fine?" Shayla tossed her shiny black hair, irritation causing her pretty cocoa brown face to pucker up. "That's the understatement of the year! You might as well kiss your hunky boyfriend good-bye."

"Shayla." Trudy intervened in her calm, no-hassle fashion. "Dae is in a tough spot here. Let's show a little sympathy."

Despite her good intentions, Trudy didn't make me feel any better. I knew Kevin would have married Ann if she hadn't had her breakdown. I wasn't sure where that left me now.

And that was the part I had to remember. I *didn't* know where that left me now. Kevin had changed a lot since he'd left Ann and the FBI behind. I was sure Ann had changed as well. They might not be able to pick up their relationship again like nothing had happened.

I didn't mean to wish Ann bad luck in coming here to find Kevin—well maybe I did. I had a vested interest in their relationship not working. Kevin and I were good for each other. What we had was special. I had a whole future planned around him.

I was going to have to bide my time. *Be patient.*

Duck residents shook my hand and thanked me for convincing Phil De Angelo, who owned the Coffee House and Bookstore, to stay in town. In truth, I had only facilitated. It was his sister, Jamie, who'd done all the heavy lifting.

But I took the credit. I was running for reelection as mayor. I needed all the goodwill I could get.

I decided against eating anything. Getting in line had only been a diversion for Kevin to get away without feeling guilty. I really just wanted to go home. Food didn't figure into it right now.

"I'm sorry. I changed my mind," I told Phil when I reached the front of the line. "Thanks."

"That's okay. It's nice to see everyone is so happy that I decided to stay here."

Despite my two years' practice as mayor of Duck, North Carolina, I couldn't summon up a happy face for him. I turned away before I embarrassed myself, and walked right into Old Man Sweeney, my next-door neighbor.

"Just the girl I wanted to see!" He hitched up his red and white checkered pants and grinned at me. "I've lost something. Horace said you'd help. I drove my golf cart all the way down here to find you. Can you help or not?"

Old Man Sweeney had lived next door to my grandfather and me forever. His real name was Mac Sweeney—I'd just never gotten used to thinking of him as someone other than "Old Man Sweeney."

I had a lot of angst leftover from him telling Gramps every time I came home late when I was a kid. He'd even lately reported every time I kissed Kevin. The man had no life besides spying on me.

"I'm sure I can try to help, Ol—Mr. Sweeney," I said, hoping he'd not noticed me correcting myself. "You'll have to tell me what's wrong."

Not that *all the way down here* from his house to the coffee shop was more than a few minutes. But I was glad to have something to distract me from trying to guess what was going on with Kevin and Ann.

The gift of being able to find lost objects had jumped from my grandmother to me, bypassing my mother. Since I was a little girl, I'd been able to find missing items by touching the person looking for them, usually by holding their hands. My mother had encouraged me, telling me I was gifted and that it was all part of giving back to my community. The idea of giving back had certainly stuck—it was the reason I'd agreed to be the first mayor after the town had incorporated.

"It's something special that's gonna make me enough money to get one of thosc big-screen TVs everyone raves about." Old Man Sweeney was still talking. "Yes, sir, there's money to be made."

"Let's step outside," I said to him. "What are you looking for?"

We sat at one of the outdoor café tables behind the coffee shop, with the yellow and green striped umbrella protecting us from the sun. It was the beginning of November, but still warm. Out here we'd be a little more alone. The whole town seemed to be pouring into the coffee shop to celebrate Phil's decision to stay in Duck.

Normally, I would've taken Old Man Sweeney to Missing Pieces, which was on the Duck Shoppes boardwalk only a short walk away. But this would do. I was starting to get a headache from trying *not* to think about Kevin and Ann.

"Well, it's the damndest thing," he started. "I found a medallion of some kind over at the Harris Teeter last week. I just needed some bread and pickles, you know. Nothing much. But here was this medallion out in the parking lot. Good quality too. Probably gold. The manager went on the intercom and asked everybody in the store if it belonged to them. No one came forward."

I nodded, listening. I'd heard stories like this before, stories that rambled more than the clouds on a hot summer day. It would be impolite to ask him to come to the point. But I could *wish* he would.

"So, I had the manager put up a little sign on the bulletin board about me finding the medallion, and I took it home."

When he didn't say anything else, I assumed he was finished. "And you'd like me to find the owner?"

That last was something new for me. I had been able to find lost things since I was a kid. I could look into the person's mind, and if they held an image of what they were looking for, I could locate it.

A life-and-death situation had changed the gift I was born with. Now I could hold possessions that belonged to other people and discern information about them. The information wasn't always what I needed or even wanted to know, but the ability to gather those sometimes disjointed facts had come in handy more than once.

"Well, I hadn't thought of that," Old Man Sweeney said. "In fact, I didn't even know you could do that. When did it happen?"

I kind of explained the basics to him. Everyone in Duck knew about the gift I'd been born with. Only a few people knew about the gift I'd acquired. "Do you have the medallion with you?"

"See, that's the problem, I guess. I can't find the medallion. And I had a phone call from the owner wanting it back. I was thinking you could do your thing and find it for me."

"I'm sure we can do that." I sat back a little to reach my hands across the table to him. "Give me your hands and think about the medallion."

"Are you sure this is necessary?" He looked around, uncomfortable, as though he was worried what others might think of us holding hands. "I didn't know it worked that way. Horace didn't say anything about *that*."

"Gramps probably didn't want to throw you off." I tried not to be impatient.

A few people were beginning to leave after the ribbon cutting for the reopening of the coffee shop. One or two saw us and waved or said hello from a distance. No one interrupted us.

No doubt everyone already knew Kevin had left with Ann, and they were wondering why. No one would ask outright—that would be rude. Instead, they'd wait a few hours until Shayla told someone who told someone else. By morning, everyone would assume Kevin and I were over.

Don't think about it. You don't know anything—until you hear from Kevin.

"What do you want me to think about the medallion?" Old Man Sweeney asked.

I took a deep breath and shut out all the people around us. The only way I was going to be able to go home and end this difficult day was by finding what Old Man Sweeney was looking for. I had to get it over with.

"Think about what it looked like," I told him. "Think about how heavy it was and what it was made out of."

"It was plenty heavy. I'll tell you that. It looked like one of those trophy things, like they give kids in school. I don't know what kind. Does that help?"

"You have to think about it," I said encouragingly. "It won't do any good to describe it to me."

Finally I got him to close his eyes, settle down and pretend he was looking at the medallion. It took a lot to keep him from talking about it as I held his worn, callused hands. He'd been a carpenter all of his life. There was no way to know how many things those hands had built. Gramps told me once that when Mrs. Sweeney was alive, Old Man Sweeney had spent all of his free time building beautiful furniture for her. He'd stopped when she died.

I looked into his mind. It was like looking into a person's attic where they stored the things that were important to them. I felt my usual reaction to being in someone else's thoughts—shaking all over for a few seconds. That passed as I focused on locating the lost medallion.

After a moment, I saw it. It was resting on the floor,

under a table near a goldfish bowl. Newspapers and some junk mail were lying on top of it. No wonder he couldn't find it.

But when my mind touched it, I knew there was something unusual about the medallion. I'd seen it before, even held it. For a moment, I couldn't make out what I recognized about it.

Then I knew—it was a gold award medallion that had belonged to a real estate broker named Amanda Sparks. She'd lost it on the road in Duck when she'd visited here in 1964.

My eyes flew open as I realized that the medallion now belonged to her son, Chuck Sparks. I'd returned it to him last year when he'd set up his business, Island Realty, LLC. "I know who this belongs to."

Old Man Sweeney's eyes popped open too as he jerked his hands away from mine. "There's a reward. I suppose you saw that too. Don't think I'm sharing just because you helped me find the medallion."

"I don't want the reward." I tried to calm his fears. "I was just surprised at finding the medallion again."

"What are you talking about? I found it."

"It belongs to Chuck Sparks. I gave it to him last year after finding it on Duck Road."

"I don't think so." Old Man Sweeney looked at me curiously, as if assessing my next move. He took a scrap of paper from his pocket and glanced at the writing on it. "He said his name is Derek. I have his phone number to call him when I find the medallion."

I really wanted to go home and tell Gramps about what had happened at the Coffee House. I knew he'd say all the right things and I'd feel better. He was good at that.

But that wasn't going to happen right away. Something about Old Man Sweeney's finding that medallion seemed off, wrong. I knew it belonged to Chuck Sparks. Why would someone named Derek say it belonged to him and offer money for its return?

I sighed and wondered how I was going to convince my neighbor to let me help him give Derek the medallion so I could find out what was going on.

Chapter 2

Old Man Sweeney's house looked weatherworn but neat on the outside. I hadn't been on the inside since I was about six and my mom made me apologize to him for writing on his sidewalk—while the concrete was still wet.

The inside had deteriorated a lot, from what I could remember. The living room looked like our house had before Gramps convinced me that I needed to open a thrift store to sell the things I'd found or collected down through the years. There had been very little room to walk and every flat surface was covered with something that had caught my attention. Some of it was valuable. Some, not so much.

In Old Man Sweeney's house, assorted items were parked and piled in every corner—from an old bicycle to stacks of books and magazines as well as crates of dishes and bottles. He looked like he needed a thrift store too.

"I don't know why you insist on being here when I turn the medallion over." Old Man Sweeney had protested all the way from the coffee shop. He hadn't let up now that we were at his house either.

"I told you, Mr. Sweeney." I laid it on thick. "As mayor of Duck, it's my monthly honor to commend one of our citizens for a good deed. I'd like that to be you at next month's town council meeting. Don't you want everyone to know what a wonderful person you are?"

It didn't work.

He still grumbled and complained, but he managed to call Derek quickly enough after I'd crawled under his table and brought out the lost medallion. I looked at it carefully before I handed it over. It was the same gold medallion I'd found for Chuck. There was no doubt in my mind who the medallion belonged to.

And that was when the vision hit me.

I was standing in the dark, empty parking lot behind the Harris Teeter supermarket. I couldn't actually see Chuck, but I was fairly sure I was seeing everything from his point of view. He was standing beside a burgundy Lincoln. The headlights were off. A single parking-lot lamppost tried valiantly to illuminate the scene.

"There! You have everything now. What else do you want?" Chuck asked someone I couldn't see. He was holding his arms up in the air as though he were being robbed.

"You're right." The voice that responded was deep and husky, as was the laugh that followed. "Thanks for adding to my retirement fund."

A second later, a shot broke the silence and Chuck fell to the ground, his mother's medallion rolling out of his limp fingers and onto the pavement. I could sense that he'd been holding it because he was scared and it made him feel lucky.

I could feel the blood and life draining from him, but

there was nothing I could do. This event had already happened. I didn't know when, but I knew it was in the recent past.

Then Chuck turned his head as though by doing so he could see me there with him. "Help her, please."

I jumped back from the memories encased in the medallion. My breath came quickly and my heart pounded. Chuck's death was in the past, I reminded myself. He couldn't have seen me there with him. Maybe he'd been talking to someone else.

But I knew I was just trying to make excuses for this new turn in my abilities. This had never happened to me before. I'd had visions of people, but they could never see me. They certainly never *talked* to me.

I heard the knock at the door and knew Derek must be there for the medallion—Derek who I realized might be the person who'd robbed and killed Chuck.

Old Man Sweeney started for the front door, probably eager for his reward. I looked at the medallion on the floor where I'd dropped it. What if Derek was trying to tie up loose ends? He must have realized that the medallion was left behind in the parking lot.

But what had happened to Chuck? I'd know if the police had found him dead at Harris Teeter. Like I said, Duck was a small town. I tried not to doubt my visions, but something seemed off about this one. Actually, *everything* seemed off about it.

Old Man Sweeney was reaching for the door handle when I grabbed him and pulled him back.

"What's wrong with you, Dae O'Donnell? I've a good mind to call Horace and tell him how crazy you've been acting today."

"Good idea! Let's give him a call right now. I know Derek

won't mind waiting." I took out my cell phone and hit speed dial to call Gramps. He was a retired sheriff of Dare County. He'd know what to do.

I hoped.

"Bah! Give me that medallion and get out of my way. I don't care if I get the mayor's award or not. I just want the *re*-ward."

The phone was ringing. I could only hope Gramps was next door. I couldn't remember if this was his day to train with the volunteer firefighters or play pinochle. Neither, I prayed.

Be next door.

"Horace O'Donnell speaking."

"Gramps, you have to come over to Old Man Sweeney's house right away. I'll explain when you get here. Hurry!"

"I can't believe you still call him that! What's wrong, Dae? I'm right in the middle of making some fish stew. I don't want to leave the stove on."

"Get over here right away, *please*!"

At that moment, Old Man Sweeney opened the front door. Derek stood on the doorstep. He smiled when he saw us. He had a pleasantly handsome face, dark brown hair combed away from his forehead. He was well dressed, even wearing expensive shoes. "Hello. I'm here for the lost medallion."

"I've got it right here." Old Man Sweeney grabbed the medallion from me. "I believe you mentioned a *generous* reward."

"Indeed I did." Derek reached inside his tailored jacket.

I panicked. I couldn't let him shoot us like he'd shot Chuck. I needed to buy some time. "Won't you come in and have some iced tea with us? I'm Dae O'Donnell, the mayor of Duck. I don't recognize you. Are you just visiting?"

As I spoke, I was pulling Old Man Sweeney backward.

He kept slapping at my hands, but I kept pulling him anyway. *Where is Gramps?*

"Nice to meet you, Mayor. I'm Derek Johnson. I'm here on business."

"And you lost your medallion," I said sympathetically. "How did you manage to do that?"

"A friend of mine picked me up at the Harris Teeter." His grin widened—it was even bigger than my mayor's smile. "I guess I dropped it there. I never go anywhere without it. It's a good luck charm."

Suddenly, Gramps came running from around the bushes between our house and Old Man Sweeney's. He was breathing raggedly, wearing his fishing overalls and straw hat. "For the love of God, Dae, what's going on?"

I realized abruptly that he didn't have a gun, like he always used to have when he was the sheriff. I didn't know what I'd been thinking when I called him. Of course he wasn't armed! I looked at both the old men and realized I'd only made matters worse. What was he supposed to do—Derek Johnson was probably dangerous.

All three men stared at me. Old Man Sweeney recovered first. "She's been acting like a fruitcake ever since I told her about finding this man's medallion. I'm sorry I took your advice, Horace, and asked for her help."

"If there's a problem, I can come back later," Derek said with a polite nod of his head. "If you'll just give me the medallion—"

"Dae?" Gramps stared angrily at me, probably embarrassed to be caught in this crazy scene.

But I couldn't forget what I'd seen. If Derek left here now, we might never know what had happened to Chuck. We were going to have to take our chances.

I drew in a deep breath, prepared to tell everyone what I knew, despite the risks. I saw Duck Police Officer Tim

Mabry out of the corner of my eye as he pulled his squad car into my driveway.

I hated to put him on the spot, but I didn't know what else to do. As soon as he saw all of us at Old Man Sweeney's front door, he started in our direction. "Hey, Dae!"

"Thank goodness you're here!" I ran to him and brought him close to the group. "You have to arrest this man." I pointed at Derek Johnson. "I think he killed Chuck Sparks."

Chapter 3

There was a general ruckus after I'd said those provocative words. It was exactly what I'd expected. The good thing was that Tim did what I'd asked of him and tackled Derek with his long, lanky body, then held him on the ground.

"Get off of him!" Old Man Sweeney shouted. "He's about to give me a reward. All you young people are just plain crazy. Horace, do something."

Gramps grabbed my arm and pulled me to one side. "Dae, what's going on? Did you have a vision or something? I hope it's something that makes sense, no offense. But you just opened the town up for a lawsuit if it doesn't."

I told him about Chuck Sparks's medallion. "You remember. I gave it to him that night at our place. He offered us a lot of money to sell the house."

"That's right." He asked Old Man Sweeney for the medallion and studied it. "You're sure this belongs to Mr. Sparks, Dae?"

I kind of stared at him. "Are you *really* asking me that?"

"Just trying to get the facts straight. Why do you think this man is guilty of anything except maybe stealing this from Chuck?"

"That would be enough, wouldn't it?" But I told him what I'd seen and heard in the vision. "I haven't heard anything about Chuck going missing or getting shot, have you?"

As past sheriff, Gramps was very chummy with the new sheriff and all the other law enforcement officials around the Outer Banks. We both knew nothing had shown up on the radar. "If you're really sure about this, honey, I'll call Chief Michaels and let him sort it out."

"I'm really sure." I shuddered again when I thought about Chuck looking at me while he lay dying.

"What do you want me to do?" Tim asked Gramps, still holding Derek on the front lawn.

"You have the wrong person," Derek said in an angry tone.

"I'm going to give Ronnie a call." Gramps made his decision and took out his cell phone. "I'd pat him down, if I were you, Tim. Just to be on the safe side."

"I assure you it's not necessary," Derek complained. "If you'll let me up, I can prove who I am."

"I don't think who you are is in question, sir," Gramps said. "But you'll have plenty of time for answers when our police chief gets here."

Tim patted his prisoner down and found a small handgun in his jacket pocket. "Not much but it would cause a little sting."

"I have a permit for that," Derek said. "A man can't be too careful anymore. I sometimes have large amounts of cash with me. It's part of my job."

"Save it for the chief," Tim said, then whispered to Gramps, "Should I Mirandize him?"

"The chief will be here soon." Gramps nodded. "Best wait until then."

"I might as well go inside and watch TV," Old Man Sweeney said. "I won't get any money out of this now. Thanks, Mayor. I won't be voting for *you* come next November."

I hated to lose even one vote, but it couldn't be helped. Losing Old Man Sweeney's vote would mean another vote for my opponent, Mad Dog Wilson. Old Man Sweeney might change his mind later if I'd saved his life.

"I still consider you a good Samaritan, Mr. Sweeney," I told him in a cheerful voice. "I still want to give you that award next month. You've earned it."

"Bah!" He slammed the door in my face.

Oh well.

Police Chief Ronnie Michaels arrived a few minutes later. He always reminded me of an older drill sergeant with his graying flattop, patent leather shoes and carefully pressed uniform. He was about ten years younger than Gramps. They'd worked together at the sheriff's office before Duck had created its own police force.

"What's going on here, Horace? I don't mind you commandeering Officer Mabry, but I hope you had good reason."

Gramps took Chief Michaels into the driveway, out of earshot of the rest of us, and presumably explained everything. The chief—like everyone else in Duck—knew about my gift. I'd helped him a few times, but he was never too happy about it. Visions and feelings weren't good police work, he always said. I suspected he liked doing it better without me.

While Tim, Derek and I waited for Gramps and the chief to return, Kevin's old red pickup pulled in front of my house. He got out and walked up the driveway toward our ever-increasing group.

I wasn't sure how to act or what to say when it came down to talking with him. What *could* I say? I didn't want to lose him. I wanted things to go on as they had between us. But clearly, that wasn't going to happen.

Kevin was an honorable man. I wouldn't expect anything less from him. He'd have to at least try to work it out with Ann. It was the only fair thing to do.

Even though I hated it.

Gramps and the chief finished their discussion. "Mayor O'Donnell, could I have a word with you?" The chief waited in the driveway while Gramps came back to the front porch of Old Man Sweeney's house.

"Can I put him in the car now?" Tim asked.

"Just stay there another minute," the chief commanded. "I'll get to you soon enough."

It was my turn to explain everything, in greater detail. I told the chief what had happened, glancing from time to time across his shoulder at Kevin. I wondered if he'd come because he'd heard about the goings-on at Old Man Sweeney's from the police scanner, or because he wanted to talk to me about Ann.

I knew that what I'd felt from the medallion was right—it had brought me there in the first place. But convincing the chief was something else.

"And you're sure you've never seen this man before?" he demanded.

"No. It was just a fluke that Mr. Sweeney asked for my help and I recognized the medallion. I knew it belonged to Chuck Sparks as soon as I saw it."

"In a vision?"

"Yes."

"There's no accident report. No missing person report

filed. Nothing that says anything has happened to Mr. Sparks."

"Fine. Let's call him then and ask him about it. Maybe Derek is just a friend of his pretending that the medallion belongs to him. It won't take more than a few minutes to check it out."

"Not a bad idea," the chief admitted, somewhat grudgingly.

He wasn't thrilled about having to follow up on one of my visions, but at least he was willing to try and make sense of it. If I was wrong about the whole thing, he could always apologize to Derek and let him go.

Me too, I supposed.

The chief used his radio to ask the dispatcher to get in touch with Chuck. When there was no answer at Island Realty, the dispatcher called Chuck's home and cell phone numbers—the police maintained a list of emergency contact information for local business owners. The chief frowned when they couldn't reach him.

"He's a real estate broker," I reminded him. "There's no way he wouldn't answer one of those phones—unless something *has* happened to him."

"You know I can't just arrest a man based on one of your visions, Mayor," he argued. "I'll send someone over to Chuck's house and office. What kind of car was that you saw in your dream again?"

I ignored the *dream* jibe and answered, "A burgundy Lincoln. Late model, I think."

The chief took it from there. He told Tim to take Derek to the police station and hold him for questioning. When Derek protested, Chief Michaels explained that it was only routine and that he'd probably be back where he wanted to be in time for supper.

"Where is home, by the way?" the chief asked. It was a

loaded question delivered in a good-old-boy drawl, but I could see the purpose in his eyes.

"I'm from the mainland," Derek responded with an uncomfortable look on his lean face. "I haven't done anything wrong. You have no right arresting me."

Chief Michaels laughed in an easygoing manner that was definitely not like him. "That's why we're not arresting you yet, son. But you better come up with some answers before I come to question you. The mainland is a big place. You think about where *exactly* you come from and why you're here for the next time I ask you."

Tim closed the police car door and got in the driver's seat. "Dae? Just so you know, I was on my way here to see you. Don't do anything crazy until you hear what I have to say."

He glared at Kevin significantly, and I knew what he had to say. There had been a misunderstanding between us for years. Tim thought the kiss we'd shared in high school meant we were destined to be together forever. In between his other girlfriends, he always came back to me.

I knew he'd heard about me and Kevin. But no matter what happened with us, Tim and I would always be just good friends. I wished he'd see that.

When everyone else was gone, Kevin and I stood there, awkwardly, not really looking at each other. I knew Gramps had already heard the news when he made a lame excuse and left us right away, glancing back once before he went inside.

"It's okay." I finally broke the awkward silence. "You didn't know this was going to happen. I understand."

"Can we sit down for a minute and talk about this?" Kevin asked. He took my hand, and we sat together on the front steps of my house.

I really hated being uncomfortable around Kevin, but there was no way to make this easy for either of us.

"I had no idea she was being released," Kevin said. "She doesn't understand what happened. It's like the last couple of years never existed for her."

"It has to be hard for her," I said sympathetically. "I can't even imagine what she must feel."

"Dae—"

"You have to stay with her," I blurted. "You were together for a long time. I know you must still love her."

He stared out at the cars passing by on Duck Road. "I don't know what I feel right now. I never expected to look up and see her standing there."

The logical, good-natured part of me *completely* understood. But the sappy, sentimental part that really wanted Kevin to be the person who'd share *my* life couldn't stand it.

I got to my feet and let go of his hand. I didn't want to. I just didn't see any other way. Better to cut it off quickly. "It will be fine. Give her, and yourself, a chance to work it out. You both deserve it. I hope she likes the Blue Whale Inn."

Kevin stood next to me. "I don't want to lose *us,* Dae. What we've shared has been important to me. You've changed my life."

I smiled and forced back the tears. "We won't lose us. I'm sure we'll still see each other. It'll be fine. You'll see."

He didn't say anything else, just got in his pickup and drove away. I sat on the stairs until it was dark. Gramps finally came outside and sat next to me.

"If it's right, it's right," he said. "Things happen for a reason, honey. You can't see it yet, but it's there. Come on in and have some stew. You need to keep up your strength or you'll never beat Mad Dog Wilson in that debate tonight."

I had totally forgotten about the first debate!

I started to tell him that I didn't care. My heart wasn't in it anymore. It felt like it was shattered into a thousand pieces in my chest.

But pride and a commitment to Duck made me glance at my watch. I had about twenty minutes to change clothes and get to the fire station where the debate was being held. "You're right. I have to go. Save me some stew. I'll eat when I get back."

Some things are just pounded too hard into your head to ignore. In the case of my family, it was community service. Gramps always made sure I understood about giving back to our hometown. I could no more sit there and sulk than I could grow gills and swim.

I changed clothes and put on a sober blue suit and white silk blouse. I wore very little makeup because I had a tan all year from being outside so much. My short, fly-away brown hair bleached out easy every summer, and that's about all I could get it to do.

I looked at myself in the mirror over the bathroom sink, blue eyes staring into blue eyes. I didn't think I'd ever been so unhappy, at least not since my mother had died. I was even starting to feel that life was unfair.

I could remember my mother telling me that life was never fair and that we made our own happiness. I never agreed with her on anything once I'd started growing up. She'd died right after one of our major arguments while I was at college on the mainland. A storm had forced her car off of a bridge that crossed from the sound to the Outer Banks. Her body was never found.

I liked to think that part of her lived on in me. Sometimes I could almost hear her talking to me. But for all of the ghosts that frequented our part of the world, she'd never come back to let me apologize for being so stubborn and saying such terrible things.

I looked at myself in the mirror again and clipped on my grandmother's pearl earrings. Life wasn't fair, but it continued, and I wouldn't let it pass me by.

"I'll drive you down to the station or you'll be late," Gramps said when I got downstairs. "You look great!"

"Thanks."

He handed me a warm corn muffin. "For strength. Mad Dog is gonna want to make you look bad tonight. Don't let him get away with it."

I wasn't sure what good a corn muffin would be in those circumstances. Plus, I felt a little queasy from everything that had happened that day. I set the muffin down on the kitchen table and drank some apple juice instead.

"Don't worry. I know he wants to be mayor any way he can. He's going to have to do better than he does at town council meetings to beat me."

The Duck Fire and Rescue Building had a large area where the fire department held classes for their recruits and the police department did training. At least a hundred chairs were set up in the open space. They all faced a podium, where Mad Dog was already standing when Gramps and I arrived.

It had been a harrowing ride on the new golf cart. It always was when Gramps drove. I hoped I didn't look as unsettled as I felt. But there wasn't time to fuss about my appearance. I patted my hair down and made sure my lipstick wasn't smudged, then I headed for the podium with fierce determination.

Most of the chairs were filled already. I waved to friends and neighbors who held their thumbs up and wished me luck. It would be my first election campaign against another candidate. I'd run unopposed in Duck's first mayoral election.

"Running a little late, Dae?" Randal "Mad Dog" Wilson taunted me. Before he'd announced that he would leave the town council to run against me, he'd always addressed me as "Mayor." That had all changed since the beginning of the election season.

At six foot four and three hundred pounds, he was a formidable opponent. He made a habit of standing close and looking down at me, and everyone else. He was the town's stock car racing hero from years ago. That was where he'd earned his colorful nickname. People said he drove like a mad dog.

"Better late than never," was the snappiest comeback I could think of. I turned to Fire Chief Cailey Fargo, who was going to be the moderator for the debate. She'd also been my fifth-grade teacher, which was sometimes a little intimidating.

"I'm sorry we could only come up with one podium," she said. "I'm not sure how you two want to do this. I guess you could sit down and debate since you're so tall, Mad Dog."

"That's not going to happen! I say we take turns answering questions at the podium. We can debate just as well that way without giving Dae the advantage."

"That's fine with me." I looked out at the sea of faces filling up the station, wishing I would spot that one special face I knew wouldn't be there. I waved to my friends Shayla and Trudy, then noticed our town clerk, Nancy Boidyn, sitting beside them. She smiled and gave me the *give-'em-hell* look she usually reserved for problems with the trash company or roadwork crews.

I appreciated the support and mentally gave myself a good shake. Kevin was handling his own problems right now. I had to handle mine. People believed in me. I couldn't let them down because I was unhappy.

"Okay," Cailey said. "I'll just stand over here and ask the questions. Maybe we should start with Dae since she's the incumbent. I think that's fair, don't you, Mad Dog?"

"What is this—the age of chivalry?" he demanded. "This is America, darlin'. Land of the free and home of the equal. I think we should toss for it."

I agreed. "That's fine." I was only reacting to whatever he said. I was going to have to do better than that. This debate was the kick-off for the political season. I had to make my mark.

Cailey tossed a silver dollar into the air. She dropped it the first time, and it rolled under the chairs in the audience. Carter Hatley, the owner of Game World, our local video game arcade, found it and gave it back to her.

She tried again with more luck. "Heads or tails?"

"Tails," I said quickly, not waiting for Mad Dog this time.

"Hey! That wasn't fair," he complained. He got louder when Cailey said that I'd won the toss. "How do I know that was even a real coin? Maybe it was rigged."

"Sit down, Mad Dog," Cailey said in her old teacher's voice. "Dae is up first."

Mad Dog grumbled, but he did as he was told. He moved the chair to the side of the podium so everyone could see him, even while I was speaking.

"Dae, take a few minutes to introduce yourself for the newbies, then I'll ask the questions." Cailey smiled and pushed her graying brown hair out of her face, using the same sweeping motion she'd perfected during her younger, schoolteacher days. I'd often wondered why she didn't cut her hair, since she seemed so impatient with it.

I smiled at the audience and focused on them, trying to

look each person in the face. My heart gave a little extra thump when I saw Kevin seated in the back row. Ann was with him. His presence gave me the feeling that he still cared about me, even if we weren't together.

"I'm Mayor Dae O'Donnell," I said finally. "I was born and raised here in Duck. I've been mayor for the past two years. I'm excited about all the progress we've made since we incorporated."

Then I proceeded to tell them all about that progress and said a few things about what we were looking forward to in the future. I thanked them, and everyone applauded.

Mad Dog, in turn, introduced himself and told everyone how long he'd been on the town council and all about his plans for the future of Duck.

When he'd finished, Cailey came closer to the microphone on the podium and asked the first question. "What's your position on the bridge controversy, Mayor?"

Before I could speak, Mad Dog lumbered to his feet and kind of pushed me out of the way. "Let's talk about what's important here, people," he rasped into the microphone. "How many murders and other crimes have happened in the two years since Dae took office?"

Chapter 4

I frowned but didn't respond.

"Too many," he bellowed in answer to his own question, making me wonder if he had any numbers to back up his claim. "I can tell you one thing, citizens of Duck, I wouldn't be so worried about sidewalks and whether or not the school is teaching Duck history, if I were the mayor. I'd be out there making sure our skyrocketing crime rate is going down. And if you elect me as mayor, I can promise you that is *exactly* what I will do!"

There was some scattered applause at his words. Anyone who knew Mad Dog had heard rhetoric like this from him before on varied subjects. He wouldn't be him if he didn't go off on some rant every now and again.

Cailey demanded that he wait his turn, and he took his seat, much to my surprise.

"Well, I guess people want to hear something about this, Dae," she said. "Would you like to respond?"

Obviously I wasn't being tough enough. I wouldn't have guessed that Mad Dog would be so nasty. In private, maybe. But not in public. He was setting the tone for the whole campaign. Who knew Duck politics would get so vicious?

"I'll be glad to respond." I took the microphone back from her. "Yes, there has been more crime. That's why the town decided to have its own police force. That wasn't my decision, but I think it was a good one. I do have a question for Councilman Wilson—where were you when crime skyrocketed? It seems to me that being on the town council put you in a position to do something about this too. Have *you* done anything about it?"

A few loud whoops and applause came from the area where Shayla, Trudy and Nancy were sitting. Mad Dog's friends frowned at them.

Mad Dog got to his feet again. "I'll tell you what I've been doing. I've been working on creating a crime task force. This is only in the planning stages right now, so I'm not at liberty to discuss it. But when I'm the mayor, things will be different."

"Yeah, right." Althea Hinson, a county librarian who worked in Manteo, heckled him. "You can't get out of your golf cart long enough to get anything done."

Mark Samson from the Rib Shack restaurant stood up. "Let him be, Althea. If there's a plan, I want to hear it."

The crowd waited expectantly for Mad Dog to speak. He floundered around, looking uncomfortable and adjusting his big green tie. "I told you, the plan is only in the planning stages."

"Well, just tell us the part of the plan that's finished," suggested Barney Thompson of the Sand Dollar Jewelry Store. "If you're going to say you're doing something, you better be doing it."

"Chief Michaels won't let me divulge those plans." Mad

Dog recovered his composure. “But even what I know now can be done, and it’s a darn sight better than what Dae O’Donnell is doing.”

“Do you have any plans to reduce crime?” Cailey asked me.

“If I did, I wouldn’t mind divulging them.” I still felt on the defensive. “But that’s not really my job. We have Chief Michaels and Sheriff Riley for that. They do a good job for us. Duck is changing, like the rest of the Outer Banks. Nobody really wants that to happen, but we’re in the middle of it now. We have to develop strategies for coping with those changes. It’s not going to happen overnight.”

“Sounds like you really don’t have anything in mind either,” August Grandin said. He owned Duck General Store, a couple of doors down from Missing Pieces.

“No,” I admitted. “I don’t have those answers. But neither does Councilman Wilson. I think appointing a group of citizens to work with the police as a community watch might be a good idea. I’ve brought that to the town council several times in the last year, but they’ve always voted against it.”

“Why is that?” August asked Mad Dog. “I remember Dae asking the council to consider that idea. What happened?”

Mad Dog kind of growled and his face turned red. “Wetnose puppies! What good would it do to have everyone in town looking over everyone else’s shoulder? It’s a stupid idea. That’s why we turned it down.”

The audience erupted into a loud discussion, getting to their feet, in some cases, to tell their neighbor what they thought about community watch programs. I wished I’d brought my gavel from town hall to quiet them down.

Cailey finally got the room to come to order—with some help from the volunteer firefighters who were present. She asked everyone to sit down again. "This is getting out of hand, people. The debate is supposed to be spirited, not rude. Let's hear what both candidates have to say—unless the rest of you plan to run for office too."

There was a chorus of groans and assurances that none of them were so stupid as to run for public office. They were leaving that part to me and Mad Dog.

I wasn't exactly sure how I felt about those sentiments. Like Gramps always said, at best serving the public was a thankless job, but it was also an important one. I always tried to see the bigger picture and not take what was said to heart.

The room was quiet after that, and we made it through the debate. Mad Dog took a few more shots at me, mostly about me being too young to know what to do as mayor. I could see a few older folks' heads bobbing up and down in agreement. That was an easy score for him. I couldn't deny that I was thirty years younger than him.

I felt like I'd made a few valid points too. Duck needed energy and vision to get where it wanted to be. Mad Dog slept through many of the council meetings, though I didn't quite say that. I did remark on his habit of not showing up for meetings, though. That was a matter of public record.

Afterward, everyone seemed to think it went very well. They came up and shook hands with me and Mad Dog. Some of them promised to vote for one or the other of us. Most held back on their congratulations. They'd continue thinking about it until next November and make their opinions known on the ballot.

"You did great, Dae!" Nancy, Shayla and Trudy chorused around me after a series of hugs. "You said exactly what needed to be said. Good job!" Trudy added.

"Let's celebrate!" Nancy said. "I'll buy the first round at Wild Stallions, if the rest of you reciprocate."

Shayla and Trudy quickly agreed. I was on the verge of agreeing too when I noticed that Kevin was waiting to talk to me. "You go ahead and I'll catch up. I have to mingle with my constituency before I leave."

Shayla glanced at Kevin and Ann, who were standing behind Trudy. "Don't get all mushy over that man," she hissed. "You don't *need* him."

"Thanks," I whispered. "My brain agrees with you. The rest of me is waiting to be convinced. Besides, he is a voter."

"*She* might be one now too," Trudy said with a frown.

Nancy outright glared at Kevin as she walked by. Trudy and Shayla scowled at him. None of them spoke to him.

Kevin was frowning as I reached him, clearly not used to being treated like yesterday's oyster shell. The women of Duck had been kind to him, welcoming almost to the point of fawning. We didn't get a lot of new single men in town. He'd been a prize worth capturing, especially since he was good-looking *and* owned the Blue Whale Inn.

Only my friends were likely to care one way or another about the latest development between Kevin and me. I appreciated their loyalty, but I hoped they'd get over it right away. Kevin didn't deserve their scorn. He was doing what he had to do.

"You did very well," he said quietly, standing close to me.

"Thanks. I'm glad you could come." We were alone, but I knew I'd seen Ann beside him just a moment ago. "Where's Ann?"

"She's outside, waiting. She doesn't like confined spaces with a lot of people."

"I hope she can adjust to all of this. I know it's a lot different than the life she's used to."

"I hope so too." He glanced around as though unsure of

what to do or say next. He grabbed the obvious. "I guess you were in the middle of all that going down at your neighbor's house today."

"I know everyone has heard about it by now. At this point, it's just run-of-the-mill for me to see dead people, or people who are probably dead. It's almost as routine as looking for antiques."

He took my hand and squeezed it gently. "Don't say that. It can never be second nature to you. You'll lose who you are, like Ann has. I can still help, if you'll let me. I don't know all the answers, like you said. But I think we've worked well together. That doesn't have to be over."

I prayed, short and fast, that he wouldn't offer his undying friendship next. That might be more than I could take for one day.

I reclaimed my hand from his, making a show of picking up my pocketbook. "I think you're going to need to focus your energies on dealing with Ann right now. I'll be fine. You know I always bounce back. Don't worry."

He put his hand into his jacket pocket. "Yeah. I guess you're right. But promise you'll call if you need me. You know I'll be there."

I said, "I know," in a voice I barely recognized. I wasn't sure if he'd heard or not.

Lucky for me, Ann came back inside, probably to see what was keeping him. I followed up with a much stronger "Good night" and thanked them both for coming.

I wanted them to leave. But when my wish came true, it left me feeling empty and alone.

My father, the one I'd recently learned I had, came up. He looked angry. "*He* has a lot of nerve showing up here tonight. I could go out right now and kick his ass, if you want me to. Nobody should do that to my little girl."

The idea that I was his little girl was funny. Here I was—

thirty-six years old—and he'd been kept from me all of my life. My mother and Gramps had both told me he was dead. For my own good, of course.

Gramps had driven Danny away from my mother when she was pregnant with me. He wasn't good enough to marry the Dare County sheriff's daughter, since he'd been in and out of trouble all of his life. That was supposed to make it okay that they'd let me believe my father was dead.

"I suggest you stay out of it, Danny," Gramps advised him, joining us. "Let them sort it out."

That struck me as funny too, knowing what I knew about the whole crazy business. I wasn't sure what to say to either of them.

Deciding I needed the company of women, I excused myself and let them know I'd be at the bar with my friends. Neither man was crazy about the idea of me going out by myself—it was almost ten P.M., after all. The streets might not be safe.

I kissed my father on the cheek and let Gramps take me down to the boardwalk on the golf cart. That was one good thing about being older—I could listen to advice but not necessarily take it.

It was a beautiful night. The moon was big and full, lending that special glow across town. It was a mile or so down to the Duck Shoppes on the Boardwalk where Wild Stallions was located. Missing Pieces was tucked between Trudy's Curves and Curls Beauty Spa and Shayla's Mrs. Roberts, Spiritual Advisor shop. The area was the heart of Duck.

Once I arrived, I knew I didn't want to sit and drink all night. Being with friends for a while was a wonderful balm for my spirit, but the moonlight was calling me out for a solitary walk on the beach.

I told Trudy and Shayla (Nancy had already left) that I

was tired and going home for the night. It was close to the truth. I *would* go home—once I'd had enough walking.

They were a little concerned about me being alone, but they handled it. I knew they'd talk about my sadness over losing Kevin and think of things to cheer me up. Shayla would offer me a love potion to find someone else, and Trudy would offer me a facial so I could look my best.

I said good night and turned off my cell phone as I left. This was just the right thing to do.

The moon illuminated Duck Road, creating a path of light through the center of town. I followed it, winding down the silent streets, until I reached the shore of the Atlantic. The sea had a hazy quality, and the waves were so calm, it was almost like looking at the Currituck Sound on the other side of town.

I stood on the shore and stared out at the water like so many of my Banker relatives had in centuries past. The Atlantic was the lifeblood of Duck and the other, older towns on the island. Our ancestors had scratched out a living here by taking in cargo from ships lost to the "Graveyard of the Atlantic."

Hundreds of ships had gone down here. Some because of the treacherous waters, others because of the local pirates, and a few here and there due to Banker tricks that caused no small amount of disaster. People had done what they needed to survive. Those weren't easy times. Cut off from the mainland—no bridges then—life had been difficult.

As I followed the horizon with my eyes, I saw what looked like an old wooden ship. It was huge and under full sail. It looked heavy and cargo rich—a Spanish galleon, if I wasn't mistaken.

"The *Andalusia*," I barely breathed aloud.

It was a legend, a ghost ship that had sunk with all hands aboard and a treasure estimated by most people to be worth over twenty-five million dollars in today's currency. The ship was destroyed in 1721, never to be seen again as a real vessel. But many people had seen it down through the years, sailing across the water. People in Duck took it as an ill omen.

I'd spent my entire life here, but I'd never seen this before. As I watched it, thrilled and terrified at the same time, I knew it couldn't be anything other than the *Andalusia.* The ship, even though it looked heavy with cargo, wasn't quite resting on the dark water. A light that wasn't part of the moon glow filled it, creating an aura around it.

I'd heard people say that seeing the ghost ship had transfixed them. They'd walked for miles looking at it. Now, I felt transfixed—captivated by the sight of it. I couldn't look away.

I started walking along the beach, trying to keep pace with the ghostly galleon. Except for the light emanating from the ship and the glow from the moon, it was very dark along the water. I stumbled into a ditch in the sand created by rain runoff from the island. The beach was still very wet from the tail end of a hurricane we'd had recently. I lost my balance and sank to my knees in the soft sand.

I put my hands out to keep myself steady. I didn't want to look away from the *Andalusia*, but I had no choice if I wanted to get back on my feet.

I looked down at the sand and saw a face with wide-open eyes looking back at me.

Chapter 5

I crawled out of the ditch as quickly as I could, my heart pounding. The ghost ship was pushed from my thoughts like yesterday's high tide. I'd almost fallen right on the person. It was hard to tell for certain in the dim light, but the face looked like Chuck Sparks.

Nothing but Banker determination made me go back to the ditch and try to decide if he was still alive. I got down close beside him. I wasn't a doctor, but I couldn't feel a pulse. He felt cold, and his body was stiff to the touch.

I used the light from my cell phone to look at him more carefully. It was Chuck. He was covered in sand, as though he'd been rolled in it. Had someone buried him and the tide had shifted the sand, bringing him back to the surface again?

I tried using the phone to call for help. *No signal.* At that point, it was a better flashlight than a phone. I didn't want to leave Chuck alone, but I had no choice. There was only so much I could do by myself.

"I'm sorry," I whispered. "I have to go. I'll be right back with someone who can help. Don't worry. You'll be fine."

As I started to get to my feet, his hand moved, clutching at my skirt beside it. His ghastly white face turned and looked at me, as he had in the vision. "Help her."

I jumped away with a small shriek, crawling until I was a few yards from him. Despite what some might term my "psychic" gift of being able to help people find things, I'd never experienced anything like this. Dead bodies normally didn't speak to me. Now that it had happened, I wished it hadn't. It was bad enough in a vision. This was so much worse.

I sat on the wet sand, shuddering, and looked up at the sky. The ghost ship was gone now, but the moon was still smiling down at me.

Did Chuck really just speak to me?

I wasn't sure. Maybe I'd imagined it. Finding a dead body, even one that didn't speak, could be traumatic enough to make someone hallucinate.

So I crawled back again, mindful that my dry cleaner, Mrs. Toivo, was going to have a few words with me about this. I felt safer near the ground, less lightheaded. I thought about standing—it might be easier to get away if Chuck decided to put any more moves on me. But my legs were shaking too much. That made fast crawling my best option.

I pulled out my cell phone and peered over the slight lip of the ditch. Chuck looked the same as he had when I'd first found him. I couldn't tell if he'd *really* moved or if I'd imagined it.

This was an awful turn for my gift to take. In the future, were recently dead people—not even ghosts—going to start talking to me? That thought made me want to run away screaming.

I took a deep breath, forcing myself to calm down. I had to focus on what to do next.

Once I saw that he was the same, I moved away and pushed myself to my feet a little farther down the beach. *So much for moonlight making everything more romantic.* This experience was definitely not romantic.

I walked up to the first house at the edge of the beach—Mr. and Mrs. Cooley's place. They'd recently retired and moved to Duck. He was an ex-corporate official from some mega-giant technology firm. I pounded on the door as though the dead were after me—which I prayed they weren't.

An outside light came on at the back deck that fronted the water. "Mayor O'Donnell?" Mrs. Cooley, a nice middle-aged woman with gray-lilac tinted hair, greeted me. "Is something wrong? Do you need help?"

Her husband came to the door behind her in his red striped pajamas. "What's wrong, Ethel?" he asked his wife. "Has she been assaulted? Should we call the police?"

"Yes!" I answered, teeth chattering, knowing they might take it the wrong way. But whatever got Chief Michaels down here worked for me. "Could I call my grandfather too? My cell phone isn't working."

"Really?" Mr. Cooley questioned. "We've always had great service here. It must be your provider."

I handed him my phone, which was also covered in sand. He hit Gramps on speed dial and the call went right through. He shrugged and handed the phone back to me.

"Dae?" Gramps answered the phone. "Where are you? Ronnie and I have gone through two pots of coffee waiting for you. There's some news about Chuck Sparks. Ronnie has some questions for you—and for Chuck."

CT Lottery

* * Starting Jan. 19, 2014 * * Turn your POWERBALL ticket into a game changer! Add POWER PLAY for $1, it multiplies some prizes up to 5 TIMES!

Term: 107993-01 19 Feb 2014 13:03
8490-0065498400-74 90fdfb2

Play 3

$0.50 - 1 Draw
WED FEB19 14
NIGHT
R

---

6 2 8 Box $0.50

8490-0065498400-74

50 50 $UPER DRAW

ONE TICKET wins 50% of the TOTAL SALES!

TICKETS ON SALE JANUARY 12, 2014
DRAWING: MARCH 17, 2014

CONNECTICUT LOTTERY CORPORATION **PH**

PRINT NAME ____________________

PRINT ADDRESS ____________________

SIGNATURE ____________________

TELEPHONE NUMBER* ______ – ______ – ______

TAX ID/SOCIAL SECURITY NUMBER* ____________________

*For Claims greater than $599 and MAIL-IN Claims Only

Lottery tickets are bearer instruments. Sign ticket upon purchase to establish ownership. Official Game Rules, Lottery Rules of Operation and all applicable laws apply. Odds of winning for each game are available at any Lottery Retailer, or at www.ctlottery.org. Winning tickets must be validated within 180 days of drawing date.

This ticket is the sole proof of wager. Examine it for accuracy. Cash single winning tickets up to $599 at any Lottery Retailer. Cash single winning tickets up to $5,000 at any High-Tier Claim Center. Present single winning tickets greater than $5,000 to Lottery Headquarters, 777 Brook Street, Rocky Hill, CT, 06067, 860-713-2700. Prizes of $50,000 or more must be presented in person at Lottery Headquarters.

To determine if this ticket is a winner, scan it using the "Ticket Checker" at any Lottery Retailer or ask the retailer to validate it. For Lottery Information, visit www.ctlottery.org or call 860-713-2000.

PLEASE PLAY RESPONSIBLY.
Purchasers must be 18 or older. Wagering on credit is prohibited.
Problem Gambling Helpline: 1-888-789-7777.
"Billions to Benefit Connecticut since 1972!"

Rev. 1/30/2013

586399231

CONNECTICUT LOTTERY CORPORATION **PH**

PRINT NAME ____________________

PRINT ADDRESS ____________________

SIGNATURE ____________________

TELEPHONE NUMBER* ______ – ______ – ______

TAX ID/SOCIAL SECURITY NUMBER* ____________________

*For Claims greater than $599 and MAIL-IN Claims Only

Lottery tickets are bearer instruments. Sign ticket upon purchase to establish ownership. Official Game Rules, Lottery Rules of Operation and all applicable laws apply. Odds of winning for each game are available at any Lottery Retailer, or at www.ctlottery.org. Winning tickets must be validated within 180 days of drawing date.

This ticket is the sole proof of wager. Examine it for accuracy. Cash single winning tickets up to $599 at any Lottery Retailer. Cash single winning tickets up to $5,000 at any High-Tier Claim Center. Present single winning tickets greater than $5,000 to Lottery Headquarters, 777 Brook Street, Rocky Hill, CT, 06067, 860-713-2700. Prizes of $50,000 or more must be presented in person at Lottery Headquarters.

To determine if this ticket is a winner, scan it using the "Ticket Checker" at any Lottery Retailer or ask the retailer to validate it. For Lottery Information, visit www.ctlottery.org or call 860-713-2000.

PLEASE PLAY RESPONSIBLY.
Purchasers must be 18 or older. Wagering on credit is prohibited.
Problem Gambling Helpline: 1-888-789-7777.
"Billions to Benefit Connecticut since 1972!"

Rev. 1/30/2013

586399232

CONNECTICUT LOTTERY CORPORATION **PH**

PRINT NAME ____________________

PRINT ADDRESS ____________________

SIGNATURE ____________________

TELEPHONE NUMBER* ______ – ______ – ______

"I have some answers for the chief. Both of you need to come over to the Cooleys' house. I'm over here. Chuck is on the beach in the drainage ditch. Dead."

"Well, I guess we won't be asking him those questions then," Gramps replied and hung up the phone.

I shivered and nodded when Ethel Cooley asked me if I wanted some coffee.

Of course, the Cooleys were concerned and disturbed that there was a dead man only a few hundred yards from their home. I dropped down on a kitchen chair, hoping they didn't mind the sand, and tried to calm their apprehension.

By that time, we could hear sirens approaching, and Mr. Cooley went to open the front door to let everyone in. It wasn't long before Chief Michaels, Gramps and Officer Scott Randall, our other full-time Duck police officer, were there.

The emergency rescue crew was immediately behind them. As soon as they arrived, we all trooped down to the beach to retrieve Chuck's body.

"What were you doing way down here?" Gramps asked. "I thought you were with your friends at Wild Stallions."

"I needed some time alone," I explained. "Then I saw the *Andalusia*."

The chief made a scoffing sound. "You and every other flaky person in Duck."

"I'm not a flake," I said, defending myself and every other person who'd seen the ghost ship. "It was there. It wasn't a real vessel. I followed it down the beach until I fell into the drainage ditch and found Chuck."

"Let's just see if this *body* is real then," the chief said.

Chuck was definitely real. As soon as the paramedics checked him and agreed that he was dead, the chief put on his latex gloves. "Looks like you were right about Chuck,

Mayor. In fact, I was at your house to tell you that something was off. No one has seen him in three days. His mail was piling up, and no one had fed his cat."

"Now maybe you'll believe me about Derek Johnson. The medallion belonged to Chuck. The only one likely to know he'd lost it would be his killer."

"Thank you, Miss Marple. If you don't mind, I think I'll draw my own conclusions. You need to get out of the crime scene area, ma'am. We'll let everyone do their jobs."

Gramps put his arm around me. "Let's get you home and out of these wet clothes, Dae. We'll find out all about this by morning, I'm sure. There's nothing else we can do here."

I saw him nod to the chief and decided that I didn't care. He was right. A hot bath and a good rest were long overdue. I was way past ready for this day to be done.

Gramps and I talked a little on the ride back in the golf cart. I still felt charged up from seeing the ghost ship. Not to mention having a dead Chuck Sparks talk to me.

"You didn't even know him that well, did you?" Gramps asked. "It's not like the two of you were friends or anything."

"No! I haven't even seen him since all of that stuff went down with the real estate scandal he was involved in last year."

Chuck had almost lost his real estate license in some shady dealings. I'd expected him to leave the area—he was new to Duck—but he'd hung on. It couldn't have been easy for him—regaining the community's trust was no small task.

But other than the fact that his mother had been in real estate too and had lost her award medallion here when he was a kid, I knew nothing about Chuck.

"That doesn't seem like much of a connection for him to reach out to you from the grave," Gramps said.

"Not even the grave yet," I reminded him. "In the vision,

he wasn't even dead yet. At least I don't think so. But it was like he could see me. No one has ever acted like they could see me in a vision. And he said the same thing both times—*Help her.*"

"Maybe he was talking about his cat," Gramps suggested. "They took a cat out of his house. People get very attached to their pets."

"Maybe. I guess we'll find out."

When I got home, I soaked in a hot bath, but I was too disturbed by the night's events to really relax. I wasn't sure if I'd done something different to make my gift behave in this new way or if Chuck himself was the reason for the change. Of course, as with all aspects of the gifts life had given me, there was no guidebook I could consult. No way of knowing what to do next.

Since Kevin's arrival in Duck, I'd grown accustomed to talking things like this over with him. He had experience in the FBI dealing with paranormal elements. Ann was a powerful psychic, according to Kevin. Her abilities had increased after she'd been shot during a case. She couldn't handle what she saw anymore.

Having Kevin as a confidant, someone with whom I could discuss things that many other people didn't understand, had been wonderful. He'd experienced so much more than I ever had. When my own abilities had grown, he'd been there for me.

But now, I didn't feel like I could just call him or go over and drink coffee with him while we talked. I was going to have to find another way of dealing with what was happening to me.

That left me with my friend Shayla. Shayla was a true medium who could readily talk to ghosts. She was from New Orleans, where her relatives were witches and other interesting occupations.

She knew a lot about the spirit world. We'd met because I'd wanted to contact my mother's ghost and find a way to put things right between us. That hadn't happened, but my friendship with Shayla had developed as a result of those efforts.

Sometimes, I was uncomfortable talking to her about my gifts. She freely scoffed at things that I found amazing. I suspected that she'd already seen so many supernatural happenings in her life, she didn't think mine were all that interesting. She never gave me the warm, fuzzy feeling the way Kevin did. I had to get over that too.

I finally climbed in bed after midnight. A wind had begun blowing from the Atlantic side of the island. I lay there for a long time listening to it, wondering where it had come from and what other places it had been.

I don't know when I fell asleep, but I was dreaming about the burgundy Lincoln again, the one I'd seen Chuck with at Harris Teeter the night he was killed.

A little girl was sitting on the hood of the car. She had a round face with chubby pink cheeks and big blue eyes. Her brown hair was in curls that looked as though they'd been mussed by the wind I'd heard before I fell asleep.

"Hello. Who are you?" she asked me.

This was obviously going to become a habit. It scared me a little when I considered all the places I'd been in my dreams and visions. If everyone could see me, that made it more personal. Maybe more dangerous.

"I'm Dae," I said finally, not sure if she could hear me.

She nodded and smiled. "I'm Betsy Sparks. I'm waiting for my daddy to come and get me."

Betsy Sparks? Chuck had a daughter?

"Where is your daddy?"

"I don't know." She shrugged, her tiny shoulders pitiful under the extra-large brown sweater she wore. "I thought

he'd be here by now. Can you find him? You're the finder lady, aren't you?"

I wasn't sure what to tell her. I wasn't sure if this was real or my imagination. I'd convinced myself that what had happened at the beach with Chuck turning his head and talking to me wasn't real. I didn't know what to think about this little girl.

"What's your daddy's name?" I decided to test her.

"His name is Charlie, but most people call him Chuck. Like that little girl with Charlie Brown, you know?"

"I know." I was confused. I didn't know Chuck well, but it seemed like I would know if he had a child. If nothing else, local gossip would've been lamenting his involvement in the real estate scandal because he had a daughter who needed him.

The only other possibility came to me slowly. In my defense, I was dreaming. "Did you just move to Duck to live with your daddy?"

"Yes. My mommy—"

Betsy suddenly held up her arms and began kicking at something, or someone. She pounded at it and screamed. She looked as though she were being lifted up and moved from the car by some unseen force. She fought as hard as she could, but she could not free herself from whatever gripped her. She called to her father over and over.

I wanted to help, but though I was substantial enough for her to see me, my hands and arms went through Betsy and the invisible entity that was taking her. I screamed at them to let her go, lending my voice to hers. But there was nothing I could do. In an instant, she was gone , vanished, and so was the Lincoln.

Chuck Sparks was still there, dying in the parking lot. He turned his head again and said, "Help her."

Chapter 6

I woke up, my chest heaving and tears streaming down my face. I had to get out of bed and go downstairs. I was too caught up in the dream to go back to sleep. It kept replaying over and over like a bad movie.

But I was convinced that it was real. Finding Chuck's body on the beach was no accident.

Gramps was downstairs watching reruns of *Gilligan's Island*. There was no way to disguise my red eyes, sniffling and tears spilling down my cheeks. When he saw me, hc turned off the TV and came to put his arms around me.

"Aw, honey. He just wasn't the right man for you. Another one will come along. I'm sorry I pushed you into meeting him."

"I'm not crying about Kevin."

"Of course you're not." He scratched his white beard. "I just wish your mama or grandma were alive to talk to you about all this female stuff. I know I haven't been much good at that. Thank God your mother was still alive when you were a teenager."

I had to laugh at that. Poor Gramps. He felt like he'd never understood. In many cases, he was right. "That's not what I mean." I told him about the dream. "I think Chuck may have a daughter."

"I don't recall ever hearing about a daughter, do you?"

"No. But we weren't close to him. We could check with the school tomorrow. She looked like she was big enough to be in school."

"But that's assuming she lives here in Duck."

"True. But she was in the Harris Teeter parking lot. And she said she lived here."

"Maybe you should mention this to Ronnie first," he said. "You know he doesn't like you to see these things and go off on your own."

"I think I should check with the school first. I mean, her name is Betsy Sparks, she said. Once I find out if she's registered here, then I'll say something to the chief."

"I'll be glad to go with you, if you need a sidekick."

"I'll be fine. I don't want you to give up your fishing charter tomorrow. Thanks anyway. I never ate that corn muffin before the debate. I'm starving now. I'll just rummage around until I find something. You go ahead and find out what happened to poor Gilligan."

He hugged me. "Don't worry, honey. It'll all be fine. Everything will turn out right. You'll see."

Someone knocked at the back door—a quiet rap, not pounding. It startled me, and I looked at the clock over the mantle. A little after two A.M. Not even the most stalwart Duck citizen would come to see me that late.

"Who could that be?" Gramps opened the drawer in the table beside his recliner where he kept his old service revolver. The Dare County Sheriff's Department had given it to him as a gift when he retired.

"It might just be the wind. It's picked up out there. I'll look."

"You're barely decent!"

I pulled my old robe closed over my shorts and tank top. "Girls wear less on the beach over the summer. I'll be fine. Better me in my shorts than you with your gun."

Before we could argue about it anymore, I yanked open the door—amazed to find Kevin standing on the porch.

"I'm sorry," he said. "But I had a dream and I just couldn't put it out of my head. Are you okay?"

I nodded, not sure what to say. We stood there and looked at each other for a minute or two. Gramps had turned back to Gilligan again as soon as he saw there wasn't a threat.

"Let's sit out here," I said, closing the door behind me.

We sat in the old rocking chairs on the porch. We could see the Currituck Sound from there with the moon as bright as day. The wind ruffled up the water and stirred the bushes around us. Chimes rang out from Old Man Sweeney's house next door.

"Is something going on with you besides that problem with your neighbor?" Kevin finally asked.

"There's been a new development in that." I told him about finding Chuck's body at the beach and about Chuck's dead, and almost-dead, form talking to me.

"I knew it." He sat back in the rocker as though he was vindicated in coming over at this late hour.

"I appreciate you coming over but—"

"I know. I shouldn't be here." He got up and leaned against the screen door leading off of the porch. "I'm sorry. This isn't easy for me either. I've grown so attuned to you that I guess I could just tell something was wrong."

I kept rocking, not saying anything, glad I couldn't see his face in the shadows.

"Maybe you could call me. I know it sounds like a bad movie line, but I wish we could still be friends through this. You know you mean a lot to me."

I wasn't sure I could put a smile on my face and deal with this in a cheerful way. *Sure, Kevin, let's be friends. I can still tell you all the strange things happening to me. You can tell me about Ann and how your relationship is going.*

"Dae?"

I drew a deep breath. "I don't want this to sound mean, but I can't do that right now. Maybe later when it's not so fresh. I know this isn't something you meant to happen, but here we are. I need some time and space to get over it."

He didn't answer for a long time. Finally he said, "I understand. I'm just worried about you. I don't know what it means that someone in a vision could see you and talk to you. It's a change in your gift. Be careful. Until you understand it, you don't know what will happen."

I closed my eyes and tried to tell my heart to stop being so stupid. It was like his words were part of me. I could feel them resonate, soothing the tension I'd felt from the dream.

When I opened my eyes, he was gone. He was out there with the wind, walking back to the Blue Whale Inn—without me. I couldn't express, even to myself, how much I wanted to be with him.

But encouraging him to want to be with me would be wrong. That poor woman had been through so much. Kevin was a good man, and I wanted him, but Ann needed him now. I hated it, and I hated myself in some ways for being willing to step aside and let him be with her. Maybe I should have fought for him.

I went inside again and thought about going back to

sleep. It wasn't going to happen. Instead, I went upstairs and put on jeans and a T-shirt. I waved to Gramps as I went out the door. "I'm going to Missing Pieces for a while. I'll see you later."

"Are you all right, honey?"

"Sure. Or if not, I will be. Love you, Gramps."

"I love you too, Dae."

I'd expected him to protest my going to the shop so late (or early), but he seemed to understand. Handling all my treasures made me happy and relieved some of my stress. It usually did, anyway. I hoped it would be the answer tonight too.

The Duck Shoppes on the Boardwalk were quiet and dark. The parking lot was empty. I ran up the stairs, a little nervous. Years ago, I wouldn't have thought anything of being here all night. I'd spent many nights on the burgundy brocade sofa in the shop.

But Mad Dog was right. Duck was changing. I didn't think it had anything to do with me being mayor. It was the times we lived in. People from outside were beginning to discover our little part of paradise. That would be fine if all of them were like Kevin, but some of them were like Derek Johnson. Duck would never be the same again. We'd have to grow and survive. But it wouldn't be the place where I grew up. It already wasn't.

I walked along the pearly gray boardwalk, the moon still illuminating the night and the waves lapping at the wood posts that supported the walkway. All the shops were dark. I knew Shayla met clients here at night from time to time. But not tonight, not this late. Wild Stallions was closed and shuttered too, only a flashing neon "Closed" sign marking the restaurant.

I slipped my key into the lock at Missing Pieces, opened the door and turned on the light before closing the door behind me and locking it. I sighed and immediately lost all my sense of panic. I was home.

I'd spent my life collecting things. Many of those collected treasures were still here on the walls and in the glass display cases. I loved all of them like they were my children. I sold them to keep the store open and bring in a little money, not because I wanted to. Finding these treasures was my true gift—my true passion. Nothing and no one could take that away.

Things had changed for me sincc my childhood when I could innocently hold someone's hand and help them find some item they'd lost—as I'd done for Old Man Sweeney.

Now those items spoke back to me, showing me where and how they were made as well as who owned them. The experience wasn't always pleasant. I'd had to sell many of the personal items I'd collected because I couldn't bear to touch them anymore. Their backgrounds were too terrible to envision every day. I had become more careful about what I picked up and purchased for the shop.

I put the teakettle on the hot plate and walked around, looking at everything, touching each piece and dusting where it was needed.

It was morning before I knew it, gray light creeping across the island. I was no closer to understanding my dream about Betsy or why Chuck could talk to me after he was dead. I had no idea who had killed Chuck. I wished it hadn't happened here.

Stan, the UPS guy, came and went. Missing Pieces was the UPS stop in Duck. I'd taken it on, hoping to attract more local customers. It hadn't worked out the way I'd planned. People came to pick up their packages and sometimes stayed to gossip but rarely bought anything. Being so dependent on tourists made it hard to keep up the rent in the off-season, which was most of the year.

I closed the shop and started back home. It seemed odd, since that was the reverse of what should've been happening. But I had to go home and change clothes so I could check to see if there was any child named Betsy Sparks at Duck Elementary School.

Trudy was just coming in for an early appointment at Curves and Curls. As usual she looked perfect with her smooth platinum hair and gorgeous tan. If she hadn't been my friend for as long as I could remember, I might be jealous. But Trudy and I had been through a lot together.

As we met on the boardwalk, she dropped her cloth shopping bags and threw her arms around me. "Oh, Dae, I've been thinking about you all night. I'm so sorry this happened to you. It's not fair. Old girlfriends aren't supposed to come back to haunt you."

"I'm okay," I lied. I didn't tell her about finding Chuck or my dream about Betsy. Trudy wasn't good at handling the weird stuff. "Kevin needs to be with Ann."

"And that's the kind of thinking that's going to make you die alone and unloved."

That's kind of harsh. "Maybe I'll find someone else. I'm not dead yet."

"But if you won't fight for him, how can you expect to win?"

"For once, I agree with Trudy!" Shayla, walking down the boardwalk toward us, chimed in. Her large dark glasses covered most of her face. "You need to get over there and kick that skinny, ex-FBI agent's ass!"

Trudy nodded in agreement. "That's exactly right. I'm sure everyone in Duck is going to treat her like something the sea dragged in. But we can't do it alone. You have to fight too."

"I don't know what the two of you have been drinking this morning," I said, hoping they weren't serious, but afraid they were. "But I want some. Where are you hiding it?"

Trudy laughed, but Shayla was dead serious. "Mock me if you want, but I can already see changes in your aura. Things are going to go bad for you, Dae, if you don't take control of the situation. I can help, if you like. I have a time-tested love spell that would have Kevin eating out of your hand."

August Grandin passed by us on the boardwalk. His face said that he'd heard some of what we'd been talking about. "Ladies," he greeted us. "Witches were never welcomed here in Duck. You recall the old tale about Maggie Madison."

"She was a witch," Trudy explained to Shayla. "I think the other Bankers may have killed her."

"Back in the 1600s," I clarified. "Not recently."

Shayla laughed. "I knew I hadn't seen any witches around here."

"Let's keep it that way," August said as he left us with the warning.

Trudy was more impressed than Shayla by his ominous words. "I've got an early appointment, Dae. Just let me know if there's anything I can do besides"—she glanced at Shayla—"magic or anything."

Once we were alone, I told Shayla of the previous night's occurrences. She ushered me into her shop, Mrs. Roberts, Spiritual Advisor. The name had been there on the shop when she'd arrived in Duck, left behind by a psychic who'd abruptly moved to Wilmington.

Unlike Missing Pieces, Shayla's shop, with its red silk curtains, tarot cards and crystal balls, exuded a feeling of mystery and magic. Enigmatic pictures hung on the walls, and unusual statues stared out from shelves—on days when I was in a bad mood, I found them positively frightening.

"So your powers have changed again." Shayla took off

her dark glasses and smoothed her hand down her coal black hair. Little silver bracelets jingled on her slim, brown arm. "It's probably this whole emotional problem between you and Kevin."

"That's ridiculous."

"Is it?" she demanded. "When did it start happening?"

"I went outside the coffee shop with Old Man Sweeney after Kevin and Ann left. But that doesn't mean I'm an emotional basket case. I'm fine."

She stared hard at me. It made me feel uncomfortable. "Let me tell you, Dae O'Donnell, you are *not* fine. Not by a long shot. You love that man, but you're willing to sacrifice that love to do the right thing. Does that about sum it up?"

I wanted to deny it, but it was true. Life would never be as good without Kevin to share it. "I still don't think that would make Chuck Sparks able to see me and talk to me."

"That's because you don't understand how all of this works." She spun slowly. "Everything magical works on emotion. The stronger the emotion, the better it works."

"This isn't magic, Shayla," I scoffed. "This is science. This is something your brain does. What does that have to do with emotion?"

"Okay. Let's talk science. A scientist will tell you that your brain chemistry is affected by emotion. You have endorphins flooding through you when you're happy. God knows what kind of terrible name they have for the bad stuff."

"I'm not saying I couldn't be affected by what happened," I argued. "But how would that play into Chuck coming back from the dead?"

"Let's take a glance in the looking glass." She sat at the small wicker table and invited me to do the same. "Can you face your demons?"

Chapter 7

"Bring it!" I said, sitting down. I was going to prove once and for all that a lot of what Shayla did was hocus-pocus. Some things, admittedly, were something else. "Magic" might be too strong a word. I was trying to make my point and not think about those other things.

We both looked into the crystal ball. It appeared to be very old, something I might have collected for Missing Pieces. Shayla said it had belonged to her great-grandmother in New Orleans.

The glass was clear when I first looked into it, but the more I stared, the hazier it got. I looked away then looked back to make sure it wasn't my imagination. The glass was still cloudy. "Do you have a mini fog machine?" I glanced under the table but saw nothing hidden there.

"Shh! We've made contact."

"With who?" And did we *want* to make contact with whoever it was?

I studied the crystal a little more carefully. An image began to form—Chuck Sparks in his suit and tie getting into the burgundy Lincoln.

"Is that him?" Shayla whispered.

"Yes. How are we seeing this?"

"Reruns from your vision, no doubt."

"I didn't see this. Maybe you should close it down now."

"It's not a TV, Dae. It sees what it wants to see."

I thought about Betsy. Maybe we could use this to our advantage. "I'm looking for a little girl. I think she may be Chuck's daughter."

As soon as I said the words, Chuck looked right up at me from the crystal ball. "Help her."

Why does this keep happening? I almost fell over trying to either push back or get out of the wicker chair. "How could he see me?"

"It's unusual, that's for sure." Shayla lazily got up from her chair. "Not unheard of. I didn't realize you were so close to him."

"I hardly knew him. I don't know why he decided to give me this message."

She shrugged. "The dead keep their own secrets."

"I wish they'd keep them to themselves."

"What? You got your answer. Go find that child. He won't rest until you do. I'm sure you wouldn't want to see his face behind you in the bathroom mirror next time you brush your teeth."

The idea made me shiver. "I don't understand any of this, and you're no help," I said accusingly. "But if he *does* have a daughter, I'll find her."

Shayla wasn't that impressed. "You do what you have to do." Her dark eyes narrowed. "Stay away from that woman with Kevin, Dae. Something bad is coming up in her future. She reeked of it yesterday. That woman will do no good."

"Then how am I supposed to fight for Kevin?"

She brought out a pink bottle. "My passion flower mixture will do it. He loves you. This will make it so he remembers that and doesn't even think about doing the right thing with *her*."

"No, thanks. Either he loves me and it works out, or not. You don't think she'd hurt Kevin, do you?"

"I don't know. She has problems."

"Okay. I'm going home now. See you later."

Less than an hour later, I had been home, eaten a little something, changed clothes and was at Duck Elementary School. Every nook and cranny of this place held memories for me. I'd fallen off of the climbing bars trying to impress Robby Maxwell when we were in second grade. I'd accidentally dumped a whole bowl of punch on myself at the fifth-grade dance. I couldn't exactly remember how that had happened, but people had talked about it for a long time.

I walked into the principal's office with a big smile and was greeted by Cathi Connor. She and I had gone through school together here. She'd been a pale, freckled girl—still was—whose mother brought her lunch to school each day. It cemented her reputation as a weird person, like me. My grandfather was the sheriff. That made me weird.

"It's good to see you, Dae!" Cathi hugged me. "We haven't seen you around much. We actually had Reading Aloud Day and you weren't here. Something up with you? Or were you just busy plotting how to kill Mad Dog?"

I laughed at that as we sat down. Who would've ever thought she'd be behind the school principal's desk? Or for that matter, that I'd be mayor?

"It's been hectic," I admitted. "You can't believe what all goes into a political campaign. Last time, no one ran against me. This time, Mad Dog has his posters everywhere."

"Well, at least *now* you won't have to worry about his smear campaign that was questioning your morals."

This was the first I'd heard of that topic. "What kind of morality are we talking about?"

"Oh, you know. That thing about you and the man from the Blue Whale Inn. Mad Dog was making you sound like a scarlet woman. Since you broke up with what's-his-name, that should take care of it. You have my vote anyway."

That was one way of looking at it. "Mad Dog can say what he wants. I don't think he'd be a good mayor even if he's been married and no one questions his morality. He's got the same old ideas, you know? We're not the same town anymore. We need new ideas."

Cathi applauded. "Brava! Nicely said. Sorry anyway, about the breakup. And right in front of everyone. People have no dignity anymore."

A subject change was needed, and since I hadn't come to discuss morality, or the lack of it, in Duck politics, I smiled and leaned forward a little. "I need your help, Cathi."

"What can I do for you?"

"I'm looking for a little girl who may go to school here. Her name is Betsy Sparks. Do you know her?"

"I wouldn't normally do this for anyone but members of the family, but since you're the mayor, I guess it's okay. Sure. Betsy Sparks is in first grade. She seems to be doing very well since the transfer."

"Transfer?"

"She's not from Duck. She looked at me, suddenly suspicious. "Why are you asking about her, Dae?"

She obviously hadn't heard about Chuck's death. I bit my lip, not wanting to be the one who told her.

And I didn't know what the chief had in mind. He might be keeping Chuck's death a secret to try and find the killer. I knew from being the sheriff's granddaughter that some information was never given out. But this was Duck—usually it was hard to contain.

If I told her, and the police *were* keeping Chuck's death a secret for whatever reason, I'd never hear the end of it from Chief Michaels. But what else could I say? It seemed to me that finding Betsy, if she was really missing, was more important.

Still I didn't want to jeopardize anything the chief was working on.

I decided to make something up. I really just needed to know if Betsy was there or not. "I heard she's read a lot of books. I was thinking about starting some kind of book club for kids who read a lot. You know, stickers, that kind of thing."

She smiled. *She doesn't know about Chuck.* "What a great idea! Let's go talk to her. Why didn't you just say so instead of sounding so mysterious?"

We walked down the quiet hallway—all the children were in class. Our shoes clicked on the shiny green tile. I hoped Betsy was in her classroom, though I wasn't sure what I'd say if she was there. I'd probably have to start a book club and buy stickers. But that would be fine.

It wasn't *rational* that she'd be here. I imagined all kinds of scenarios that would allow her to be at school, despite her father's death. Perhaps she didn't yet know that Chuck was dead. Maybe she didn't even live with him. Maybe she'd been visiting her mother, who'd dropped her off this morning. Anything would work for me.

Please let her be here.

"You said Betsy transferred recently," I said to Cathi.

"Yes. She came to live with her father. I haven't met her mom, so I assume she's out of the day-to-day picture."

"Do you know where she transferred from?"

"Somewhere on the mainland. I don't remember right

now. Chuck didn't want to talk about it when he enrolled her."

We got to a classroom where the little sign card on the door read "Miss Ames—First Grade." Cathi smiled, knocked and opened the door.

"Ms. Connor!" Miss Ames looked a little frazzled to see her there. "What can I do for *you*?"

"The mayor wants to see Betsy Sparks. Is she here today?"

Both women and all twenty children in the classroom looked around. There was one empty desk with a nameplate on it that read "Betsy."

"No." Miss Ames frowned. "She wasn't here yesterday either. I haven't heard anything from her father. I suppose someone from the office should check on her."

Cathi thanked her, and we left the classroom, walking back toward the office. "I really don't like it when teachers don't follow our student-absence procedures. She should have called home yesterday. Putting it off on the office isn't the answer either."

I was too stunned, wondering what I should do next, to reply. *Help her.* Chuck's words brought fear stealing into my soul. I knew he was talking about Betsy now. Something had happened to her when he'd been killed. Had she been with him that night?

"Dae, what's going on?" Cathi demanded.

It took me a moment to realize that she'd stopped walking. "I'm not sure yet. I'm sorry. I can't tell you any more right now. I will when I know something definite."

I left her there with her mouth compressed into a very thin line. I wanted to tell her what I knew, but Betsy's disappearance might be the very reason Chief Michaels had kept Chuck's death quiet. It seemed likely Betsy had been kidnapped.

Chapter 8

I called Chief Michaels. He wasn't at the office. Scott Randall said he'd gone to Manteo to talk with Sheriff Riley about Chuck's death. I asked if the chief was purposely keeping Chuck's death a secret. Scott didn't seem to know anything about that—or about Betsy.

If the chief didn't know about Chuck's daughter, telling him I saw her in a vision wasn't going to make a big impression. I could use the fact that she hadn't been at school for two days. I could save the chief some time by seeing what else I could find out.

There was only one thing to do. I could go and take a look at Chuck's house. I needed some proof, besides visions and dreams, if I was going to convince Chief Michaels to search for Betsy right away.

I wasn't sure what that proof would be. I hoped it would be something obvious. Chuck was dead. Betsy appeared to be missing, though I couldn't know for sure she wasn't with her mother. I didn't how those two things fit together. But if there were any answers, I was sure they'd be at Chuck's.

I drove the golf cart up to Chuck's cozy little brick house on Sand Dollar Lane. There was no car in the driveway, no sign of the burgundy Lincoln—*if* that was Chuck's car.

The yard was neat, grass and bushes carefully trimmed. Everything outside seemed to be in perfect order. The front door was locked, of course. Mail was sticking out of the box, like no one had checked it for a few days. Apparently, the police had left it as they'd found it.

I walked around the back, hoping to find the back door open or an easily accessible window. I didn't relish the idea of climbing up a trellis in my suit and heels to access a window, but I was going to get into Chuck's house no matter what.

The back door was locked too. No matter how much I shook the handle and threw myself against it, the portal wouldn't budge. I was fairly sure I'd injured my shoulder, though, from the way it hurt. Who knew they made doors so solid?

There were also no windows conveniently left open to catch the sweet morning breeze from the ocean. It took me about ten seconds to decide if I should break one of the windows. It seemed like it was the only way I was getting inside.

I picked up a decorative rock from the garden and wrapped it in my scarf, preparing to pitch the whole thing through the glass. As I put my arm back in throwing position, a hand stopped me.

"You know, this is how we first met—with you breaking into someone's house."

Kevin's voice and his hand on mine made me drop the rock. My heart zoomed up into my throat. "I wasn't planning on breaking into Miss Elizabeth's house that day. We didn't know for sure what had happened to her. I was going to call the chief for help, which I did."

"So what makes this different?"

I didn't have an answer. I was very glad to see him. He looked so tall and handsome standing there. Still this was an investigation. "Why are *you* here?" I asked, falling back on that time-honored tradition of answering a question with a question—even though Gramps had once told me that was a surefire way to tell if someone was guilty of something.

"I saw your golf cart in the driveway as I was going by. I thought you or Horace might need some help. But you haven't answered my question. What brings the mayor of Duck out on a nice day like this to engage in breaking and entering?"

I knew he wasn't going to go away until I explained, so I gave him the basic information I had. "That's why this is different. We know Chuck is dead, and I'm pretty sure his daughter is missing. I need some proof."

"I guess that makes sense." He shrugged and looked at the window I was going to break. "Let's see if we can find a way inside without breaking anything."

I tried not to look at him or admire his dark hair and ocean blue eyes. I tried not to remember that he tanned easily and he'd had sunburn only once while he was replacing the roof on the Blue Whale Inn.

"This door doesn't look too sturdy," he decided. With a quick jab of his shoulder against the wood, it swung open. I massaged my shoulder, which had obviously loosened it up for him.

I started to go in, but he held me back. "Are you armed?" he asked.

"No. I'm just looking around. You know I don't carry a gun."

He pulled a pistol out from beneath his blue hoodie. "We don't know if anyone is in there. Chuck is dead. His killer could be living in here, for all we know. I'll go in first."

"Won't that just scare them back at me?"

"If it does, I'll turn around and shoot them. But usually people run the other way when they see a gun."

As soon as we entered the house, it was easy to tell something was up. Everything inside had been trashed. Dishes, forks and glasses were thrown everywhere. Tables and chairs were overturned.

"Someone was looking for something," Kevin whispered. "Keep your eyes open, Dae."

He didn't have to tell me. I picked up a broken chair leg and brandished it before me like a club.

"No blood. No signs of a struggle. What are we looking for?" Kevin stood in the middle of the room.

"I don't know. Something that proves Betsy Sparks was here and that something happened to her when her father was killed."

"Okay. That's a tall order."

"I know."

We went slowly from room to room. Every room was demolished, like a hurricane had blown through. We went carefully across the living room and into Chuck's bedroom. Kevin paused and examined a laptop thrown on the bed. "They took the hard drive. That might be a clue about what happened to Chuck."

"There has to be something else."

"Not to put too fine a point on it, Dae, but you're the one who finds things. I'm just backup."

"My amazing finding abilities seem to be on vacation right now."

We finally reached a little pink and white room that I guessed was Betsy's. Even this was ripped apart—bedclothes tossed around and stuffed animals torn to pieces. "What were they looking for in her teddy bears?"

"Drugs. Jewels. Flash drives. There are plenty of things you can hide in a stuffed animal. I've seen a lot of things hidden in them."

"Well, we know she was here."

"But was she here when Chuck was killed?" Kevin asked.

"I don't really know if she was with him. I feel fairly sure he was killed at the Harris Teeter and someone tried to get rid of his body in the Atlantic. I didn't see her in the original vision set off by the medallion. I don't know where her mother is. All I really have is my vision about Chuck and my dream about someone taking Betsy against her will. And, of course, dead Chuck telling me to help her."

We'd reached the living room again. Kevin stopped walking. "I think you have enough to bring in the chief, Dae. Looking at this as a professional, I'd want to know where the little girl was in these circumstances, even if she's with her mother. You should call him."

I knew he was right. I just wished I had something more definite so we didn't have to go through the chief's usual *Oh, Dae had a vision* kind of thing. It would be nice to justify what I'd seen before the police ripped it apart.

Out of the corner of my eye, I saw something move, and went to investigate. I had to navigate through overturned furniture, broken knickknacks and torn-up books to reach the front-door area.

I was pretty sure that whatever had moved wasn't Betsy—too small. But as I searched through all the debris, I saw a doll that had been dropped by the front door.

I carefully picked up the well-loved doll and realized that this was a key to what had happened. Betsy had been holding it when someone took her away. I dropped it on the floor again before I could feel anything else from it.

What if she's dead? What if her last memories are imbued in this doll? The idea made my hands tremble and my mind almost numb with fear.

"What's wrong?" Kevin joined me in the entryway. "What did you find?"

I told him my thoughts. "I'm scared to hold it." It was blunt and brief but horribly true. I'd seen some terrible things since my original gift had changed and increased.

He put his hands on my shoulders as he leaned in close to me. "I'm here, Dae. I'll pull you back. I won't let you go."

Just for a moment, I had a brief vision of him saying almost the same thing to Ann. They'd been very close as partners. That was how they'd become romantically involved. They'd been with each other all the time.

Kevin was a very supportive person—very hands-on and empathic. Had he been drawn to me because I was gifted like Ann?

I forced myself back to the problem at hand. "I can do this, but thanks for being here."

"Always."

There was no hesitation on his part as he said it. I sighed and forced myself again to address the issue I was facing right now.

I started to pick up the doll again when something hissed and bit me. For a minute, I thought it was a snake. Gramps had been bitten by a cottonmouth out in the garage one day. He'd been sick for a while after, but he'd pulled through.

When I looked again, I saw that it wasn't a snake but a small black kitten with bright green eyes. It was backed into the corner, crouched on part of the doll. That was the movement I'd seen.

"It's a kitten," Kevin said. "Poor thing. It's probably starving and terrified."

I looked at the tiny but bloody wound it had inflicted on my finger. "I heard they took a cat from here. Probably didn't realize her kitten was still in the house. We'll have to get it out of here. I wish I had some gloves. That would make the job a lot easier."

The kitten kept hissing and snarling, all of its black fur standing on end. I didn't want to hurt it, but I didn't want it to hurt me again either.

Kevin came around from the other side with a pillowcase. He managed to sneak up on the kitten while it watched me. He scooped it up neatly into the cloth sack. I could still hear the kitten hissing and see it clawing at the material.

"There you go."

"Thanks. Don't tell me the FBI catches wild animals too."

"When the occasion warrants it," he replied. "Still want to do your thing?"

I nodded and tried to prepare myself for whatever I might see from the doll. No matter what, it would bring me another step closer to understanding what had happened to Betsy.

I picked the doll up and looked at her pretty china face. She had brown hair and blue eyes like her owner. The resemblance ended there because Betsy's face had been so vividly alive.

I felt the vision pull me in like a whirlpool until I was under it, inside it.

I couldn't open my eyes at first—or at least I thought that was the problem. Then I realized that my eyes were open—it was just so dark that I couldn't see anything. "Betsy?"

"Is someone here?" her tearful voice asked.

"Can you hear me?" I tried again.

"If someone is here," she cried, "please tell me. I'm very scared. Please don't leave me here alone anymore."

I tried again and again to talk with her. It was no use. I couldn't see her—she couldn't see or hear me this time.

I tried to pay attention to everything around me. The place smelled of wet sand, and somewhere nearby, water was dripping, but I couldn't hear anything else. What kind of place could this be that was so dark and silent? It seemed like a tomb. And what kind of horrible person would put a child here?

I came back out of the vision feeling cold and sick. I leaned against Kevin for a long time trying to absorb some of his strength and warmth. "I don't know anything more than I did a few minutes ago."

He held me close and whispered, "You have to let this go now. Let's call Chief Michaels and let him take care of it."

"He's not gonna like it."

"I can't think who would."

Chapter 9

I made the call that brought Tim and Chief Michaels to the house on Sand Dollar Lane. Kevin waited with me. We didn't talk much—just a few comments about the weather and other innocuous topics.

I felt awkward being with him now that we weren't in the throes of trying to find Betsy. I didn't know if I should ask after Ann or not. Obviously, he felt the same and didn't bring her up.

"What's going on here, Mayor?" Chief Michaels asked in a tired way, as though he was exhausted by the effort of having to ask yet again.

"I had a dream about Betsy Sparks. I went to Duck Elementary and then came here looking for her." I tried to stay on a narrow path of explanation. He didn't like the funny stuff, as he called my visions. I told him about the place I'd seen Betsy when I'd held her doll.

"Betsy Sparks? His daughter?" He rocked back on his heels. "Are you sure?"

"She's his daughter. I think she's about six years old. Her mother might have dropped her off with Chuck."

I explained what I believed to be true—that someone had murdered Chuck and possibly taken Betsy with them. I told him that she'd been absent from school and that Chuck had recently come to have custody of her. "I don't know who or where her mother is."

"That's super amazing!" Tim said. "Dae, you can see anything."

"Easy with the flirting, Officer Mabry," the chief reprimanded. "Is a dream the same thing as the vision you had about Derek Johnson? Because if so, I gotta tell you that it's not much help. As far as we can tell, Johnson is a two-bit errand boy for some high-powered folks on the mainland. They come down here, get all liquored up and do some things they regret later. I have a feeling that's what happened to Chuck."

"The house was a mess when we got in here," Kevin added with the smooth, no-nonsense tone of a professional. "You can clearly see someone was looking around. It must have been after your men checked it. Something is up here, Ronnie."

"You could just find out if Betsy is with her mother," I suggested. "Principal Connor didn't seem to know much about the mother, but I'll bet you can find out about her. Then we'd know if she'd been kidnapped."

Chief Michaels glared at me. "I didn't realize there was a child involved, Mayor. Now that we think there *might* be, we'll do whatever needs to be done to ensure her safety. Believe me, we will take this very seriously. You can go home and rest assured that we won't need you to break into any other residences. You know people pay our salary to keep those things from happening."

"I'm afraid that was my fault, Chief Michaels," Kevin cut in. "I was riding by and stopped to see what was going on. I tripped on the back step and fell into the door, which opened. I'll be glad to pay for any damages. But I think you've got bigger problems on your hands."

Chief Michaels looked at me, then studied Kevin. "No, sir. I think *you've* got bigger problems, Brickman. And I hope you didn't hurt your shoulder falling into the door."

"Thanks, Chief." Kevin smiled. "I hope all of it works out."

I stormed out of the house, angry to be excluded from the investigation. I tried to remind myself that what mattered was that the police were looking for Betsy. I couldn't do it by myself. Chief Michaels would do a good job, like he always did.

But he hadn't seen Betsy as I had, desperately fighting off some invisible abductor. He hadn't heard her voice echoing in the dark hell where they were keeping her. That was all on me. I was frustrated at not being allowed an active part in the search. I wanted to find Betsy *now*.

Maybe Shayla had been right about my emotions working overtime. Maybe the best thing was to go back to the shop and do what I was supposed to do.

"Dae?" Kevin caught up with me. "What do you want me to do with the kitten?"

He was still holding the flowered pillowcase. "Maybe you could use him at the Blue Whale to catch mice," I suggested.

"You know I've already got three cats that you 'rescued' for me. I don't think I need any more right now. What about you?"

"I've never had a cat." I considered the idea. "I don't think he liked me."

"You could bring him to the animal shelter."

I didn't like that idea very much either. "I'll see if I can find someone else to take him," I said, gently taking the pillowcase. "Thanks again, Kevin."

"Sure. I'll let you know if I hear anything else about the girl. I hope you'll do the same for me."

"You know I will." There it was again—that terrible awkwardness. We were both going to live in Duck. We'd have to get over it.

I smiled, my real feelings hidden behind it, and put out my free hand. "You've been a real help to the people of Duck, Kevin. Thanks for everything."

He hesitantly shook my hand, his much warmer fingers closing around mine. But I think he understood. "You're very welcome. I was glad to do it."

We parted ways—no long post-mission wrap-up over coffee at Missing Pieces or lasagna at the Blue Whale. It was sad, but things changed.

I went back to the boardwalk and stopped at town hall. Nancy helped me find a box that the kitten couldn't jump out of. I watched him for a while when I got to Missing Pieces as he tried his best to get out.

"You know I'm not feeling very friendly toward you right now," I told it. "You bit me really hard. That wasn't very nice, since I'm only trying to help Betsy."

I called around to find out what had happened to the other cat that had been taken from Chuck's house by the police. No one seemed to know. I asked Tim to check on it.

A customer came in to ask about the Christopher Haun lead-glazed pitcher displayed in the shop window. "What an interesting piece! What do you know about it?"

I ignored the kitten while I talked to the white-haired

woman, who was dressed casually but carried an expensive purse. "Christopher Haun did only a few pieces with this unusual compass star and a handle. He was a Union sympathizer from Greenville, Tennessee, who was hanged by the Confederacy in 1861."

"Oh my!" The woman looked uncomfortable at my description. Of course, she couldn't know how lucky she was not to have lived through Haun's experience herself, as I had the first time I'd touched the pitcher. "I don't think I want anything with that kind of dark history. What about these baskets?"

I explained about the sweetgrass baskets made by a woman I'd met who lived in Nags Head. "She was brought up making them, taught by her mother and grandmother. They're an exclusive design made only by members of her family."

She sneaked a peek at the baskets, probably looking for a price tag, but I never tagged items. "What do you want for them?"

I named my price. The woman was surprised but not in a good way. "I never expected such eclectic pieces—or such high prices in a shop way out here."

I smiled and watched her leave Missing Pieces. "I guess it was too much for her," I told the kitten. "She's not the right buyer. Wait and see. Someone will come in who doesn't mind that Christopher Haun was hanged or that sweetgrass is expensive."

I realized I was talking to the kitten again and went to put on the kettle and make some tea. I wasn't sure what I was going to do with the little animal. I didn't feel comfortable leaving him at the shop, but Gramps had never been a pet person.

The kitten meowed and kept circling the bottom of the box.

"You know, I bet you're hungry. You haven't had a mommy to feed you in a while. Let me see what I can find."

I closed the shop for a minute and walked down to Wild Stallions. Cody Baucom, one of the owners, was wiping water spots off of glasses. "I have a little fish he could have. And some milk," he offered. "Careful on the milk, though—it can make cats sick."

"Thanks for your help. I don't want him to starve while I try and find his mother."

He laughed. "He's not that young—must have teeth if he bit you, Dae. You don't have to worry about him. He'll eat when he's ready, when he trusts you."

I asked him if he'd like to take care of the kitten for a while, since he obviously had experience. He said he had three cats at home already. He wasn't open to taking this one.

I went back to the shop to feed the kitten and found the door open. It wasn't that unusual, since Gramps had a key and a habit of dropping in unexpectedly. It *could* be him.

Recent circumstances had made me a little less trusting, however. I picked up one of the small flowerpots from the boardwalk. I wasn't sure what kind of weapon it would make, but I felt somewhat safer holding it.

The shop seemed empty. The kitten was meowing like crazy but still in the box. I found a chipped saucer and put some milk into it.

"You like cats?"

I jumped, dropping the saucer and milk as well as the flowerpot. Everything crashed at my feet, milk flying on me and the box.

It was Ann. This was a moment I'd been expecting—and dreading. I knew she'd want to talk to me because I wanted to talk to her. Maybe "wanting" was the wrong verb. I felt like I *should* talk to her.

"No. Not really. Well, I don't know. I've never had a cat. Or a dog for that matter. I lived with my grandfather when I was growing up and he didn't care for pets." I was babbling, but I couldn't seem to stop.

"I was raised by a father in the Army. He never wanted to have pets either. Less to move around, I think."

Ann reached her hand into the box with the kitten before I could stop her. The kitten bit her too. She sucked on the little spot of blood that appeared. "Maybe this one needs to be put down."

At least it's not just me. "I don't think so. He's just scared and alone. He needs his mother."

"You talk to animals?" Ann sat back on her feet. "Kevin told me you were gifted. I've known others who did."

"No. I don't do that. At least not right now. It's always possible, I guess."

The kettle began to whistle. I switched off the hot plate and offered her a cup of tea. "I have Earl Grey, chamomile and peppermint."

"I'll have some chamomile, I think. Thank you."

She looked around the shop as I worked, then went to sit on the burgundy brocade sofa. I was nervous with her there. She seemed to be watching everything I did. I spilled some water, which hissed on the hot plate, and burned my finger. If I was trying to impress her, I was failing miserably.

"This is a wonderful place." Ann looked around at all my treasures. "I can see why you'd be happy here."

Her smile—her whole face—was filled with deep sadness. It created hollows in her high cheekbones and furrows in her brow. The world had not been kind to this woman. I knew some pretty tragic things about her, but there was still so much Kevin hadn't told me.

Has he told her everything about me?

"Thanks. I love it here. Do you find things too?" I asked.

"No. Well, not like this. Not since I was a child. My gift changed as I got older. It became more precise. That's how I got recruited into the FBI in college. I wanted to use my gift to help someone besides myself."

I felt very useless and selfish as I handed her a cup of tea. She was right. When I was younger, I'd thought about going out into the larger world and using my gift to really help people, but those thoughts had died away when I left college. I'd never even tried to control my gift or hone it. People in Duck had always been happy about it. That had been good enough for me.

"Everyone is different." She thanked me for the tea. "I didn't mean your gift is less important. You found the dead man. It's possible your gift is still maturing, Dae."

I sat at the other end of the sofa and studied her. She reminded me of a piece of driftwood that had been scoured by the wind and the sea. She seemed scrubbed clean of any emotion. Her eyes were flat and dull. I'd been careful not to touch her hand as I'd given her the tea. I didn't want to know the stories behind her eyes.

We were nothing alike except for the gifts we shared. *And Kevin.*

Kevin had been her salvation, a shining light in her dark world. Finding him again was the only thing that had kept her alive.

"You're not trying to read me, are you, dear?" Ann asked, interrupting my thoughts. "Trust me—it would be a waste of time. I've spent most of my life keeping myself safe from people like you."

"No. I'm sorry. It just comes and goes." I sipped my Earl Grey, trying to be a little less eager to rattle off my life story.

"Kevin said there's a child missing."

It was one of those "aha" moments. *So that's why you're here.* "Yes."

"How long?"

"I'm not sure. A few days, I think." I put my cup down. "Why?"

"I thought I might help. That was my expertise before." She got to her feet in one lithe movement, like a dancer. "The inn practically runs itself. Kevin doesn't need me to do anything. Not that I've *ever* been domestic. I thought this might be something I could do."

"I know what you did before."

She frowned. "I suppose you do. Kevin probably told you everything. He's got a dear heart, but he likes to talk. Lovers are like that, aren't they?"

In his defense, I wanted to tell her that I'd had to pry information out of him. It hadn't been easy. But I smiled and sipped my tea.

"Can you help me?" she asked. "With the police, I mean. They know you."

I shrugged. "Probably not. They wouldn't let *me* help."

"I see."

There was a wealth of meaning in those words, hidden nuances in her tone. The kitten kept watch in the box, staring intently at me.

"Do you have any ideas about where the child could be? I know you saw *something*, Dae."

The question made me feel like she'd go out looking for Betsy regardless of what the chief said. I realized that I could be doing that too. *When did I get to be such a stickler for the rules?*

Maybe Ann *could* help, even if she was doing so out of longing for her past glories rather than out of real concern for Betsy. Kevin said she was the best. I couldn't let my feelings about her, colored by my relationship with Kevin, keep someone from finding Betsy.

I thought about the dripping water and unrelenting darkness. *Not really much to go on.* I told Ann the little I knew. "They don't know who killed her father yet, but that might be a good place to start."

"What about the mother? Could she be involved?"

"I don't know. Chief Michaels is finding out what he can right now. He's not very psychic friendly. He'll put up with it to get someplace he can't find on his own, but he doesn't like it."

"Many of them never do. I was blessed to have Kevin as a partner all those years with the FBI. Even though he wasn't exposed to it earlier in life, he just seemed to understand."

The long moments ticked by. Ann finally put her teacup down on the table. "It was very nice meeting you, Dae. I'm sorry about what happened between you and Kevin. I didn't guess he'd be somewhere like this—that he'd given up the FBI. But we can make it better again. You'll see."

She didn't say good-bye. Just kind of wandered out of the shop.

It was drifting into late afternoon. There was a town council meeting that night. My suit was a little messed up from my breaking-and-entering project. I decided to call it a day and head home for a shower and change of clothes. That meant introducing Gramps to our guest.

I turned off the lights and got everything situated before I picked up the kitten's box. A look outside showed some dark storm clouds riding the horizon of the Currituck Sound. I knew I'd better move if I was going to keep the kitten dry.

As I turned back to pull the door closed, I saw Chuck Sparks sitting on the burgundy brocade sofa. "Help her," he said. "Help her."

Chapter 10

I stepped back into the shop, closed the door and put down the box. Desperation made me brazen. "It would be a lot more help if you'd stop saying that and tell me where she is. You're dead. You probably know. Tell me and I'll go get her."

He looked at me but didn't respond.

"You know, Shayla is probably right next door. Maybe she could talk to you. Don't move!"

I interrupted Shayla's weekly tarot-card reading with Mr. Davenport, who was looking for his third wife. Shayla had told me that he thought he needed her help to find the perfect mate, since the first two wives had left him.

I dragged her back to Missing Pieces, but it didn't matter—Chuck was gone.

"I could've told you if you'd given me a chance," she said. "He's contacting you, not me. Why didn't you talk to him when you had the chance?"

"I tried. He keeps saying the same thing over and over. There's no conversation."

"Maybe that's all he can say," she argued. "Did you ever think of that? Not every spirit has an easy time talking to the living. I'm surprised he can say anything to you since you're not related. Now excuse me while I go back and try to help this poor man find a lady who will make him happy for a while."

I was sorry I'd bothered her. This time when I was ready to leave the shop, I didn't look back as I closed the door.

The kitten settled back in the box as we went down the boardwalk. The new kayak shop at the end of the walkway was cutting new stairs that would lead to the sandbar right off the boardwalk. This would allow people to push off from there and into the sound after they'd bought or rented their kayak. It was an ingenious idea.

For as long as I could remember, the town had held parties on the sandbar when the tide was very low. All kinds of bottles and other artifacts from the 1920s and 1930s had been found there. Apparently the hunters who'd visited Duck at that time liked their rye whiskey.

The first raindrops started to fall as the kitten and I reached the golf cart. I was glad I had transportation for once. Usually I liked walking and the cart was a nuisance for the short trip home. Not today since there were two of us, especially since the kitten was terrified once he heard the first raindrop hit the box. He started hissing and tearing at the cardboard.

"It's okay," I told him and risked putting my hand in the box again.

This time, he calmed down right away and started staring at me again. His mouth moved but no sound came out. The great green eyes were almost hypnotic. I thought about what Ann had said about people communicating with animals.

"Hi, Dae." Tim startled me. I hadn't noticed his police car in the parking lot until then. "Whatcha got in there?"

"A kitten. Want it?"

The kitten started wailing loudly, narrowing his eyes and swishing his tail.

"No thanks. What are you going to do with it?"

"I'm taking care of it for a friend. No word on the cat from Chuck Sparks's house yet, huh?"

"They probably took it to the shelter at Kill Devil Hills. Who knows if it's even still alive."

"Don't say that. I think this kitten needs its mother." I looked down at the kitten again, but his agitation had eased and he was sitting back staring at me again.

"Well maybe you won't have to keep it for long." He leaned close with his hand on the top of the golf cart, ignoring the raindrops that splattered on his uniform. "I heard they found the girl's mother."

"Really? Is she somewhere around here?"

"Nope. We found an address for her in Richmond. There was no working phone, so we couldn't contact her directly. We contacted the Richmond Police about it instead. The chief didn't want to drive up all that way to question her. You know how the town council keeps track of how much we spend on gas each month."

"Good idea. I hope she's with her mother."

"Of course she is. Sparks probably only had that girl for visitation. She's probably up there with her mother right now. Problem solved."

I wished I thought it was that easy. But if Chuck had her only for short visits, she wouldn't have been enrolled in Duck Elementary. I didn't say anything to Tim about my vision of her. I hoped I was wrong about the darkness and the dripping water. I didn't want Betsy to be in that awful place.

I waved good-bye and hurried through some light traffic, trying to keep the kitten dry as the raindrops kept coming from the Atlantic side. With no doors, the golf cart offered limited protection from the elements.

We finally made it home. I pulled the golf cart into the shed and ducked in through the back door. Gramps called out that he was making chili—"You'll need it tonight at the town meeting. You know Mad Dog will try every way he can to upstage you."

I was trying to move away and up the stairs to my room as we talked, hoping he wouldn't notice the box. "I don't need chili to take care of him, but thanks for making it."

He laughed. "What have you got in there? It must be one of your treasures that just couldn't stay at the shop. Let's see it."

"I have to clean it up," I replied. "It's really dirty. I wouldn't want anyone to see it this way. That's why I brought it home. But I'm sure it's going to be a real treasure."

At that moment (of course) the kitten started howling and hissing again. There was no way to hide the fact that something alive was in the box.

Gramps's scowl looked as angry as the gray skies outside. "Is that a *cat*?"

"A kitten, actually. He belongs to Betsy Sparks. He couldn't live at that house all alone with nothing to eat. Kevin couldn't take him. I didn't know what else to do."

"You could take it to the shelter."

"I didn't have time. Maybe you'd like to run him down there for me tonight."

He held up his hands like he was fending off an attacker. "Not me! You can take it tomorrow. You know how I feel about pets, Dae. Remember that time you tried to keep that fish you caught? Pets just don't work out. They're smelly, mean and unpredictable."

"Okay then. Just for tonight. I have to change clothes for the meeting. I'll see you in a few minutes."

"Make sure you lock that critter in your room," he was saying as he went back into the kitchen. "I don't want to see it sneaking around trying to steal food all over the kitchen."

I took the box up to my room and put it on the bed. I was a little angry at Gramps's attitude, but it wasn't like he'd changed. He'd always felt that way each time I'd brought home any animal that I'd found somewhere.

The kitten was going to have to stay here for the night. Gramps didn't really want to throw him out on the street. We could decide what to do in the morning.

"You know, you're really beautiful," I told him, running my hand down his thin body. "But you need to eat, don't you? I'll find you something. Don't worry."

As I looked into his green eyes again, he started purring loudly and rubbing against my palm. I sensed something from him—not a vision like those I experienced when I touched an inanimate object—more like feelings or emotions.

Beautiful!

The word seemed to come back at me from the animal.

I jumped away. This wasn't happening. I was just stressed and influenced by Ann talking about people who communicated with animals.

I couldn't waste any more time thinking about it. I stripped off my dirty clothes and jumped in the shower. It wouldn't help my election bid to be late for a town meeting.

I dried off quickly, thinking about Betsy and Ann, me and Chuck. The whole thing was almost like a bad joke. I hardly knew Chuck, yet here I was with his kitten, looking for his daughter and hoping to solve his murder.

Ann was the wild card, coming out of nowhere into a

situation she thought she could understand. I wondered if helping find Betsy would make her feel normal again.

I pulled on a nice blue cotton skirt and found a clean jacket that matched. I couldn't find a dressy blouse, so I wore a new white Duck T-shirt from the summer. We had new ones made every year.

The outfit looked okay, I decided. Like I was trying to make a statement about Duck and what it meant to me. I hoped that's how it would look to everyone else.

I combed my hair and slipped my feet into sling backs, grabbed my straw pocketbook and headed back down the stairs—after closing the bedroom door, of course.

Gramps was in a better mood, since I wasn't dragging the kitten around in the box. He told me all about his fishing excursion on his charter boat, the *Eleanore*. The man he'd taken out on the sound was a well-to-do investment banker from Raleigh who'd booked another trip for later in the year.

"You should've seen this young fella's face when he pulled in his first fish. He was as happy as a kid at Christmas. You never know how people are going to react."

"I'm glad it went well for you."

"Ronnie told me about you and Kevin breaking in over at the Sparks's place looking for his daughter. I know you know better. Kevin sure knows better. You're lucky Ronnie didn't want to cause you any trouble. If you want to be mayor again, honey, you gotta be more careful."

"Finding this little girl is important to me. I can't let it go—even if it hurts my chances to be mayor again."

He hugged me. "I understand. There were too many cases like that for me when I was sheriff. What about you and Kevin?"

I put my bowl in the sink. "There is no Kevin and me

anymore." I started to tell him about my visit from Ann, but there wasn't enough time. "I have to go."

"I think you're wrong about Kevin, honey," he yelled after me. "A man like him doesn't go around breaking the law for a woman who's just a friend. Mark my words."

Chapter 11

By seven P.M., the town hall meeting room was packed, as always. There might be only 586 full-time residents in Duck, but they were all interested in what went on and wanted to know how and why things happened.

The problem was that town hall was very small—two offices and the meeting room that could hold about a hundred people, and then only if they were squished in like sardines. We needed more room to grow, but money was tight.

I'd sat through a lot of meetings about grants and loans to build a new town hall without breaking our budget. Nothing had materialized yet—but when I saw the twinkle in our town manager's eyes, I had a feeling that was about to change.

"Good evening, Mayor," Chris Slayton said to me. He held a large roll of plans under his arm. He was an energetic man in his late thirties who was always coming up with new ideas for Duck. He wasn't from here, but we were lucky to have him and his experience.

"I think you must have some good news for us," I said as I took my place behind my nameplate and gavel.

"You'll have to wait and be surprised."

I was glad to see he was wearing a Duck T-shirt with his sport coat and pants. We almost looked like twins, with our similar height and our brown hair. It gave the appearance of a conspiracy between us, both of us showing our Duck side.

With people standing in the outer offices, peeking in, I banged my gavel to bring the council meeting to order.

The finance committee, planning and zoning board, and waste management department gave their usual reports. Chief Michaels wasn't there to present his monthly update on police activities, but Officer Randall did an excellent job filling in. As usual, there'd been a few break-ins and thefts of big-ticket items like flat-screen TVs and boats. Most of those incidences had occurred at the houses that sat empty during the off-season while their owners stayed on the mainland.

Officer Randall went quickly through Chuck's death, only mentioning the homicide in the barest terms. I knew the chief had briefed him. There would be plenty of questions from citizens during the public-comment portion of the meeting. Surprisingly, the audience waited patiently without any outbursts until we got to that part of the agenda.

Just before the line of questioners could begin asking about what had happened to Chuck and where the police were with the investigation, Mad Dog requested a five-minute recess. I'd noticed him looking around as though he were upset about something. He'd been suspiciously quiet throughout the beginning of the meeting, then restless during the next part.

"What's wrong with him?" Nancy whispered. She sat

beside me at the council table taping the minutes of the meeting and taking notes for her write-up.

"You're asking the wrong person," I muttered back. "I don't understand most of what he does."

But a few minutes later, when Mad Dog returned wearing the same Duck T-shirt Chris and I had on, it was easy to understand what had been bothering him tonight. Obviously he'd been upset that Chris and I were wearing the T-shirts. He'd excused himself to put one on in place of his usual shirt and tie.

"Good grief!" Nancy chuckled so just the two of us could hear. "Is he for real?" There was some muttering and a couple of cackles from the audience, then we got on with the rest of the town's business.

Most of the questions and concerns from our citizen speakers had to do with Chuck's death and how it affected them. Two people said they didn't feel safe in Duck anymore and wanted to know what the police were going to do about it. Officer Randall answered their questions the best he could, never showing impatience or irritation with them. The chief wouldn't have been so calm.

Most of the residents just wanted to have their concerns heard, especially the older residents. Twenty years ago, when I was growing up, there was no such thing as a murder in Duck. There were the occasional thefts and a few fishermen who went missing. But no terrible crime like murder ever happened in Duck. People were proud of that.

I didn't know what to say—except that growth had a price. The police did their best, but with twenty-five thousand people living here during the summer, bad things could happen. Not that I was sure the person who'd killed Chuck—and probably kidnapped Betsy—had come from outside the town.

Unfortunately, even if we wanted to, we couldn't just

shut down Duck and keep the place to ourselves. We were going to have to find ways to deal with change.

Two older ladies—Mrs. Fitzsimmons and Mrs. Daniels—were concerned that there was no library in Duck. They had to go to Corolla, a few miles up the road, to get books at the library. They wanted to know when Duck was going to get a library.

Mad Dog rolled to his feet, pulling down hard on his T-shirt, which was about a size too small.

It was time for him to do some grandstanding. He told the ladies it was a shame that they had to use the library in Corolla, and if they'd vote for him for mayor, he'd see that a library was opened in Duck. "It's high time," he pronounced with a *humphing* sound. "Someone should've done something about it long ago. Duck residents aren't second-class citizens!"

I saw librarian Althea Hinson roll her eyes. We all knew the county library system had barely enough money to maintain its current branches. If someone would've called Mad Dog on his campaign promise, he would've looked silly.

But the two older ladies simpered and smiled at him and thanked him for his time. There was no hope for situations like these, and I refused to lie to people just to get their vote. Maybe I'd be sorry later, but I didn't want that kind of lie coming back on me six months after the election. Sometimes things just didn't work the way you wanted them to. I couldn't produce a Duck library any more than I could guarantee all the fresh produce people wanted at the stores in January!

Finally, it was Chris's turn to give his report. I was so glad, I almost thanked him when I announced it.

He had a slideshow presentation that went along with his bundle of maps and pictures. "I've found a way for the town to build a new public building that will give us more room to conduct town business," he began, excitement in his face and voice. "And I believe we can throw in a new feature that will not only be exciting for residents and tourists, but will also add the vital function of taking some of the foot traffic off of Duck Road."

This was more for residents, since all of us on the council had seen the presentation many times before. Contracts and project plans had already been formalized. We were just waiting for the go-ahead on the money.

It was a long presentation, showing where the funds to build the new town hall would come from. The building would be erected on town property that was part of Duck Municipal Park. The proposal was to create a boardwalk that would link the park, town hall, the Duck Shoppes and most of the commercial property in town. Chris reminded everyone that the North Carolina Department of Transportation had rejected the idea of pedestrian crosswalks across Duck Road.

"In the winter when there aren't so many people, it's not a big deal," he said. "But when we're full of twenty-five thousand people in the summer, it becomes a major hazard getting all those people up and down safely."

I noticed that Mad Dog's eyes were slowly closing as he rested his head on his hand, pretending to be listening. When the audience burst into spontaneous applause after the presentation, he jerked his head up, startled.

"Well," I announced after the audience had quieted, "I think we're all in favor of this plan already. All we have to do is vote to accept the money for the project. Would you like to vote on that, Council?"

Of course, having seen the residents' enthusiasm for the project, the council members voted unanimously in favor of it. Everyone seemed delighted.

The meeting was over soon after Chris's presentation. I

was glad to see that he was immediately swallowed up by residents of Duck who loved his ideas. Mad Dog pushed his way through the crowd and stood close to Chris as though the project was his idea too.

I noticed a professional photographer taking picture after picture of Mad Dog. Maybe my opponent even had a campaign manager too. He was really serious about winning the election.

"You need to get down there," Councilwoman La Donna Nelson pointed out to me. "He's going to hog up all the glory."

La Donna was Chief Michaels's sister. With her flowing gray-white hair and bright blue eyes, she could not have looked, or been, more different from her brother. La Donna was an artist who had a strong voice for keeping Duck small and under control. She'd begun the first drive to incorporate when the big stores started pounding on Duck's back door.

"He can take all the pictures he likes, but what's he going to do with them?" I asked. "I don't see a newspaper reporter or anyone from a TV station."

"He could send them to the media, Dae. Don't be so sure of the fact that he'll be ignored. And don't take it for granted that he won't beat you. I want to see him retire from Duck government next year—not take your place."

I realized she was probably right. I didn't really consider Mad Dog a threat, but I probably should. He'd lived here longer than I had, was probably better known because of his glory days and definitely had a bigger mouth.

But jumping in on the group congratulating Chris didn't seem like the appropriate time to shine either. "I'll do something later."

She gathered up her folder and briefcase. "Don't wait too long. Maybe you should be holding press conferences about the dead man and his missing daughter. That could get some attention."

"Attention from whom?" I asked, but she uttered a few more words of wisdom and was gone. And what would I say? I wasn't sure I could purposely use that as a campaign strategy. First of all, it could backfire, with Mad Dog accusing me again of being soft on crime. Second, I could be thought of as insensitive.

That wasn't me. I'd have to think of something else. Maybe I could bake brownies for the whole town and give everyone an antique.

That sounded worse than doing nothing. La Donna was right. I needed a strategy.

I was getting ready to leave when Officer Randall stopped me. "The chief would like to have a word, Mayor, if you have a few moments."

"Of course. Where is he?"

"He's at the station, ma'am. With the FBI."

Chapter 12

"The FBI?" I asked as we walked out of the meeting room together. Most of the citizens still wanted to stand around and talk. We had to excuse ourselves all the way to the door on the boardwalk.

"Yes, ma'am. We found out earlier this evening that the little girl isn't with her mother in Richmond. It looks as though you may be right and she might be in harm's way."

I glanced back at all the excited Duck residents. Too bad I couldn't parlay his words about me being right into a campaign slogan. "Thanks for telling me."

He nodded a little awkwardly, holding the patrol car door for me to get in. We drove down to the Duck Fire and Rescue Building, which housed both the police and volunteer fire departments. It made sense to situate both groups at a single location, since they complemented each other in many cases. Also, though the two forces had a massive number of volunteers, each employed only a few paid professionals.

I was surprised to see so many cars in the parking lot. Usually only two were here at this time of night—one for the fire department, one for the police.

But that was nothing compared to the changes inside. Dozens of laptops were set up on several tables. Groups of men and women in dark suits hovered around them like bees after honey. Phones were ringing, and large boards full of diagrams and pictures were propped up on desks.

"Come this way, Mayor." Officer Randall led the way to the chief's office. He knocked once on the closed door (I'd never seen the chief's door closed before), and the chief called for us to come in.

As soon as I saw the weeping woman in the corner, I knew she was Betsy's mother. The chief was sitting behind his desk, scowling, while another man paced the floor with a cell phone to his ear. Yet another man sat opposite the chief, watching his pacing colleague.

"I hope you were able to make it through the meeting," the chief said. "I called Scott and let him know what happened. Bad enough I couldn't be there. I didn't want to interrupt everything. Did he do a good job?"

"He was great. People were worried, but I think he put their minds at ease. As much as anyone could right now."

I sat down in the nearest empty chair, next to the man already sitting. He nodded absently and introduced himself. "Agent Dawson, ma'am." He was an FBI agent specially flown in from Richmond because he had experience finding missing children.

Ignoring the interruption, the chief went on. "That's good. That's very good," he said. "I don't know how much Scott told you about what's going on here—"

"I'm sure he didn't say anything he shouldn't."

"Of course." The chief looked at the man on the cell phone, who was still pacing the floor, and stood up. "Let's find another room to talk."

There were only so many other rooms in the building. Frustrated with finding every nook and cranny full of people, the chief opened the door to the break room and we went in there.

"I'm sorry about this mess, Mayor. I was hoping not to drag you into this any further, but we just learned that Chuck Sparks *was* killed in the Harris Teeter parking lot. We found traces of blood that we believe belonged to him. That makes you a witness, in a manner of speaking."

"I understand." *He's trying to protect me.* And here I was angry at being cut out of the investigation. You never knew what people were thinking. "What can I do?"

"Well, it seems the mother, the former Mrs. Sparks, left her daughter with Chuck about two weeks ago. She was moving from Raleigh to Richmond for a new job and was uncertain of where she was staying. She'd planned to come back and get the girl when she was settled."

"So that's why none of us knew anything about Betsy," I said. "If she'd been here a little longer, everyone would've known her."

"Exactly. That leads us to believe, as you said at the house today, that the people who killed Chuck could have the girl. There haven't been any ransom demands—at least not to the mother. It's still early days, although the FBI likes to get involved in these cases during the first few hours. No reason to panic yet."

"But whoever killed Chuck might not have known about Betsy's mother. They might've been as surprised as us that he had a daughter."

"That's true. But we can't assume anything. At this point, we're working on the theory that she's alive and with the people who killed Chuck."

"I believe she's alive, Chief. I've seen her." I explained again about my vision of where she was being kept.

"And that *could* be accurate," he admitted. "But the best way to find her is probably to find the people who killed Chuck. If she's alive, they'll know where she is."

"What do you need from me?"

"Well, I was thinking that since your vision of Chuck being killed at Harris Teeter was accurate, you might be able to recall some other details about the assailants."

I thought back to the vision I'd had from the medallion. I couldn't see the person who killed Chuck—just the store and the burgundy Lincoln. "I'm sorry," I told him after I explained what I'd seen. "That's all there is. Betsy was sitting on the same car in the first vision I had about her."

"Let's take a look at the DMV files and see if that's Chuck's car. Last time I saw him, he was driving a baby blue BMW—but you know how those real estate people like to change cars."

We went back into his office. The man on the phone was sitting down now in the chair I had vacated, nervously drumming his fingers on the chief's desk with Agent Dawson beside him. "This is a bad time to disappear, Chief Michaels," he said. "We need to get all of our ducks in a row."

"That's exactly what I was trying to do, Agent Kowalski," the chief explained. "This is Mayor Dae O'Donnell, the *gifted* woman I was telling you about."

Before I could shake his hand, Betsy's mother ran over to us and all but threw herself on me. "I'm Melinda Lafferty, Betsy's mother. Have you talked to her? Have you seen her recently? Is she still alive? Please tell me she's still alive."

"As far as I know, she's still alive," I blurted out, wishing I could take it back when I saw the look of relief on her tearstained face. How much worse was it going to be for this poor woman if Betsy was dead now? It had been hours since my vision of her from the doll. I felt like she was alive, but I knew I could be wrong.

"Thank God! And thank you!" She hugged me and sobbed into my shoulder.

Agent Kowalski quickly asked Agent Dawson to lead Melinda back to her seat in the corner. He stuck out his hand and introduced himself. "I'm Agent Pat Kowalski, Mayor O'Donnell. I'm in charge on this case. I've heard you are very talented in this area—finding lost things. I hope you'll be willing to work with us to find this little girl."

Agent Kowalski was tall and very thin. He looked as though he'd recently lost weight—his suit was too big for him and hung badly. Even as he was speaking to me, he was kind of shaking his arm and leg. I thought he might have a nervous twitch. He asked me to sit down again and couldn't seem to stop shaking his leg.

"I'll do what I can to help."

"Would you be willing to meet one of our sketch artists and help him come up with a face?" he asked.

"I'm afraid I didn't see the killer's face."

He briefly looked surprised. "Okay. I probably don't understand your process. What *did* you see? Can you find a way to express what you *saw* so we can use it to find the girl?"

I told him about the Lincoln. Besides Betsy and Chuck, that was all I'd seen. I was sure he didn't want a picture of dead Chuck. I didn't mention that part either.

"Okay. Okay. We can work with that," he rattled off in his nervous manner.

Tim came in and winked at me as he handed the chief a note.

"Well, this confirms it." The chief read the note. "DMV has only one car registered to Chuck Sparks—a light blue BMW. I guess the Lincoln doesn't belong to him."

Was it my imagination or did the chief look annoyed because I didn't have better information to share with the FBI? Was he embarrassed that I didn't know more?

"But it might belong to the killer." Agent Kowalski studied me as he gnawed on his lower lip. "How would you feel about being hypnotized, Mayor O'Donnell? We might get something from that. Sometimes it helps nonprofessional psychics to wrap it up better. Maybe there's something more that you saw and didn't realize was important."

He made some awful air quotes with his fingers when he said "saw."

"I don't think so. I'm not exactly sure how my process works either, but I'm sure some other visions will come to me. They always do."

"Okay. I understand. That's fine. We can work with that."

I glared at Chief Michaels, wondering if he knew what Agent Kowalski had been planning on putting me through. I wished at that point that he'd change his mind again and decide he didn't want me to be involved. I was beginning to feel like a lab rat.

Another agent peeked his head through the door. "There's someone to see you out here, Kowalski."

"See me? What does that mean? I'm not 'seeing' anyone right now. This isn't a social—hello!" Kowalski left the room abruptly.

I looked through the blinds and saw Ann and Kevin. Agent Kowalski was shaking Kevin's hand. He greeted Ann with a hug. She caught my eye, and I looked away.

"Who is it?" the chief asked behind me. "That's Brickman—who is she?"

"His fiancée," I answered, hoping my words didn't sound as tight as they felt.

He raised his eyebrows but didn't say anything. I was surprised when he patted me on the shoulder.

Agent Kowalski came striding back into the office, a big grin on his face. "You're fortunate, Ms. Lafferty. This is Ann Porter, one of the finest psychics who ever worked for the FBI. We were at Quantico together. It was a terrible blow for us to lose her. But she's willing to be a private consultant on this case. And this is Kevin Brickman. He was an agent too before he decided to quit and make lasagna full-time." Kowalski patted Kevin heartily on the back. "We're gonna find your little girl."

Melinda brightened considerably, wiped her eyes, and tried to stop crying. "Thank you. Bless you all for being here."

Agent Kowalski spoke to the other agent in the room while Melinda eyed Ann and Kevin with a mixture of hope and desperation. Agent Dawson, apparently Kowalski's aide, came close to me and said, "If you'll come with me, Ms. O'Donnell, I'll have someone take you home. I don't think we'll have need of your services after all. Thanks for coming in."

His tone was so smooth—so rote—I knew he'd said it many times before. "That's fine," I said, trying not to look at Ann or Kevin. They were the experts. I felt awkward and unwanted. I couldn't even tell them what the killer had looked like in my dream.

I left the office. Scott was waiting for me, hat in hand. "I'll take you home, if you like, ma'am."

Considering it was late and a long walk home from the

station, I agreed. I could only hope this meant that dead Chuck and Betsy would start showing up in Ann's dreams and visions—or whatever her *process* was.

It was mean and a little spiteful of me, but I was tired and that was how I felt.

Scott dropped me off in the driveway, and I entered the house as quietly as I could. I knew Gramps would probably be in bed by then.

To my surprise, he was asleep on the recliner and the little black kitten I'd left locked in my room was curled up in a ball, asleep on his lap.

I shook him awake. "What's this? I thought you hated pets."

Gramps looked down at his lap. "The thing kept howling up there, Dae. I couldn't hear the TV. I let him out and he was quiet. I don't know what he's doing on me."

But he didn't throw the kitten down either, I noticed.

"How'd the meeting go? Mad Dog give you a hard time?"

I told him about Mad Dog's Duck T-shirt and the new town hall. We talked about the boardwalk idea—then I told him about the unexpected turn of events that had taken place after the meeting.

"You're best out of it anyway, with the FBI involved," he said. "They play hardball, Dae. Let Ronnie handle it."

"You're right. I have plenty to do campaigning against Mad Dog and running Missing Pieces. I'm sure they'll find Betsy without me. After all, they have the best psychic in the FBI helping them." I leaned down and kissed his cheek. "Good night. What are we going to call the kitten?"

"Nothing. We aren't naming anything. We're just keeping it until the little girl comes home, right?"

"That's right. And I hope that will be soon."

He shook his head. "I hope so too, honey. I only worked one kidnapping case in my whole career. It was the wife of a millionaire who lived in Nags Head. They say every hour the victim is missing makes the chances of finding them that much lower. We never found that woman from Nags Head. I don't like to think what might be happening to that little girl out there all alone."

Neither did I—but it was all I *could* think about.

I got ready for bed and started to pull back the comforter—only to find the kitten lying on it.

"Oh? You don't want to sleep in the box now?" I asked him.

He flexed his claws on my pillow and settled in a little deeper. I managed to get in around him and tried to settle down for the night. My mind wouldn't let me.

Where could she be?

Perhaps the dark, silent place I'd sensed in my last vision was a cave near the water. But as far as I knew, there were no caves around Duck.

It could be a leaky basement, I thought, punching my pillow and rolling over. There were plenty of those in the area—storm cellars and root cellars as well. Too many possibilities to count.

I finally fell asleep and found myself at Harris Teeter again.

There was no sign of a blue BMW in the parking lot, at least not from my vantage point. Only the burgundy Lincoln was there.

Had Chuck brought Betsy with him to meet someone here this late at night?

No—even though I'd seen her here with the Lincoln—I knew from touching the doll I'd found that she'd been taken from the house. Why do I keep seeing her here?

Betsy was standing in the parking lot, holding her doll. She was crying. "My daddy is dead. I want my mommy. Please let me call my mommy."

I looked around as carefully as I could. There was no one else with us. The car. The doll. The girl. That was it. Not even dead Chuck—thankfully.

"Can you help me?" she asked, staring right at me.

"Your mom is here in Duck." There was no point in pretending she couldn't see me. I'd have to worry about why and how later. "We don't know where you are. Do you know? Do you know who took you?"

"A man. He drives this car."

"Where did he take you?"

"I don't know. I-I fell asleep. I woke up and it was dark. I don't know." She started crying again.

"It's okay." I tried to comfort her. "We're going to find you."

"Am I dead like my daddy? Is that why I can't come home?" The horror on her face broke my heart. I wanted to hold her and bring her back to her mother.

"We'll find you," I promised, hoping I was right. "Can you show me the place again where they're keeping you?"

Instantly, it was completely dark. The sound of dripping water along with the smell of mold, dirt and maybe rotten garbage filled my senses.

"Don't stand up," she whispered. "It's very small in here. You might hit your head like I did."

I'd thought I already was *standing, but at Betsy's words, I realized I was lying in a shallow indentation in the ground.*

I screamed—and found myself back in my bed.

The kitten hissed at me as I threw back the comforter and reached for the phone. Then he curled up on my lap.

The other end of the line rang repeatedly before it was finally picked up.

"Hello?" Chris Slayton asked in an uncertain tone. Probably not used to getting many phone calls in the middle of the night.

"Chris? It's Dae."

"Mayor?"

"That's right. Do you have a map or chart that shows all the houses in Duck that have basements? What about commercial property?"

"I-I don't know. I could look—"

"Great! Let's do it right away."

"Now?"

"There's no time like the present, Chris. I'll meet you at town hall in ten minutes."

Chapter 13

We huddled over the maps together in the meeting room at town hall. The first map had been drawn up by a group of engineers at the request of a dozen Duck residents who'd worked tirelessly toward the town's incorporation. They'd wanted to prevent several big-box stores from opening and destroying everything we loved about our community. This map had been the first serious step toward that goal.

In addition to including all of Duck's geographic features, the mapmakers had done their best to show every existing house lot in Duck, so we'd have a model to work with as the town grew. They'd used a map legend to indicate whether each house was raised on stilts—a common style for beachfront homes—or had a basement.

A newer map, created just two years ago, left out some of the details from that first map, such as the basements and even Rodgers Pond. James Millford's old shed, which he claimed his great-grandfather built a hundred years ago, wasn't on it either. His grandfather ran a popular rye whiskey still out of it for fifty years. Gramps had told me stories about that place.

"Which one do you want to use?" Chris asked, yawning. "For property values, the new one is better."

"I think the old map would be better in this case." I told him briefly about Betsy and my desire to find her. He deserved some information—poor man, out at this time, still in his pajamas.

"You're right." He traced the old map with his finger. "How are you going to check all those basements for her?"

"I'm not going to check all of them—not if you'll help. If I check some of them and you check some, it won't be so bad. We could get the guys from public works to help too. It could work."

He looked skeptical. "Shouldn't we call the police? People might not like it."

I knew he meant Mad Dog. I probably should've stopped right then. There wasn't much Mad Dog could do to me, but he could cause Chris to lose his job.

But I'd come this far in my effort to find Betsy; I couldn't give up now. I knew I couldn't do it alone, though, and that law enforcement wouldn't be on my side. After Anne threw her hat in the ring to find Betsy, I didn't blame them. Anne was more experienced.

But I knew Duck better.

"I can't explain why right now, but it's not a good time to call the police. And if we tell people we're looking for something important—like the ancient riverbeds you were telling me about when the geological team was here last year—that might be just the trick to get them to let us explore their basement. No one, who isn't hiding something, wants the foundation on their house to shift because it's sitting in an ancient riverbed, do they?"

"No. Of course not." He smiled. "You know that would be a lie, Mayor."

"Yes, it would. But it would be a lie that might save a little girl's life. If someone refuses to let us look at their basement, we can assume they have something to hide. That might be the time to call in the police. And I won't blame you if you don't want to do it. It's up to you."

"I know. And I'd like to help."

By seven A.M., we were ready to start. Chris and I had gone home to put on old clothes and wading boots. Our three public works guys were onboard. We all had flyers explaining that we were checking for sliding foundations due to ancient riverbeds.

It *kind of* made sense when I looked at it on paper. Most people probably wouldn't question it—or understand it—for that matter. I hoped it was enough to get the job done.

We divided the map of Duck between us. That gave each of us about twenty-five houses to check. These were homes that had been here a while, not renters that were used only in the summer. We'd get to them later. My plan was to check all the basements first. If we didn't find Betsy, I'd figure out a way to search all the root and storm cellars. I knew there were a lot of those—like the one under the Blue Whale Inn.

"Okay. Everyone keep in touch. If you suspect anything, call the police. Don't try to apprehend anyone by yourself. Whoever has this little girl is probably armed and definitely dangerous."

Everyone nodded when I finished my little pep talk. I hoped I wasn't sending anyone into harm's way. I wanted desperately to find Betsy. This seemed like a good plan. All we needed was a little energy and a little ingenuity.

And a lot of brass.

It was cool and foggy outside with a chance of rain, according to the radio. I hoped the weatherman was wrong. Not that nice weather would make this any easier. I just didn't want it to be any harder on the public works guys, or Chris, than it had to be.

My first house was Elmore Dickie's. He used to run the skee ball place when it was just skee ball and pool tables. Now it was Game World and had more sophisticated amusements. Carter Hatley had replaced the pool tables and skee ball with video games. Kids used to stand around smoking when I was growing up. Now they stood around texting on their cell phones.

I explained to Mr. Dickie why I was there and what I was looking for. Of course he trusted me and led me downstairs to his basement. I thought it was a waste of time—Mr. Dickie probably wasn't holding Betsy prisoner in his basement. But he was an elderly man who had a lot of relatives who came to stay with him. One of them could be involved with taking Betsy and Mr. Dickie might not even know about it.

"You know, I was talking to my son-in-law about the new town hall. How does that geothermal stuff work anyway? Does it send hot water gushing up through the pipes?" Mr. Dickie asked.

I didn't know much about geothermal anything, so I answered his questions as briefly as I could, and then I referred him to Chris. "He'll be able to tell you all about it."

We were down in his cramped, damp basement. It had the same smell as the place in my visions with Betsy. But other than some mildewed old life preservers and other watersport equipment, the area was empty.

I shined my flashlight along the edges of the floor anyway. Millions of dead bugs were pushed into the corners.

Ugh. "No. I think you're safe, Mr. Dickie. I don't see any sign of your foundation sliding."

He looked at me with the same incredulous expression he'd used when I was a kid and told him that I'd lost my quarter in a game. That look had made me turn in all the quarters I'd ever found left behind in the skee ball games. "No offense, Your Honor, but that seems like a quick inspection for such a big problem."

I rattled off statistics and figures, explaining how I could tell right away that the foundation was fine. I stared matter-of-factly back at him, wondering if he'd buy it.

He shrugged and took a puff from his cigar. "Okay. Just wondering. Everything is so fast these days. Nothing takes any time at all."

I shook his hand. He promised to vote for me. We parted on friendly terms. But once I was outside, I had to stop and catch my breath. This had seemed like a good idea at two A.M. Now, in the bright sunlight, I realized I was risking a lot to do this. Chris and the public works guys were risking even more.

If anyone else found out about it, the consequences would be bad.

I finally got myself together by drinking a double-shot mocha latte at the coffee shop. I saw Kevin and Ann sitting in a corner, looking at a map that was probably of Duck. It hurt to see their heads bent so close together. Ann reached up and absently stroked the side of his hair. I turned away.

I hoped they wouldn't see me, but no such luck. "Dae!" Kevin called my name when I was halfway to the door. "I'd like to talk to you a minute."

I tried to think of something to say, something airy, an excuse to leave right away. There were important things afoot in Duck. I needed to be somewhere else.

But I couldn't think of a single excuse. My tongue felt

stuck to the roof of my mouth as I stood there in my big rubber boots.

Kevin was coming my way. Ann stayed at the table. The door to the coffee shop opened and Chris came in. He was holding an old sign that looked like it had been out in the water for a while, all messed up and falling apart.

"Mayor, I found this out in the park next to the pier," he said. "I thought public works cleaned up in that area yesterday."

I seized his lead like a lifeline. "You are absolutely right. I'm going to get right on it. Sorry, Kevin. I hope whatever you have to say will wait until later."

Kevin frowned, and I thought he might not agree to wait. Then he relented. "Fine. We'll talk later, Dae. But we *really* need to talk."

His last few words were spoken in a quiet but meaningful tone. His mouth was tight, and his more-gray-than-blue eyes were intent on mine.

I smiled and nodded, then walked quickly out of the shop. I didn't even care that it was pouring rain.

Chris nodded and dropped the sign into a Dumpster. "I really *did* find it in the street."

"Thanks. I feel kind of stupid. *Everyone* knows."

"You're right. *Everyone* knows." He grinned. "But sometimes that's a good thing. I know what you're going through, Mayor. I've been there myself. How's your basement search going?"

I told him of my visit with Mr. Dickie.

"If I can make a suggestion." He pulled out one of the maps from town hall. "I think we're wasting our time on the people we know. I guess one of them *could* be a kidnapper, but it's probably an outsider, if it's anyone. Maybe we should concentrate on rental places. We have twenty-five hundred newer rental houses here in Duck. But not many people build houses with basements anymore. Maybe it could be one of the older houses that's rented out by the owner."

It was a good suggestion. I wished I'd thought of it. But the important thing was that someone had. I didn't want to go through another visit with an old Duck resident like Mr. Dickie, if I could help it.

Chris and I reviewed the list of the houses with basements, circled the ones we knew were rentals and divided them between us. He called the public works guys with a few addresses too. We'd have to go back to the town clerk's office to look up the houses we weren't sure about, but we decided we'd wait to do that until we finished inspecting the ones we already had.

I could have called Nancy at town hall and asked for help, but I knew she wouldn't agree to be part of the search—unless I was more explicit about why the police weren't involved. She had a thing about not getting herself, or anyone else, in trouble. I wouldn't have asked her unless I was willing to call Chief Michaels at the same time.

I knocked at the first door on the new list. A big, tough-looking man with dark hair and a tattoo across his forehead answered. He was young—maybe in his late twenties. I had never seen him before.

"Can I help you?"

"Yes. I'm from the town of Duck, and I'm checking basements for problems." I handed him the flyer. "It won't take more than a few minutes."

He glanced at the flyer, then handed it back to me. "There's no basement here, love," he said in a cool British accent. "Maybe you should try the next house."

"Maybe you haven't been down there yet." I smiled. "But our records show that there's a basement here. Believe me, it won't take that long to look at it."

"No." He slammed the door in my face.

I knocked again and rang the doorbell. This time, a young woman with very black hair and a lot of eye makeup answered. "Yes?"

I gave her my speech. "I'm sorry to bother you, but we need to check these foundations. It's part of a government survey. You know how it is."

"Sure." She sucked hard on a lollipop. "But we don't have a basement. An upstairs—but not a basement. Sorry."

Could this be the place? They were certainly reluctant to let me in. I checked the address on my list against the one on the house.

The woman had already closed the door. I knocked on it—again—unsure when I should call the police. I really needed to have something substantial before I told the chief what I'd been doing. I hoped Chris and the other guys weren't having the same problem.

"Are you crazy?" The man with the tattoo emerged again, much angrier this time. "What's it gonna take to get rid of you?"

From behind him, the woman's voice called out, "Give her some money. Civil servants are always underpaid and looking for bribes."

The man reluctantly pulled out his wallet. "How about a hundred? Will that work?"

I was too astonished to be offended. No one had ever offered me a bribe before. That was one for the record books.

"I really don't want your money." I tried to reason with him. "I'm just trying to do my job. You're making this much harder than it should be. Are you hiding something in the basement?"

"What are you insinuating?"

"I don't really know. But if you're hiding something,

now would be a good time to leave before the police get here. We don't have a big jail, but it would hold the two of you until you could be transported to Manteo to stand trial."

I wasn't sure if this was the right way to handle the situation, but being nice hadn't worked. I wondered how he'd take my warning—until he pulled out a gun and held it on me.

"I think this chick is onto us," he yelled back to the woman, who I assumed was his girlfriend. "We're gonna have to do something with her until we can get the stuff out to the boat."

Now smuggling, I understood. Every family from Duck had a smuggler or two in their family tree. At one time, it had been the only way to survive out here. The tradition continued.

"Oh, if you're just trying to get something out to a boat, that's fine. We understand that around this town. Smuggling is kind of a way of life, so to speak. I'll leave you to it."

But of course, it was too late. I'd already played my trump card—the police. People involved in illegal activities didn't like to hear that word.

I ended up a few minutes later with a thorough view of the basement I'd wanted to see. I was sharing it with some marijuana plants.

The woman had tied me to a chair, with apologies. It seemed she was from Duck and her family owned the house. Her boyfriend was involved in some questionable activities. She wasn't happy about it, but she loved him and wanted to be supportive. He'd promised a trip to Antigua. I told her I understood.

After she'd left me, I heard the door to the upstairs slam shut and a lock turn in place. Thankfully, the rope she'd tied me with was old and came apart easily. I got up from the chair and looked around—might as well examine the basement since I was there.

But this basement was very clean, empty, and well lit with plenty of grow lights for the plants. This wasn't where Betsy was being held. It was all for nothing.

I was beginning to question the wisdom of my plan when my cell phone rang in my pocket. Fortunately, the couple weren't experienced at taking prisoners. They'd kept my clipboard and flyers but hadn't check to see if I had a phone.

"Hello?"

"Dae?" It was Kevin. "I want to meet you somewhere so we can talk. Are you free?"

The question made me want to giggle. *Yes, I'm free—since I managed to get out of the ropes.* "I'm a little busy right now. Maybe later."

"You're avoiding me."

"Not really." I started looking around for a door out of the basement that wouldn't lead me past my captors. I *really* didn't want to tell the chief about this. "I've just been very busy, Kevin. I promise I'll find some time." *As soon as I escape.*

"You sound strange. Where are you?"

"Out working for the town." It wasn't really a lie. "If this is about what happened with the FBI, don't worry about it. You and Ann are experts at this. You'll find Betsy."

"I'd like you to be part of the team. Ann is having a hard time picking up on the girl. We don't have time to waste. You've had contact with her. I think Agent Kowalski was wrong to dismiss you. Let's talk."

The basement had only the one door, the one the woman had locked. There was a window about six feet from the floor, but I wasn't sure I could fit through it, even if I could manage to reach it. I looked around for a stepladder or boxes to stand on.

"It's better this way," I told him. "I have a few ideas but nothing substantial either. I think I'd only hold you back."

"A few ideas?" He sounded suspicious. "Like the one you had about searching Sparks's house? Exactly where are you right now, Dae?"

"I'm in the basement of one of the newer houses on the Atlantic side. Everything is going to be fine, Kevin. Don't worry. I can get out of this without your help." I saw another call was coming through. It was Chris, thank goodness. I could tell him exactly where I was. "I'll talk to you later."

"Wait, Dae! Don't hang up!" Kevin sounded a little frantic. I hoped I hadn't said too much.

I answered the other line while I found a wooden crate that I thought might hold my weight. "Chris! I think I might need some help. Where are you?"

He was across town on the Currituck side. "What kind of help? Should I call the police?"

"No! Don't do that. The chief won't like it." I explained the situation to him. "I think I can get out of this window. Once I'm outside, I'll call Tim and let him know what's going on here. That way, it doesn't require any further explanation."

"Mayor, I think we should call right now. You're in danger. We can explain everything else later. You said we shouldn't take chances."

I didn't tell him that I hadn't known I was taking chances until I'd seen the gun. By then, it was a little too late. "Don't worry. I'll call you back in five minutes.

"Mayor! *Dae!*"

I had to hang up. It wasn't going to be easy pushing myself up to the window and getting through it. I needed both hands. I didn't want to attract any attention from the people upstairs. I picked up the crate, ready for a storm of facts from it when I touched it—where it was made and how it got here.

Instead, it floored me with a vision.

The crate had held illegal whiskey at one point. That's how it got into Duck. I heard laughter and the faintest sound of someone crying. At least ten men were standing around outside a building, with several of them keeping a lookout for someone else.

The man they were expecting drove up in a burgundy Lincoln, exactly like the one in my earlier vision. He got out of the car, hailed by his men. He was accompanied by a woman, beautiful and elegant, who followed him into the clearing near the beach.

"You have some blood on you," she said, taking a tissue out and dabbing it on his tie. "Can't you do anything without getting it all over?"

He looked down at her and I saw his face—craggy lines, square jaw, icy blue eyes. "Get back in the car. I'll clean up later. We've got work to do."

She started to protest, but something in his face made her back down. She turned to go back to the car, looked right at me and said, "You better be careful. He doesn't fool around when it comes to business."

I came back to myself at that point. I was freezing, shaking with cold and shock. I got up off the floor, pulled myself together and carefully aligned the crate again so I could get out of the window.

I heard a disturbance upstairs and worked a little faster. Who knew what was going on up there? They could come down for the plants, and me, anytime. They didn't seem like killers, but what were they going to do with me? I had seen their faces and their large, pot-growing organization.

I could just reach the window standing on the crate, but

I couldn't get it open. It was probably painted or nailed shut. My only chance was to break it and hope my captors didn't hear.

I got down to look for something to do the job. The door to the upstairs opened, and I hid behind the furnace. A large mallet lay on the floor beside me. Even though the head was covered in rubber, it would do for a weapon, if I needed one. I hoped I didn't.

Someone came down the stairs. I couldn't see who it was without giving away my hiding place. Whoever it was looked around, moved a few things, then yelled upstairs, "She's not down here. The basement is full of plants but no sign of Dae."

It was Kevin. I came out from behind the furnace, clutching my mallet. "You must've known I was about to break a window. It's amazing how fast the grapevine works."

"Are you okay?" He frowned. "Are you looking for drug dealers now?"

"Very funny. How did you know where I was?"

"I told him." Chris came down the stairs. "I'm sorry, but I was really scared, and you asked me not to call the police." He looked around the basement greenhouse and whistled. "But I think this changes everything."

I put the mallet on the floor. I felt ridiculous holding it now that they were there. "Not really. We'll have to tell the chief about this, but we can go on with our *other* project."

Chris shook his head. "Sorry, Mayor. I already spilled the beans on that. I know you want to do this on your own, but maybe it would be better if you had help. The real kind—not me, Roy, Shelton and Harry. We don't have a gun between us, and I think you might need one for this work."

His eyes reflected sympathy for my situation with Kevin and Ann, but I could tell he was ready to pass this off to more experienced hands. "The police are upstairs now. They have the people who are staying here in custody. The man pulled a gun on him. Bad move."

"I probably shouldn't have involved you anyway. I'm sorry. I won't let you take any heat over this. If the chief asks, I told you that you had to help me."

The door going upstairs squeaked open again. "What's everybody doing down here in the basement?" Chief Michaels demanded as he came down the stairs. "What's going on? And why did I find out about it from one of the public works guys?"

Chapter 14

No one said anything for a minute or two. We all stood around, probably looking guilty. I didn't want Chris to get in trouble, so I spoke up. "I was down here checking out the basement and I found these pot plants."

The chief eyed the plants with less excitement than I'd hoped. "There's not that much down here. Why were all of you out checking basements anyway? Roy told me Martha Segall ran him off with a broom. He's lucky she didn't tear a strip off his back."

I started to explain, but Kevin stepped in. "Dae is working with Ann and me looking for Betsy Sparks. She had an idea about the girl being kept in a basement. That seemed to be important town business, so she involved Chris and the public works guys."

While I appreciated his backup, I'd let him speak up for me at Chuck's house. I wasn't comfortable allowing him to fight my battle this time. "Thanks, Kevin, but I can answer this myself."

I raised my chin and looked into the chief's stern eyes. "I think it's possible Betsy is being held someplace like a basement or an old root cellar. I didn't want to waste your time until I could check things out. I asked Chris and the others for their help."

The chief nodded and made a snorting sound. "I'm not the one to judge you on this, Mayor. I'm sure the council will want some explanation. That's not my problem. But I want you to stay out of this from here on in. You could've been seriously hurt today, or we could be looking for another kidnap victim. I know Horace wouldn't approve of you being out here checking basements and whatnot. I need your word that you won't go off on your own investigation again."

In situations like this, Chief Michaels reminded me a lot of Gramps. Years ago, when I was a somewhat wild seventeen-year-old and the chief was still just a sheriff's deputy, he had pulled me over for speeding. He'd given me a similar speech and called Gramps, who was sheriff at the time. I never again drove a car too fast down Duck Road.

"You have my word, Chief. I won't investigate on my own. I'm just concerned that we're going to find this little girl too late."

He kind of patted me on the back, then cleared his throat. "We're all worried about that. And truth be told, it would be a darn good idea for you to help Brickman here with his investigation. I'm sure he could use all the help he could get. And that way, he doesn't have to keep chasing after you."

Kevin nodded. "You're right, Chief. I've asked Dae to help us. Ann is good at what she does, but she doesn't know the island like Dae. Maybe you can help convince her."

The chief raised his eyebrows. "I'll leave that to you, son. Dae, stay out of trouble."

He looked at the pot plants again and shook his head before he went upstairs. I heard him yell at Tim to bag up all the pot plants in the basement. No doubt the combination of the pot and the gun drawn on the chief would be a jail sentence for the young couple. Chris excused himself with another apology, telling me he was going to work.

That left me and Kevin in the basement. Was it me or were these encounters getting more difficult?

"What have you seen so far?" he asked.

"I don't know exactly." I was reluctant to tell him anything about my visions, knowing he'd take the information to Ann. I knew it shouldn't matter—we were all trying to save Betsy's life. I wished I didn't have so many conflicting emotions about her . . . him . . . us.

"I meant what I said, Dae. I want you to work with us. It may be the only way we're going to find that little girl."

"I want to help, Kevin. I'm sorry." I glanced around the room, anywhere except Kevin's face. I began to realize that Shayla was right. Giving up Kevin and then having my heartstrings tugged by Betsy's plight was an emotional nightmare for me. The terrible part was, I didn't know how to let go of either one of them. I couldn't seem to do anything about either problem, except dig myself in deeper.

"I know this is hard," he said. "It's hard for me too. I envisioned spending the rest of my life with you here in Duck, working at the Blue Whale. I didn't expect to see Ann again."

Here in Duck? Is he leaving? "Is Ann unhappy here?"

"Miserably so. She wants to go to New York and open up a private consulting firm to find missing children. The Bureau won't take her back after her meltdown. The best she can hope for is consulting work. That's why she latched on to this situation. She needs to know she can still do the work."

"I see." That's why she'd talked to me at Missing Pieces and then found a way to get involved. I hadn't told him about that visit.

"Can we find a way to work together on this? I have a feeling you know a lot more than you're giving away right now. Maybe with what Ann has sensed so far, we'll be able to bring Betsy home today."

How can I say no?

He was right. I knew more now than I had. I'd seen the face of the man who'd killed Chuck. I didn't know for sure that he had Betsy, but it seemed a good bet. Since I knew what he looked like, maybe there was some way to identify him.

"Okay. What do you want to do first?" I hoped he wouldn't want to go back to the Blue Whale and sit at his kitchen table eating lasagna and drinking wine while we talked things over—without kissing and holding hands—like we'd always done.

"We've set up a kind of command center at the Blue Whale. I have the truck here. Do you want to drive over with me?" he asked as we walked out of the house.

It was just my luck. Someone was obviously testing me. Pushing me as far as they could—seeing where I'd break. I looked skyward for the culprit, but no sign came from the puffy clouds riding across the dark sky.

We didn't talk as we drove through town. Before Ann's arrival, we'd had a hard time being quiet, crowding in our thoughts around each other's words. The storm seemed to be chasing us, just like my dark thoughts.

"What does he look like? No one you recognize, I guess," he said finally.

"Excuse me?"

"The man who killed Chuck. He drives the burgundy Lincoln, right? You've seen him by now."

"Just a while ago when I touched that old whiskey crate." I sighed. Maybe Kevin was psychic too. He always seemed to know what I was thinking. It was good that he was keeping us on track—finding Betsy.

"Would a sketch artist help?"

"Maybe. I'm not sure. He was very striking. I can tell you that. Someone you'd pick out in a crowd. I'd know him anywhere now."

"Let's hope you don't see him again until he's in custody."

"But we still don't know for sure that he has Betsy. We might be chasing the wrong person when we have so little time—although his girlfriend said—"

"Said? To you? Do you know her?"

"No. I don't know her. She was in the Lincoln with him in my last vision. She said he wouldn't let anything get in the way of his business. She was referring to some bloodstains on his tie that she'd wanted to clean. I think it was probably from shooting Chuck."

"How's dead Chuck doing today? Any visits?"

"No. Just as well. He always says the same thing." I told him about Chuck's visit to Missing Pieces and his quick departure. "With all the energy Shayla says it takes a ghost to come back, you'd think he'd want to say something more important."

"Maybe now that we understand what he was trying to say—that we needed to help his daughter—he can rest in peace."

"That would be okay with me. Although I'm not really sure that dead Chuck is a ghost. But when I see him, I don't feel like I'm having a vision. And almost everything about Betsy has come from a dream. I'm not sure at this point if I'm coming or going."

"How are you coping with all of it?" He looked over at me in a measured way as he drove slowly into the circle drive that led to the Blue Whale. "You look—good."

"I'm fine," I answered a little defensively. "I can handle it."

I watched his mouth tighten. It was the same strained look he'd worn when he'd first come to Duck. In the last few months, he hadn't seemed so tense. I knew this was a difficult position for him too. At least I *hoped* it was. I hoped he was a little miserable without me.

Right next door to the Blue Whale Inn was the new Duck Historical Museum. Some workmen were in the process of hanging a large sign on the side that faced the inn. It featured a close-up of Mad Dog's face, smiling like he'd just won the lottery.

Across the full color picture, it read, "Vote for me. I won't fool around all Dae."

"That's new," Kevin said. "How's the campaign going?"

"I don't know," I admitted. "I guess the Duck Historical Society has made their choice for candidate. I don't have any big posters, if that's what you mean. And I'm spending all of my time talking to dead Chuck and his daughter. Mad Dog seems to be devoting all of his time to the campaign."

"Don't worry." He turned off the truck and absently laid his hand on mine where it rested on the seat between us. "You'll do fine. You still know more about Duck than he does. Everyone could see that at the debate."

"I hope that's enough." I was feeling the effects of a long, sleepless night, disappointment and embarrassment.

"It has to be enough, Dae. You can win this election *and* find Betsy. I have faith in you."

When he squeezed my hand, I thought I'd blubber like a baby, but I managed to keep it together, thank him for his confidence in me and get out of the truck before I completely fell apart.

I walked past the new mermaid fountain that I'd helped Kevin pick out after a storm had destroyed the old one. The wide veranda with its rocking chairs and flowerpots all looked the same as they had the last time I'd been here. I ran my hand across the antique hitching post where gentlemen in the 1920s had tied their horses when they went in for dinner and a drink.

Ann opened the front door and ran out to greet Kevin with a big kiss. She kind of wrapped herself around him, then faced me.

"I hope you're not too disappointed about the girl," she said.

"You mean because the FBI said it was okay for you to look for her?"

She smiled tightly. "Kevin, didn't you tell her?"

He looked away. "Ann, you know how I feel about this."

"Kevin has always been an optimist. What he was *supposed* to tell you is that the Sparks girl is dead. I'm sorry. But there it is. We all have to face the truth."

Chapter 15

I glanced at Kevin, but his face was expressionless. I stared instead at Ann with her equally expressionless face and cold eyes. "What do you mean? Do you have some information I don't?"

"Let's go inside," Kevin suggested. "I have two guests staying here that love to gossip."

"Not that it matters." Ann took his arm. "Everyone will know the truth soon."

I followed them inside, passing the two older ladies Kevin had been talking about. I didn't recognize them, but they were probably here visiting family or friends. They certainly didn't need to hear and spread what Ann had just told me.

I was furious with Kevin for bringing me here. Had the FBI given them some heads-up? Why hadn't someone told me? Why was I at the Blue Whale?

We went into the big kitchen where two staff members

were making lunch for the ladies who were still out on the veranda. Kevin had hired a few people from Duck to help him run the three-story inn. It may have been shut down for more than thirty years, but it hadn't taken long for people to find out it was open again.

"Would you like something to drink, Dae?" Kevin asked quietly.

Why is he acting so normally? "No. Not really. I want to know what's going on." I felt as though someone had punched me in the stomach with no explanation. How could they be so detached?

"What's going on," Ann said, leaning toward me, "is that Kevin could never stand an unhappy ending, right, sweetie? He always wanted us to find the kids while they were still alive, even though that didn't happen very much."

"I think that would be preferable," I remarked impatiently.

"Of course. But it can't always go that way." She picked up an apple from the basket on the table and bit into it.

I rounded on Kevin, ready to spew out fire and brimstone, as Gramps used to say. "Is Betsy dead or not? If so, how do you know about it? Where did they find her?"

"Please sit down, Dae, and let's sort through this." As though to encourage me, Kevin grabbed a bottle of water and sat down.

I refused to go along with any of it. Besides, I didn't think I could sit still until I'd heard it all.

"What Ann is trying to say," he explained, "is that she *believes* Betsy is dead. She feels that all the signs are there. She thinks Betsy has been dead the whole time you've been talking to her, which is why you've been able to communicate with her."

I sat down. *"What?"* I glared at Ann, who was happily

munching away like a child who doesn't know any better. "What signs?"

Ann swallowed the apple she'd chewed. "I picked up on your little dreams. I'm good at attuning myself with other psychic connections. *I saw what you saw*."

"That's crazy." I glanced at Kevin for support. I felt sick and violated. *What else had she seen*?

"It's part of psychic warfare these days." Ann smiled maliciously. "She has the doll in your dreams. You found it in the house. She can't have it physically. The only way you could see her with it is if she manifested it after she died. It happens with children and their favorite toys. The second thing is that she knew her father was dead. Children who are still living don't know things like that much less accept them rationally. When you were talking to her and saw yourself in a grave—in my experience—that was *her* grave."

Her voice was so cold and analytical. Chills coursed down my spine as I listened to her describe the reasons Betsy had to be dead. I felt betrayed, as I had when Ann had come to the shop to take over looking for Betsy. Her conclusions were all based on invading my mind.

"I don't believe it." I glared at her again for good measure. There had to be some way to keep her out of my head from now on. I just had no idea what it was. "I'm not giving up on such a small amount of evidence and some bad experiences you've had."

"I don't believe it either," Kevin said. "I think we can still find her—*alive*."

"You can believe what you want," Ann said. "But you'll be wasting your time. I'm going to tell Agent Kowalski my findings. It's up to him after that."

"How can you be this way?" I demanded, still angry.

"That's a real person out there who needs us. We can't just give up because you think she's dead."

"You're a little crusader, Dae," she retorted. "Just like Kevin described. No wonder the two of you were an item for a while. You're a perfect match."

She smiled and kind of floated out of the kitchen, not looking back.

"This isn't like her." Kevin sounded apologetic. "When we worked together, she never gave up until she had no choice. Sometimes I thought she was part bloodhound. She's not thinking clearly. That may be why she's so defensive."

I got slowly to my feet. "I'm sorry, but I don't think I can work with the two of you. I know you want to help her get her groove back, but this is new to me. I don't think I can handle all the drama. I feel like I need aluminum foil on my head or something to keep her out. I need a clear, Ann-free brain if I'm going to help Betsy."

"I know it doesn't seem possible right now, but the three of us working together is the best bet that little girl has. Ann may not seem like a resource, but she is. Like you said, you don't have much experience, Dae. She does. But you have the inside track on Chuck and his daughter. Don't throw all of this away because of how you feel about what's going on between us."

He sounded so sensible—*like he always did*. It drew me in, *like always*. He was a calm center in the eye of any storm.

But he was wrong this time.

I didn't need Ann or her jaded point of view to find Betsy. I didn't need his daily presence reminding me of my heartache either. That pain was clouding my judgment. I needed to be clearheaded. This was the most important thing I had ever used my gift for.

"I'm sorry, Kevin. This isn't going to work for me."

"Look, I know this is hard. I know you don't want it to work because we'd have to be together. I'm sorry it has to be this way, more than I can say. But what if you're wrong? What if you refuse to work with us and the girl isn't found until it's too late? Give me a chance to pull your and Ann's strengths together on this. I know it will work."

I wanted to believe. I wanted him to be right. And it was true, I was just fumbling around, not sure what to do. He obviously had a plan.

I managed to push aside my feelings and prepared to hear him out. "What did you have in mind?"

Kevin brought out a big whiteboard that he sometimes used to announce specials in the dining room. He put it up on the steamy kitchen wall while the aromas of broccoli and cheese casserole and apple pie wafted around us.

"For now, let's get everything up here that you've experienced, Dae. When we see it as a whole, it can make a difference."

So we started from the beginning—the medallion that had belonged to Chuck's mother.

"I don't understand why they didn't arrest Derek Johnson," I complained.

"He had a perfect alibi," Kevin explained. "The police in Wilmington were questioning him about another crime they thought he'd committed when Chuck was killed. Time of death from the medical examiner's office confirms that. As far as the medallion was concerned, he said he saw the sign in the store, was interested in it and made up the story about being its owner and offering a reward. No one can really argue with that. It's plausible."

"That doesn't explain why he had a gun when he got to Old Man Sweeney's house."

"He's been in and out of jail since he was a kid. People like that tend to carry weapons."

"Or he was cleaning up after the person who shot Chuck. Maybe they were worried about the medallion giving them away."

"That's possible. I don't believe Derek's story—neither do the police. But they can't prove otherwise."

We talked about seeing dead Chuck the first time—and after. Then we focused on Betsy.

While we were working, Ann came back to the kitchen and sat down. Kevin went to check on the cheese sauce for dinner that night.

"I don't know why he doesn't trust me," she muttered. "He knows I understand these things better than he does."

"Maybe he's just not ready to give up."

"It's not giving up." She turned to face me. "It's being realistic. Do you have any idea how many of these cases I've worked?"

"No, I don't. And you're right—I haven't been doing this for very long. I definitely don't have your experience. But I also don't have your fatalism about it. I can *feel* that she's still alive."

"The earmarks are all wrong."

"I don't care about the earmarks. This is only one little girl, not the ones you've worked with before. Until I see her dead body, I'm not giving up."

She shrugged. "Suit yourself. I'll play the little game. I don't have anything else to do."

Kevin returned, looked at both of us, then went back to the whiteboard. "We have a visual on the suspect Dae thinks is responsible for Mr. Sparks's death. If he's been arrested before, Dae will be able to ID him from police photos."

Ann didn't say anything. She doodled on a piece of paper while Kevin went over everything we had talked about.

I looked at the paper she had in her hands. A man's face was emerging from her pencil. Thick dark hair, craggy, deep lines in his face, a square jaw and piercing eyes.

"That's him!" I said, almost jumping out of my seat. "She drew him from my thoughts. I didn't even tell her what he looked like. I can't believe it!"

Kevin looked at the sketch. "I don't recognize him. Ann, do you get any kind of vibe from him?"

She continued to doodle. "He's a powerful man, used to giving commands and having them obeyed. He's spent his whole life in and out of trouble. He's not from this area, but he's interested in working here."

"Good." Kevin added those characteristics to the whiteboard. "If you'll give me that sketch, I'll make some copies of it. We'll give one to Agent Kowalski."

"How did you do that?" I asked Ann after he was gone. "How could you see that in my brain?"

"I don't know. Like you, I was born this way. Unlike you, my parents wanted me to do something with my gift. They sent me to a school in Europe where I received specialized training. While most kids were playing with blocks, I was developing my abilities."

I continued to watch her. She was now drawing on a second piece of paper. It was another face. "Who is that?"

"I'm not sure. He's in your head. You don't know him?"

"No. I don't recognize him. I've never seen him."

"You will." She handed me the sketch and smiled. "Like I said, you have a lot to learn, Dae. But you're very talented. Maybe if you joined the FBI, you'd pick up more."

I looked at the sketch and wondered who the man was. "I don't think so. It's not easy doing this on my own, but I don't want to make a career out of looking for missing children. I like where I am right now, helping where I can. I don't know if I'm cut out for more."

"I don't blame you. So what if your full potential never develops. You aren't out to impress anyone, are you? I wish I felt that way. It must be nice to have a home somewhere. No matter where I go, I'm never home."

Except with Kevin.

The words came to me like a whisper, but not from her lips. I wasn't sure whether I'd actually heard her thoughts or only imagined that she felt that way.

Kevin came back with the copies, and we decided to go to the FBI hub at the police station. We were getting into his pickup—Ann in the middle—when my cell phone rang.

"Hi, Dae." It was Trudy. "There's a man here who says he has something for you. It's about some kind of gun. I told him you still own Missing Pieces—you're just never here."

"Thanks, Trudy. I'll be there in a few minutes."

Ann and Kevin were looking at me when I closed my cell phone. "I have to go to the shop. I could meet you at the station later, but I made an appointment before all of this came up. I just forgot about it."

"Not a problem," Kevin said. "It will probably take some time to research this man's face. I'll call you if it goes faster."

"Thanks."

"I'll see you later, Dae," Ann said. "Kevin and I will take care of the big, scary stuff. You can go on with your normal little life. We'll let you know if there's anything else you can do."

I turned down a ride to Missing Pieces. Kevin was right about Ann. She was very good at what she did, finding missing children, *and* needling me. I needed some time to get my thoughts in order.

They were very professional together. It was easy to imagine them working at the FBI, and falling in love. They made a striking couple. It was like they knew what to do and say without even discussing it. It made me feel a little insignificant, even though a lot of my information had led to the new discoveries.

I walked from the Blue Whale toward the downtown area. Kevin waved as he and Ann passed me in the truck. I wasn't sorry I wasn't going with them.

I noticed Mad Dog at the corner setting out a few smaller signs, pounding them into the sandy ground. I hoped he wouldn't notice me, but what were the chances? Even though there was a good crowd of walkers out on Duck Road, I'd never blend in that well.

"Hello, Dae!" he sang out. "It's a lovely day, isn't it? How do you like my little poster next to the inn? Very impressive, right?"

"I didn't notice," I lied with a pleasant smile. "I do hope you aren't violating any sign ordinances. You know the public works guys are always on the lookout for that."

"Speaking of the public works department, I heard the most vicious rumor about you and Chris Slayton. Did the two of you *really* hire our workers to dig for some treasure you're looking for? Because that would be a total violation of your power as mayor of Duck. I don't think the other members of the council are happy about it either."

In other words, he'd heard the rumor and called everyone else on the council. *Digging for treasure.* That's what happened sometimes when the grapevine went haywire.

"It's been a while since I dug for any treasure, Councilman. Excuse me. I have to run over to Missing Pieces. I'll see you later."

"Indeed you will!" he yelled after me. "I'm going to ask for a special meeting of the council to discuss all of these goings-on. Enjoy being mayor—while you can."

I guessed Mad Dog was conspiring to become mayor

without an election. It was possible. He was the mayor pro tem. Should the council issue a vote of no confidence against me, he would automatically take my place. A special election would have to be held later but not until after he'd been mayor for a while. It was too late for new candidates to file for office. We have an early filing period in Duck.

I hurried by him, through traffic, up the stairs and down the boardwalk. Nancy was outside town hall, smoking, as I went by. "Hey! We need to talk, sweetie. There are some bad things coming down the pipeline that you should know about," she called out.

"In a few minutes," I yelled back, already aware of the bad things coming my way. "I'm late!"

I was a little breathless by the time I got to the shop. Trudy and my seller were out on the bench in front. They seemed to be hitting it off.

"Sorry I'm late," I apologized.

The man beside her stood up and held out his hand. "That's okay. It gave me a chance to meet your friend and ask her out for dinner."

I shook his hand and looked into his face. My whole body went cold.

He was the second man Ann had sketched from my thoughts.

Chapter 16

People from across the Southeast frequently contacted me—usually via the Internet—with items to sell. Buyers looking for specific items did the same. It was nice when they matched up. I got a fee for brokering the sale, or sold the piece outright. Not to mention the thrill of seeing and holding some very old and expensive antiques. Very sweet!

In this case, the buyer who'd contacted me was looking for a single-shot Flobert pistol with an original fruitwood grip. It was very rare, only a few left in good shape. I just so happened to find the Flobert last year at an antique rally in Charleston.

Port Tymov was a nationally known antiques dealer. We'd never met, but we'd spoken on the phone and worked together through the Internet. When I told him I had the Flobert he was looking for, he told me he'd come to the shop with the money.

He was a good-looking man, probably in his early forties, but his features were sharp and his eyes struck me as being greedy. There was a lot of money to be made in antiques. Many dealers weren't in the business for the thrill of finding the rare items. They just wanted to make money. I didn't hold it against Port.

After Port had confirmed that Trudy would meet him at Wild Stallions that night, we went into Missing Pieces and I took out the pistol case.

I was still trying to process how Ann had seen him in my thoughts even before I'd seen him—when I noticed him staring at the pistol case. It was emblazoned with a gold swastika. "If it offends you, I can get rid of it."

"No. I'm just surprised to see it. The buyer will be thrilled to have the original case."

"Well, you know many people get upset when they see that symbol, some enough not to buy it."

"I know," he agreed. "Believe me, my buyer isn't one of those people."

The Flobert was like a toy, but I knew it was real. It had belonged to a Nazi officer who'd managed to escape Germany at the end of World War II. It was considered a parlor pistol, pretty and useful, easily tucked into a pocket or a drawer.

"Would you like to hold it?" I asked, stretching it out to him.

Fortunately, this was an occasion when slipping on a pair of gloves didn't look odd. I wanted to hold the weapon but wouldn't dare without the gloves to protect me from the memories trapped inside of it. Even so, I shuddered as I picked it up again. Just imagining who it had belonged to was scary enough.

The pistol was very delicate, almost a work of art. It meant a nice sale for me too, and I was excited to work with

Port. He could help me broker other sales in the future with his wide range of contacts. Altogether, a very good deal.

He gave back the pistol after examining it for only a minute or two. "It's in wonderful condition."

"The daughter of the SS officer who'd owned it took very good care of it for the brief time it was in her possession," I explained as I put the pistol back in the case. "When the daughter found the pistol and some other Nazi effects in her mother's attic after her death, she was horrified to learn she had a relative involved in all of that. She got rid of everything at a wholesale price. I scarfed it up."

"I'm glad you did. It would be a shame for it to be lost, despite the background."

"I understand her feelings." I told him about a carved wood mirror I'd had—until I'd learned it had belonged to a slave. "I didn't feel the same way about it after that, and I let it go for a lot less than it was probably worth."

He looked at me as if I'd lost my mind. "It's one thing to give things away that belonged to your family, Dae. But this is business. You won't stay around long if you sell things for less than their value. How did you find out about its history anyway? There's not much left in that category."

He wasn't from Duck, and I didn't feel obliged to make him understand about my gifts. "I don't remember, but it was a good source. I know the history was accurate."

"Well, give me a call next time you have something worth that much money that you want to get rid of cheap." He scanned the shop. "Mind if I take a look around?"

"Please do. I can't promise a cheap sale, but I'm sure we can work something out."

"Is this what I think it is?" he asked a few minutes later in an excited tone. "Tell me you don't have one of the three silver church bells that were buried at St. Augustine to keep them from being taken by the English soldiers."

"Yes. That's what it is." I wondered how he knew. I knew what it was when it came to me via another seller because I'd touched it and was immediately transported to that time. The monks had worked frantically to hide the three silver church bells. They had planned to come back and dig them up, but the English soldiers had killed all of them.

"What do you want for it? And do you have the other two?"

"I only have the one. I'm not going to sell it. At least not until I get the other two," I told him.

His sharp, thin face, so much like the image Ann had drawn, registered his disbelief. "Are you serious? Do you know what this is worth? You might have to wait a lifetime for the other two bells, if you're ever lucky enough to see them. I'll write you a check for this one right now."

"No thanks. I appreciate the offer, but I know the other two are coming this way. I don't mind waiting to see all of them together."

He looked at the bell in his hand and shook his head. "You're never going to stay in business, Dae. You're too romantic. I've sold off dozens of single treasure parts. Keeping this bell for the reason you describe would be like expecting to gather together all of Blackbeard's treasure here and intact. Not a good business decision. You can take that from someone who's been in the business for a lot longer than you."

"You may be right." I shrugged. "But I am who I am. I have a lifetime to wait for the two other bells. I'm very patient when it comes to things like that."

Of course, he didn't know what I knew from holding the bell. I knew the other two had a resonance with this one. They wouldn't be separated for long. I didn't know how they'd come here or who would bring them, but I knew they were on their way.

"I hope you're well insured." He put the bell down reluctantly. "I can't believe you have something this valuable sitting out here like this. I guess I'm going to be here for a while looking at everything else. Who knows what else you have?"

"How did you know about the bell?"

"I research missing treasure like the bells. I study them so I'll know if I come across one." He smiled. "It's intuition too, I have to admit. You develop a sense for these things after a while. Don't worry. It will be like that for you one day too."

I returned his smile. "Like I said, I'm patient. I can wait."

While Port rummaged carefully through Missing Pieces for another treasure he might persuade me to sell, I unfolded the picture of him that Ann had drawn. Either she could see into the future or she had the ability to summon a picture from a name. Port's name was in my brain. What he looked like had been a mystery to me. But not to her.

Kevin was right—she was very talented. And scary. But maybe between us we would be able to find Betsy.

Yet these moments were leading into hours and days. How much longer would Betsy's kidnapper keep her alive? He wasn't asking for a ransom—probably realized that Betsy's mother didn't have the resources to provide anything worthwhile. It was surprising that he hadn't already killed her. Maybe if we understood that part, we might understand it all.

Port left Missing Pieces about an hour later, after perusing everything in the shop except for my Duck souvenir collection. And leaving me a nice fat check. He didn't remark on anything else the way he had the silver bell. He did ask about a brass scale weight used for weighing real silver coins, but didn't offer to buy it. A scale weight had been a business necessity in the distant past, when silver coins were the common currency—the scale prevented a buyer from filing down the coins and thus cheating the seller.

I shook Port's hand again when he left. I saw an image of the woman I thought was Chuck's killer's girlfriend—the woman who'd cleaned the blood from the killer's tie. I didn't understand the connection between Chuck, Betsy and Port.

Was it possible Port was involved with the killer's girlfriend? Maybe that was the connection Ann had sensed, enabling her to draw his face. But even if there *was* a connection, I had no way of knowing the nature of the relationship—the girlfriend could be Port's sister, or maybe they were lovers. I certainly couldn't ask Port about the woman—I didn't even know her name.

I was going to have to be that patient person I'd told Port I was. In this case, that was a very difficult thing.

A while later, Ann and Kevin came in, between customers. I thought it was more important for me to stay at Missing Pieces and try to make some money. They could handle the FBI and the search for Chuck's killer.

I'd managed to sell a nice Spanish porcelain statue of a Madonna and child that had been taken from a shipwreck in the 1800s. The treasure finders who'd located the shipwreck had been interested in the Spanish gold and nothing else. But the Madonna statue was worth a pretty penny too. They'd kept it as a souvenir and passed it down through several generations, until a descendant decided to do some spring cleaning. It was a consignment piece, so I didn't make as much on the sale as usual, but I was sure the seller would be as happy as I was with the price.

"Looks like you've been busy," Kevin said.

"Yes. It was a surprise. There's not much going on during the week right now."

Ann had already taken a spot on the burgundy brocade sofa. I decided I'd stay where I was, behind the counter.

"How did it go with the sketch?" I finally asked.

"Fine if you count the fact that the man's face was recognizable, so we know who he is," Ann said. "Not so good because Agent Kowalski doesn't believe he's involved."

"I don't understand," I said. "If you told them everything and the man is a criminal, what's the problem?"

"The problem is that the man in the sketch is Dillon Guthrie." Kevin grabbed a Sun Drop from the mini-fridge, as he always did. "He's a well-known smuggler who has trafficked everything from drugs to cars, art and antiques. He's been around a long time and has never been arrested for anything. No one has been able to touch him."

"That makes him the perfect suspect, right?" I didn't like what I was hearing.

"Too perfect." Ann took a bottle of water from Kevin, who'd joined her on the sofa. "The FBI doesn't believe a big player like Guthrie would be out here in Duck killing a nobody like your real estate broker. He's never been known to have anything to do with kids, so no reason to kidnap the girl. In short, they probably won't even bother questioning him."

"What?" I got down from the stool behind the counter and, despite my earlier reluctance, went to sit with them on the sofa. "That's ridiculous. He's a bad guy. Wouldn't he be capable of doing anything bad?"

"I'm afraid the FBI doesn't work like that," Kevin explained. "No profiler would believe that Guthrie would suddenly change professions and start kidnapping little girls. Criminals don't work that way. They follow their own set of rules. That's what eventually gets them caught. They're slaves to their own routines."

"Plus, Agent Kowalski reminded us twice that even if

Guthrie killed Chuck, that isn't their mission. He's only here to find the little girl. Because Guthrie doesn't track for this type of crime, he won't even discuss him." Ann took a long sip from her water. She looked pale and exhausted.

"So we're on our own," I surmised. "What do we do now?"

"I don't know about the two of you, but I quit." Ann got up from the sofa. "I don't know how you people live down here with all the sand and the salt air. It drains me."

"But I had something happen to me while you were busy." I pulled out the sketch she'd given me. "This is Port Tymov. I've never met him before today. He came to buy a piece I found in Charleston. This is the sketch you did of him, Ann."

She yawned. "So?"

"When I shook his hand, I saw Guthrie's girlfriend from the other visions. They're connected somehow."

I thought she might be excited about the news, but Ann just stared at me.

"His connection to Guthrie's girlfriend doesn't seem to matter much since the FBI won't go after Guthrie," she reminded me.

"But don't you see?" I looked at Kevin. "This means we could get to her if we can find out who she is. She could be a relative of Port's—"

"Or she could be some hot chick your dealer ran into and her face stuck in his brain," Ann interrupted impatiently. "You need a lot more training in how to apply your abilities effectively in a criminal investigation."

"Dae has a natural gift for using her abilities to help other people," Kevin said. "While you were trained as a child to use your abilities, Ann, Dae has always been motivated solely by a desire to assist those she knows and loves."

Ann glared at him. "It doesn't matter. I *know* the girl is

dead. You know I'm not wrong about these things. Why are you fighting me on this, Kevin? You can't let your feelings for Dae get in the way of making a rational judgment on the case."

"You could be mistaken," Kevin reminded her. "You haven't done this in a long time. Your abilities may be rusty or affected by your breakdown."

Ann didn't say another word. She turned and walked out of Missing Pieces, closing the door silently behind her.

Kevin leaned back against the sofa. "We've been arguing about this all the way back from the police station. I don't know if she'll go on with the case."

"I'm sorry. Maybe you should give up on it too. Maybe she just can't do this work anymore."

"Or maybe she's right. I don't know. But the FBI made it clear we won't get any more help from them if we're going to pursue Guthrie."

"So what do we do now?" I asked him.

"What we've done before. Find what's missing."

Chapter 17

I felt the first thing we should do was talk to Chief Michaels. I owed him that after my efforts to find Betsy without him. I knew it always upset him when I struck out on my own. Sometimes, I just couldn't help it. It was going to mean getting another lecture, but I was going to have to suck it up. No matter what, he was a good friend of the family and a good police chief. I couldn't imagine Duck without him.

I had to remind my fast-beating heart that this was just a working partnership with Kevin. Nothing had changed in that matter. I hated the awkwardness between us as much as the breakup itself. It was difficult to find something to say that didn't involve Ann's arrival in Duck and its emotional aftermath. We drove from the shop to the police station in Kevin's truck, not really having a conversation. Lucky it wasn't a long drive.

"So where do people in Duck vote?" he asked.

"We're headed there. Once the new town hall is finished, we might vote there. We'll have to see."

"I heard there might be another storm coming our way," he added.

"It's possible." It was the worst conversation in the world. I was glad when we finally reached the police station.

The FBI agents in dark suits were swarming around their computers. One of them stopped us at the door. "Can I help you?"

"I don't think so. We're here to see Chief Michaels." I didn't like his proprietary tone, as though he belonged here and I didn't. No matter what, this was *my* town.

"He's very busy right now, ma'am." He didn't even bother looking back toward the chief's office, as though trying to tell a convincing lie. "I'll be glad to take a message for him."

I threw my shoulders back and faced him down. "First of all, I'm a citizen of this town and I have every right to be here and to talk to the chief. And second of all, I'm the mayor. I'll wait right over here until the chief can see me."

He wasn't impressed. "That's fine. But I can't tell you when that will be, Mayor. It could be a long wait."

"He has to go home sometime."

Kevin and I went to sit in the row of chairs positioned against the wall. "You can't expect much more from them," he said. "When the FBI or any federal agency gets involved in a problem, they take the lead. It's the way things are done."

"Well, it's rude and disrespectful." But that was all I said on the matter—only because I noticed Melinda Lafferty, Chuck's ex-wife, sitting by herself in one of the same plastic chairs.

I admit that, at first, I thought of her only as an important person to talk to about Betsy. She was the girl's mother. She could probably share some insights into Chuck's life too. I wondered if anyone would notice if I sat beside her and asked her questions.

But the more I observed her, the more I realized that she was in terrible shape. She looked as though she was about to fall on the floor with exhaustion. Her face was pale, and her eyes were glazed over. She probably hadn't eaten or slept since she got here. That was no way for a visitor in Duck to be treated.

"I'm sorry, Ms. Lafferty." I approached her with a smile that I hoped was sympathetic. I couldn't let my annoyance with the FBI affect her. She was the true victim in all of this. "I'm Dae O'Donnell, mayor of Duck. We met yesterday. I'm sorry you've been through so much. If there's anything I can do, please let me know. Do you have a place to stay? Have you eaten?"

She ran her hand through her bright red hair. "I just don't know what to do. They brought me down here and said I could help them in some way. I've been sitting in this chair, or somewhere in this station, since I got here. They gave me a blanket last night and some crackers this morning. I can hardly think anymore. How can I help Betsy like this?"

Questioning her about her ex-husband and her daughter fled from my mind like clouds dispersing after a storm. "Never mind. You come with us. We'll find you something to eat and a place to lie down for a while."

"What about Betsy?" she whispered. "What about Chuck?"

"There's nothing you can do right now, Ms. Lafferty," Kevin assured her, following my lead. "Dae is right. You need some food and some rest. If they need you, they'll call you. We'll make sure they know where you are."

She was still unconvinced and scared she might miss something. I knew I'd feel the same if I were in her position.

"You have to stay strong and take care of yourself for your daughter. We don't know where any of this will lead. She needs you to be in fighting shape for her, Melinda. Come with us. Let us take care of you so you can take care of her when we find her."

It was a good speech. It worked on Melinda. But she was near collapse with anxiety and fatigue.

It didn't work as well on Agent Kowalski when we started to help Melinda leave the police station. "Where do you think you're going?" he demanded, thundering toward us, his face red like he'd been in the sun too long. "I didn't authorize Ms. Lafferty to leave this building."

"We're taking Melinda out of here so she can rest and have something to eat," I replied, explaining the obvious. "Shame on you! She can barely hold her head up! What are you thinking?"

He looked slightly abashed for a moment—long enough for Chief Michaels to come out of his office.

"Is there a problem out here?" the chief asked Kowalski. The agent reiterated that he didn't want Melinda to leave.

"We're taking her to the Blue Whale," Kevin said. "She's not going to do anyone any good if she collapses."

I stared at the chief, hoping he'd understand my appeal for this bit of humanity.

"All right. We'll know where to find her," he finally said.

Kowalski was furious. "I didn't give permission for that!"

"You don't have to give *me* permission in my own town to be civil to a guest, Agent. Kevin, Dae—you take good care of Ms. Lafferty, but keep a phone handy. If this breaks, it could happen very quickly."

I agreed to those terms. I was proud of the chief for standing up to Kowalski, who threw his hands in the air and walked away.

"Could I have a few words with you?" I asked the chief when we were alone.

"I have just enough time for a few words, Mayor. That's about it." He walked back into his office.

"Don't worry," Kevin assured me as he walked Melinda to the door. "I'll take her to the Blue Whale. She can stay with me while she's here."

"Oh, I couldn't do that," she protested weakly. "I don't have any money until I start my new job. That's why I left Betsy with Chuck." She covered her face with her hands.

"Not a problem," Kevin told her. "We'll talk about it later."

"I'll catch a ride over when I'm done," I said cheerfully. "Thanks."

I hadn't planned on taking Melinda to the Blue Whale. I was going to take her back to my house. But I couldn't complain, since Kevin was ready to shoulder the responsibility of getting her settled somewhere else. He definitely had more room than we had.

I gave Melinda a hug and told her that she'd be all right with Kevin. Then I walked past Agent Kowalski, who'd taken a stance, arms folded against his chest, in front of the chief's door. I resisted the urge to poke my tongue out at him, and slammed the door to the chief's office in his face.

"What's going on?" I demanded when I was alone with him. "Why aren't the FBI taking the sketch of Dillon Guthrie seriously? I thought Agent Kowalski didn't mind working with gifted people. He seemed to like Ann a lot."

"I don't really know. I've never heard of this Guthrie fellow before," he admitted. "They say he's worked around these parts for years as the head of some big smuggling ring. Too big for us to be more than a blip on his radar, I guess."

Chief Michaels sounded a bit disappointed that Guthrie hadn't considered Duck a worthy spot to do "business." I, on the other hand, thought it a good thing that Guthrie didn't normally work around here.

"What do we know about him?" I asked, hoping he'd share some helpful information.

"He's a bad guy, Mayor. Got a rap sheet longer than your arm for some terrible things. But Agent Kowalski and his superiors say kidnapping, even murdering Chuck, isn't something a man like Guthrie would do. It's beneath him. He'd have someone else do it—and he'd make sure he could not be linked to the crime. My hands are tied right now. And I'm afraid the clock is ticking."

I sat down in one of the chairs in front of the chief's desk. "You know me. You know I don't see random images. I'm the one who led everyone to Chuck and knew that Betsy was missing. I'm telling you this man killed Chuck in the Harris Teeter parking lot, Chief. He has Betsy—somewhere. If we don't do something to help her, she'll die."

He rocked back in his chair and stared at the ceiling with his hands behind his head. "You know I'm not real comfortable with all this stuff, Dae. But I know you have the gift. I've seen you use it your whole life. I saw your grandmother before you do amazing things. No doubt about it."

He sat forward. "But that other woman that used to work with the FBI told Kowalski she believes the girl is dead. He isn't exactly taking her word for it, but I get the feeling he thinks too much time has gone by and that she may be right. He's still working on the case. We'll have to see what happens."

"Maybe it would be for the best if the FBI left so the Duck Police could look for Betsy without them."

"We don't have that kind of experience, Dae. You know

that. I'm sure Horace didn't work more than one kidnapping in his whole career. We need their help on this. I'm not saying we'll give up if they leave, but we stand a better chance of finding that little girl with them."

"There has to be some link between Chuck and Guthrie," I insisted. "It can't hurt to check that out."

He nodded and tossed a stapled group of papers toward me. "Chuck had gotten himself in a mess. His financial records show that little stunt of his, getting involved in trying to cheat Miss Mildred last year, cost him a lot of business. I'm surprised he even stayed here. Between that and the downturn in the real estate market, it must've been all he could do to stay alive."

I flipped through the last twelve months of Chuck's business statements. "Then he started bringing in some good money."

"That's right. I think it's possible he was involved with Guthrie's smuggling operation. I can't prove it. Maybe he crossed some line with Guthrie and he was killed. All of this is speculation. Agent Kowalski says my theory is too unlikely to be worth pursuing. But Chuck got that money somehow. I keep hoping we can make sense of it all and find his killer, before it's too late for that little girl."

I gave him back the statements. "I might have a way to connect Guthrie to Betsy. I don't know yet. I'm working on it."

The chief stood abruptly. I was afraid he was going to jump right over the desk. "Don't mess around with this, Dae O'Donnell. Do you hear me? That's my only warning to you. I'm going to pick up the phone and call Horace as soon as you leave. These are professional killers we're talking about. That pretty smile of yours and a whole batch of your grandfather's fish stew won't keep you alive if you meet up with him. You go and tend to your store. We'll find Chuck's killer and his little girl. Leave this to the professionals for once."

He glowered at me. He was more serious than usual about warning me away. I didn't smile or make fun of his demand as I might have done at another time. "I'll stay out of it," I told him. "You don't have to call Gramps."

He sat down again. "Good. Now go and check on that nice lady. You were right to offer her some hospitality. I'm sorry I didn't notice it sooner. I'll be by the Blue Whale later to check on her myself."

"Thanks, Chief."

I didn't smile when I left. But I knew I was lying when I promised to stay out of it. Until Betsy was found, I was involved.

I caught a ride back to my house but didn't stay long. I decided to head over to Chuck's house again. I wanted to make sure Betsy was still alive. Despite Ann's disparaging remarks about my abilities, I really believed that if I could contact the girl again, I would know if she was dead or alive.

Since the police had taken her doll away from me, I needed something else that would give me the same connection. It might not reassure anyone else, but I'd feel better.

Crime scene tape stretched across every entrance to the house, but the back door wasn't locked. Seeing all that tape reminded me of the time I'd gotten hold of Gramps's crime scene tape and wrapped it across every doorway and around every piece of furniture in our house. That adventure had ended badly for me, despite the initial fun. Gramps was fair, but he was strict.

After ducking under the tape, I entered through the back door and walked through the house, ignoring the mess this time. The police and FBI had made it even worse. I tried not to look too long at Chuck's personal items strewn about. I didn't want him showing up dead again.

I let my instinct guide me to a pink teddy bear with a black bow tie that I found outside Betsy's room. Half of his body was torn away (what kind of person does something like that?), but I could feel her on him. It was a strong connection. I knew she loved him and had frequently held him close.

I sat down on her small bed and clutched the bear tightly to me. Instantly a deep, bitter cold swept through me. I heard the sound of water dripping again—and Betsy's voice.

"Please. If you let me out, I'll be very good. I won't say a word. Please don't leave me here alone again."

A voice said something in return, but it was muffled, incoherent. I couldn't tell whether a man or a woman had spoken.

"No! Please don't leave. I can be good."

But despite her appeals to the visitor I couldn't see or understand, she was left alone. There was another sound—wood against wood? A tree branch scraping? I wasn't sure. Maybe it was just a door closing.

Betsy was crying. I tried to find her in the dark but couldn't. I called her name, but this time, it seemed she couldn't hear me. The only thing I could do, until this vision came to an end, was focus on the area around me.

The floor wasn't smooth and even, like concrete. It was bumpy. There were patches where something was sticking up. It wasn't sand, as it had appeared in the other vision. I reached out to try and touch the walls. They were rough, with what felt like gaping holes. Not large enough for a child to climb through, but openings nonetheless.

I reached my palms against the flat ceiling above me. It was just inches above my head. It was rough too, with a few holes in it. These were jagged, not like they had been cut, but gouged.

There was a distinct smell of old wood and the ocean. It was very strong—maybe on the beach?

The vision was over as suddenly as it had begun. I was sitting on the bed again with the ripped-up pink teddy bear. Beside me was dead Chuck. I jumped up and ran to the door.

"Help her," he said again.

I left the bedroom. I had nothing to say to him. I was doing the best I could. But wherever Guthrie had Betsy stashed, it wasn't easy to define or locate.

I *knew* Betsy was still alive, though. Let Ann think she was dead, if she wanted. I *knew* better. What I didn't know was what to do with that information. I didn't want to hurt the investigation by trying to find her myself, but I'd brought some good leads to the table. I knew I could be of use.

The chief was worried that the FBI would pull out. I couldn't be sure Betsy was in Duck either, as he'd said. We didn't have the resources to go all over the Outer Banks looking for her. It was hard to decide what to do.

Kevin, even working with Ann, might still be my best shot, although I wished that wasn't the case.

I wondered again why Guthrie was keeping the girl alive. He hadn't asked for anything in return—didn't seem to plan on giving her back. But what *was* he planning?

Maybe if I could figure out why Dillon Guthrie had killed Chuck, I might gain some insight into why he'd taken and was still holding Betsy. It seemed like the best way to start that process would be to break in on Port's dinner with

Trudy. Whether he realized it or not (and I hoped he didn't), Port was involved with what had happened to Chuck and his daughter.

Three might not be company, but it might help find Chuck's killer.

Chapter 18

I'd seen enough murder mysteries on TV and heard enough stories from Gramps that I thought I understood how the connection between Chuck and Guthrie had originated.

Chuck's bank statement showed that he was getting extra money from somewhere. Guthrie was a smuggler—it stood to reason that Chuck was working for him.

Chuck was under a lot of financial stress. His ex-wife was between jobs. He had to take care of Betsy by himself. His business was already failing after a terrible real estate scandal that had driven most local people away. He needed money like never before and was desperate enough to consider doing something illegal.

But something had gone wrong between Chuck and Guthrie, as happens many times in this type of relationship. Guthrie had killed Chuck. I had no doubt about that—despite Guthrie's top-dog status, which seemed to make the FBI afraid to question him. Then Guthrie had taken Betsy.

How is Port involved?

That was the part I couldn't figure. I'd have to spend more time with Port if I was going to answer that question. A handshake wasn't going to do it. I needed prolonged contact with him or to hold something that belonged to him. I had no idea how I was going to manage either one.

I took Betsy's teddy bear with me, hiding it in a paper bag in case I ran into some law enforcement official ready to accuse me of taking things from the scene of a crime.

I also picked up Chuck's electric razor—my hand protected by a glove I'd begun carrying around in my pocketbook. The razor would be close and personal to him. I might need that too if contact with Port didn't work out.

Beyond my not-well-thought-out plan to glean information from Port, I was as clueless as the FBI. Why would a big-name smuggler who had killers on his staff (I felt sure I'd seen them in my dream) kill a lowly real estate broker?

It seemed to me—à la *Law & Order*—that Guthrie's hands-on involvement indicated a personal motivation. Maybe it'd had nothing to do with business. Or maybe Guthrie had wanted to make an example of Chuck.

Betsy?

If she was with Chuck when he was killed, why wouldn't Guthrie kill her too? That would make sense. Hanging on to her was stupid and dangerous for him. What if someone found her?

But maybe Guthrie didn't kill children. Maybe he'd assigned one of his henchmen but the henchman couldn't kill her. Maybe the henchman was like the huntsman in *Snow White* who couldn't kill the pretty princess and instead had let her run away. In Betsy's case, though, maybe the henchman had put Betsy someplace he felt she would be safe until he had a chance to let her go.

I didn't dare express this theory to anyone else. I knew I'd be laughed into next week as soon as I mentioned *Snow White*. I knew it didn't really make traditional police sense, but it was all I had—at least until I could get more (hopefully) from Port.

I walked the rest of the way back to my house with my purloined items safely tucked away. No one had tried to stop me or even noticed what I was doing. The FBI probably felt they'd gotten all the evidence they could from Chuck's house.

Lucky for me. I really wasn't up for another visit to the police station.

Just as I reached my house, Kevin's pickup pulled next to me. "I've been calling you for a while. Where have you been?"

"Just out walking. I needed some space."

"Betsy's mother wants to talk to you. She trusts you. There might be something everyone else is missing that she could show you."

I glanced at my watch. I had plenty of time to interrupt Trudy and Port's dinner. Maybe talking to Melinda would help. "Okay. Let me put this in the house. I'll be right out."

As I walked away from the pickup, something caught my eye. It was as though a beam of sunlight was shining through a crack in the clouds, illuminating something unusual in Old Man Sweeney's driveway.

Like a magpie, I couldn't resist it. I had to see what it was. Probably nothing. A piece of gum wrapper or a dropped coin. But it *felt* like something important.

It was a matchbook—wet from the rain and slightly mangled. The name on the cover was "Sailor's Dream," the little bar and grill near the beach where my father worked. There was a bit of blue glitter on it.

I couldn't be sure, but I doubted Old Man Sweeney frequented the place. As soon as I picked up the matchbook, I knew how it had come to be here.

Derek Johnson had dropped it in the driveway, probably when he was being arrested. The matchbook also revealed that Derek spent a lot of time at Sailor's Dream—waiting to meet with Guthrie.

"What is it, Dae?" Kevin joined me in the driveway. "What did you find?"

I showed him. "Derek Johnson had it when he was arrested trying to reclaim Chuck's medallion from Old Man Sweeney. That's where this all started for me. When I touched the matchbook, I saw Derek waiting at Sailor's Dream for Guthrie."

"Dae—"

"What? We all know Johnson didn't just see the sign for the medallion and decide to retrieve his lost property. He didn't kill Chuck—that was Guthrie—whether the FBI believes it or not. Derek was probably just covering for Guthrie. They meet at the Sailor's Dream. He works for him. If I go to Sailor's Dream, maybe I can pick up on something else."

"You can't go alone," he said. "These men are killers. You shouldn't be there at all, but if you have to go, I'm going too."

"You can't go with me." I pocketed the matchbook as I dismissed the idea. "They would know you were a Fed a mile away."

"I'm not a Fed anymore." He laughed. "And you watch too many crime shows on TV. I can blend in as well as you can. Neither one of us needs any excuse to be there. Danny is your father and my friend."

I considered his suggestion. He was right, of course. I'd

probably *feel* safer being there with Kevin, whether I was or not.

"All right. We'll go tonight. I want to talk to Melinda first, and then I have to meet a few friends at Wild Stallions. I'll give you a call."

I ran inside to put down the razor and the bear I'd taken from Chuck's house. Actually, I hid them under my bed. I didn't want to take any chances.

The black kitten started purring as soon as he saw me. He sat down on my foot, staring up at me in a dreamy way. Since I'd never had a pet, I wasn't sure what to expect from one. I picked him up, and he snuggled into my hand. An incredible feeling of joy radiated from him.

"I bet you need some food," I said to him. I brought him up close to my face and was lost in his bright eyes. "I don't think there's any cat food yet, but I'll see what I can find."

Gramps surprised me again by having cat food and a bowl in the kitchen for him. I put some food down, and the kitten jumped on it. Apparently Gramps had undergone a major change of heart while I'd been out and had decided the kitten was welcome after all.

I scratched the kitten behind one ear. "I guess Gramps likes you. That's a good thing because you aren't going anywhere else, are you?"

He made a tiny meowing sound and purred while he ate. I didn't know anyone could feel this close to an animal.

I ran back out and got in the pickup with Kevin. There was very little traffic on Duck Road, which made for a quick trip to the Blue Whale. We talked the whole way about what we might find at the Sailor's Dream later. Suddenly, the awkwardness between us was gone. It was just like old times.

Then Ann was waiting for us on the veranda. "I might

have known you two would be together. It's not just the little girl, is it, Kevin? You can't stop thinking about Dae."

"Let's go somewhere private to discuss this," he said.

"Never mind." She sipped what smelled like a mint julep. "I know all of this has been a shock. You never expected me to come back and ruin the perfect little life you created with Mayor Smiley-face."

"You're drunk." Kevin took her arm and pulled her out of the chair. "Let's go inside."

"Maybe I am drunk," she agreed. "But I'll bet you haven't told her all about us, have you? She doesn't know the things we've done together, what we meant to each other. Maybe she wouldn't care so much about you if she knew."

Ann reached out quickly and grabbed my hand. Her eyes were like cold steel tearing into my brain. I thought I screamed as thousands of images flooded into my brain. They packed in so fast that I couldn't handle it. It was a massive overload. I couldn't distinguish one image from another.

I thought Kevin broke us apart. When I looked at him, I saw him holding a gun, shooting a man who'd refused to surrender. Kevin didn't know if the man meant to kill him or not. Ann consoled him after it was over. The images of the two of them in bed together burned into my mind. I squeezed my eyes tightly closed and let myself drift away.

When I came back to myself, Ann was gone. Kevin was sitting beside me on the bed in one of the inn's rooms. I loved the lilac walls and the gossamer curtains, through which the sun shone bright every morning.

"Are you okay?" He took my hand. "Ann is *very* powerful. Even more so now. I didn't realize—I'm sorry."

"I'm fine." I sat up. My brain felt like a piece of fiery mush, but I'd survived the attack. "You could've warned me."

I said it, but I knew no warning could've prepared me for what Ann had just put me through. The idea of her attacking me with her thoughts and memories seemed too much like science fiction. I doubted I would've believed it was possible if I hadn't lived through it.

"I'm sorry." He got up and paced the room. "I thought maybe this would work—that she'd learn to love . . . Duck . . . like I have."

"But she doesn't." I didn't mind telling him about her visit to Missing Pieces now. "I don't think she ever will."

"I know." He looked around the room that faced the ocean. I knew he was thinking about all the time he'd put into the Blue Whale, believing it was his new home. His eyes were wistful. "I think I should leave. Ann isn't stable. I don't know if she'll ever be if we stay here. There's too big a gap from where we were. For her, it's like everything is still the same as it was when she went into the hospital. Nothing has changed. In her mind, the last few years never happened."

I wanted to ask him to stay and we'd find a way to fix it. That was me—always looking for a way to make things right. But I didn't speak. Intuition told me he was right. If he was going to stay with Ann, out of guilt or love, he'd have to live somewhere else.

It was one of the saddest moments of my life.

But I had to keep going. I couldn't let this stop me from finding Betsy.

I pushed to my feet. I still felt shaky, but the active memories Ann had thrown at me were fading. They'd left behind a headache—and a distaste for Ann and Kevin's love life—but otherwise, I knew I'd be fine. "I'm here. I guess I should talk to Melinda."

"You should sit down for a while," he suggested. "Let me get you some tea, and I'll take you home later. Is chamomile okay?"

I said it was fine just so he'd leave. It wasn't his fault Ann had attacked me, but what she'd shown me was too fresh for me not to be affected by it. I didn't know if I could ever look at Kevin the same way again. Maybe that's all she'd really meant to do.

I needed to find Melinda.

Talk to her.

And get out of there.

I waited until I was sure Kevin would be in the old iron-lace elevator, on his way to the kitchen, then I left the room.

It wasn't hard to find Melinda. I saw her from an upstairs window, sitting on a bench in the back of the inn, staring at the ocean. I looked around carefully as I walked through the ballroom and out the back door. I didn't see Ann anywhere.

I sat down next to Melinda on the bench. She turned toward me, her eyes red and swollen. "I wish there was something—*anything*—I could do to help. I feel so useless. My daughter, my baby, is out there somewhere. Maybe she's still alive. Is anyone still looking for her?"

"Everyone is looking for her," I reassured her. "We'll find her."

"I don't think they're going to find her. What was I thinking, leaving her here with Chuck? He's always been irresponsible."

"You were doing what you thought was right." I took a deep breath to steady myself and push away from the mental abuse I'd suffered at Ann's hands. "I may be able to help you find Betsy."

"How?" She was clearly bewildered. "What else can you do?"

I tried to explain about my gift. Her eyes grew wide as she stared at me in disbelief. "I don't know for sure it will work. I've been finding lost things for people since I was a child. If you think about how much you love Betsy and that she's lost, maybe it will work."

It hadn't been my intention to offer her what might be false hope. First of all, Melinda hadn't technically *lost* her daughter. The girl had been, essentially, stolen. I wasn't sure my gift would work if the seeker didn't have some sense, at least subconsciously, of where the lost item could be.

Still, it was worth a try, I thought as I watched Melinda's reaction. If it didn't work, we were no worse off than we were before. If it did work, Betsy might be home soon.

Melinda clearly didn't understand or believe what I'd told her. Time had taught me that her belief wasn't necessary. When she finally nodded to let me know we could try the experiment, I took her hands and closed my eyes.

The sandy grass behind the Blue Whale faded away with the sound of the ocean and the cry of the gulls. As in my previous visions and dreams of Betsy, I was enveloped in blackness. I stood perfectly still, waiting, listening, hoping for the off chance I'd detect another clue as to where she was being held.

The constant drip of water was annoying and no help at all. The smell of wet sand and decaying sea life surrounded me. There was nothing new here.

I was about to call her name when suddenly a door opened from above me. It brought in weak light—maybe a distant streetlight or light from a nearby house.

I studied the square shape of the opening above me. I was sure it was a thick wooden door, only enough room to allow in one person at a time. But no one came through.

"Are you there, little girl?" a masculine voice called out. "I brought you something to eat. Come and get it so I don't drop it in the sand."

In response, Betsy moved toward the light. She looked

like a little ghost, her nightgown torn in places. She lifted her hands for the food. Her tangled brown hair slipped back from her shoulders. "Please let me out. Please don't leave me here."

The food came down in a narrow basket dropped by a rope. "You know I can't do that. But I think your time is coming. I think you'll be out of here soon. Just be a good girl a little longer. Jackie is going to get you out of here. Wait and see."

Betsy looked at me squarely in the face before she took the food from the basket. "Can you see? This might be the last time. Can you find me?"

I was pulled from the spot, trembling and crying. Maybe another instant and I would've been able to identify the place or the person who was lowering the food. Maybe another moment—

"Did you see anything?" Melinda was shaking me. Or was I just shaking? I couldn't tell. "Did you find her?"

My teeth were chattering too hard to speak. My whole body felt as though it might fall apart. I wanted to reassure her, but the words wouldn't come.

Through my mental fog, I sensed Ann rushing toward us like a vortex of raw energy. I wanted to run, but I couldn't get my legs to work. I tried to yell for help—I couldn't possibly face her this way. Another blast of her awful venom might keep me from ever using my gift again.

I was surprised when she helped me sit upright. Her cold blue eyes stared into mine. "You're a stupid little fool, aren't you? You don't know when to stop. How have you survived all these years like this?"

"I-I was fine until y-you came," I managed to get out.

She laughed, and a breeze from the ocean caught at her pale hair, blowing it across her sculpted face. "I guess it doesn't matter. You could've killed yourself, or at least never regained consciousness trying this little stunt after I blasted you. But you've convinced me. I don't know why I couldn't feel that little girl—until now. Maybe I was too afraid to let myself feel her."

"A-and now?" I dared.

"Now we find this little girl—this little girl who's still alive and needs rescuing."

"You mean you know Betsy is alive now?" Melinda asked, sobbing.

"That's right," Ann said abruptly. "Now stop crying and help me get Dae inside."

Chapter 19

After about an hour, I was fine again—but confused. I sat in the kitchen with Kevin and Ann. Kevin was chopping mushrooms for his famous homemade mushroom soup. Ann was looking at a magazine full of shoes.

"So what happens now?" I croaked. Somehow all of this psychic energy had made my voice hoarse.

"Now we figure out where they're keeping the girl." Ann didn't look up from the magazine. "Kevin said you're going to look for some guy at a bar tonight. Is that a personal thing or part of the investigation?"

I explained about Derek Johnson and the matchbook I'd found. "I think that may have been his voice I heard speaking to Betsy in the vision."

She shrugged. "We need proof."

"Maybe we can get that from Derek, if he's taking care of her."

Ann didn't respond.

"There's the name—Jackie—too. He said Jackie was going to let Betsy go soon. That might be something. I haven't heard that name mentioned before."

"Wait!" Ann tossed the magazine across the table and stood up. "I think I may have some ideas on that." She started sketching on a napkin, but Kevin got her a piece of computer paper and she began again. "I keep seeing this woman. Maybe she's Jackie."

Her sketching was fast and furious, like everything else she did. Where I was slow and methodical, she was a human dynamo.

"Look familiar?" She held out the crude sketch.

"That's her! I think she's Guthrie's girlfriend! You think she's Jackie?"

"It's possible. I got this resonance from you when you said the name."

"But I don't know if the girlfriend's name is Jackie or not."

"It doesn't matter," she said impatiently. "This woman is the key. Maybe someone at the FBI knows her. We should all go down there again."

I glanced at my watch. It was nearly time for Trudy and Port to meet at Wild Stallions. "There's something else. I have to see where it leads me. I know the information I got from Port is important and it involves this woman." I explained the situation to them.

"Fine. We'll go there, get something to eat and scrape this guy's mind."

"I can't leave right now," Kevin said. "I have to get this soup on."

Ann shrugged her narrow shoulders. "We don't need you. We're big girls, right, Dae?"

I wasn't sure how to answer. Despite Ann's newfound spirit of cooperation, I didn't trust her. Clearly, Kevin was uncertain about us going off together too. After our talk earlier, I wasn't exactly in fear for my life, but I was still on edge.

What if Ann's mood swings changed her again? I didn't know if I could handle another mental onslaught right now.

"I'll go up and change. Meet you there in about an hour?" she suggested.

"Okay." I glanced at Kevin. "In about an hour."

"It will only take me another minute and I'll be done with these mushrooms, so I can run you home, Dae," Kevin said. "I'll come back for you, Ann."

"Not necessary." She breezed by him. "I can find my way. You just make sure Dae doesn't take on any other challengers until after she gets through this evening."

With that, she was gone, running up the stairs with the energy of a teenager.

Kevin put the chopped mushrooms in a large pot on the stove. "All right. Let's go."

I felt like I'd been on a roller coaster the last few hours. I needed a lot more than chamomile tea (which I'd had in the kitchen) to fully recover from my most recent vision of Betsy. But there wasn't time.

Instead, Kevin and I got back in his truck and headed for my house.

"Well?" he asked as we started toward Duck Road. "I know you have questions."

"I don't know. Is she always that way?"

"She wasn't. She was calm and methodical when we first met. Finding all of those missing children, the ones we couldn't save, changed her. She's nothing like the woman I fell in love with. I don't know what's going on with her anymore."

"But she's obviously dangerous. Can we work together?"

"I don't know. I'm worried it might not be safe for you. On the other hand, the two of you make a good team. You complement each other. You might still be able to find Betsy Sparks against every scrap of FBI protocol. Just don't go *anywhere* alone with her."

"How did she learn to do that—throw her memories at me?"

"She was brought up learning things like that. You haven't developed the survival instincts to defend yourself. That's why you couldn't ward off her attack."

"I see." But I really didn't. What had happened at the Blue Whale was completely out of my realm of experience.

He stopped the truck to wait for traffic, then turned to face me. "You don't want to learn how to do those things, Dae. Look at what it's done to her. She'll never be able to lead a normal life as someone's mother or positively contribute to society like you will. I'm not sure how far she can go without completely falling apart again."

I was flattered by his words. They made me sound much stronger and more competent than I felt at that moment. Maybe I would never work for the FBI, but I didn't have to be completely useless either.

"I think it's worth the risk, working with her. Together, we might be able to figure things out."

A few moments later Kevin pulled the pickup into the driveway, behind Gramps's golf cart. "Just promise me you'll be careful. Don't trust her. I'll stay close to you."

I nodded, not trusting myself to speak either. I could see it pained him to agree that I should work with Ann. I knew him well enough to know when something wasn't right for him. This plan was one of those things. I just couldn't think of any other way. Apparently neither could he.

Gramps was inside making supper for his pinochle

group, which would be meeting at our house later. I explained briefly about my plans for the evening, though I didn't mention what had happened between me and Ann that afternoon. I didn't need him trying to protect me too.

"Watch your back with Kevin's fiancée," he warned, proving that his instincts for trouble were still good. He stroked the black kitten as it rubbed up against him. "I don't think that woman knows what she's doing. She might lead you into danger."

"I'll be careful." I smiled at the picture of contentment he made with the cat. "I never thought I'd see the day."

"Me either. But I like the little devil. I must be going crazy in my old age. Tim called and told me he'd found the other cat that was picked up at Chuck's house. I think she may be this one's mother. I told him to bring her on over and we'll sit both of them until you find that little girl."

"You might not want to get rid of them," I warned.

"Never mind. Just go get ready—try not to stay out too late."

I laughed and went upstairs to change. I felt better after a long, hot shower. The attack had left me feeling like I had the flu—sore throat and all. It seemed like an odd reaction to what had happened, but maybe it was common. I would definitely research the idea on the Internet when I had a free moment.

I picked out a black velvet dress that I liked. It was a little old-fashioned, but it always made me feel beautiful. I'd learned why after my gift had changed, allowing me to sense emotions from objects. The dress had belonged to an older woman who'd had a wonderful life. I could feel her happiness every time I wore it. I hoped it would give me confidence tonight.

I brushed my short hair and put on some plum-colored lipstick that I'd bought at Trudy's last makeup party. Thinking about my friend triggered a feeling of uneasiness about what I had planned for the evening.

I realized at that point that I didn't *really* have a plan. Interrupting Port and Trudy's romantic dinner was going to be bad enough. But how was I going to take something personal from Port or touch him long enough to get the information I needed? Kevin and I could just ask him about Jackie, I supposed, but what if Port had some role in what had happened to Chuck? We couldn't take that chance.

I said good night to Gramps as I walked out the front door. I really didn't need Kevin's help at Wild Stallions, but it was still nice to see him waiting for me in the driveway.

He'd showered and changed into brown slacks and a casual tan sport coat. His dark hair was still damp, and he smelled like soap.

When I looked at him, I realized that I loved him. It was embarrassing, especially since we weren't together anymore. But there it was. Tears formed in my eyes, despite my best attempts to stop them. I had never been in love this way before.

"That was fast." I kept my face averted as I blinked away those telltale tears and kept the conversation light. "And you even walked back."

"Not exactly."

He pointed to a deep blue golf cart—the same shade we'd painted the Blue Whale Inn. It was pulled next to Gramps's cart. "I bought it last month, remember? It was just delivered today. Shall we go?"

"That's it. You've finally succumbed." I smiled at him. "You're a Banker now for sure."

"I definitely think there's a little pirate in me," he admitted with a slash of a smile. "Maybe I was meant to be here. Maybe an ancestor of mine came from Duck. Who knows?"

The night was very fine—not a wisp of a cloud to hide

the stars, making them seem closer. The moon was smaller, off in the distance, peeping over the horizon. A warm November breeze stirred the trees around us.

I could imagine it could always be this way. Kevin and I, going through life together.

"Have you got any idea how you're going to get the information you want from this guy at Wild Stallions?" he asked.

"None at all. I guess that makes this an adventure."

"All right then." He opened the door to the golf cart. "What do you need?"

"Maybe his keys or some other personal object he keeps with him. Or I thought I could hold his hand for a while or even kiss him. Maybe a hug would do it."

"Either one of those things are sure to put you on Trudy's hit list. Maybe I can get you his wallet."

"How would you do that? Do you have a hidden talent for picking pockets that you haven't told me about?"

He smiled. "Let me take care of that."

The closer we got to Wild Stallions, the more nervous I became. I knew Trudy would not take kindly to our crashing her romantic dinner. She hadn't had a date in months. I wouldn't have done it for less than someone's life. I dreaded our conversation afterward, but I couldn't let that concern stop me from helping Betsy.

Maybe Kevin's pick-pocket plan would work. It was definitely preferable to my having to hug and kiss Port. I was certain Trudy would feel the same.

Wild Stallions was busy at the end of the boardwalk. The walkway was alive with lights and music thumping from a live band. People were strolling around, looking in dark, closed shop windows. What a pity no one was open.

I hadn't realized there was business here at night. I

thought I might look into being open a few late nights and see if I could catch the interest of the crowd that wasn't here during the day.

The Currituck Sound was smooth as glass, reflecting the gorgeous flares of sunset color. Lights twinkled on across the water, probably in Corolla or Kitty Hawk. The lighthouse beacons weren't on as yet, but they would be soon, sweeping the night with their thick beams.

I thought again about seeing the *Andalusia* the night I'd found Chuck's body on the Atlantic side. Maybe it was a bad omen, as many older citizens of Duck claimed. Certainly nothing good had happened to me since I'd seen it.

Kevin and I parted company before we reached Wild Stallions. He thought it might be best if we weren't together when we went in. I didn't know what his plan was, but I hoped it would work.

Maybe this time, when I held Derek's wallet, I'd see the place where Betsy was being held.

Let this be the moment, I prayed silently. *Let this be the last night Betsy has to spend out there alone.*

I cleared my throat and squared my shoulders before I walked into the restaurant. I saw Trudy and Port right away. They were seated at my favorite booth, back away from the noise and crowd.

Trudy was sitting very close to Port. She was smiling in an adoring manner as he fed her pasta. They weren't taking their eyes off each other.

I started deliberately toward them, pasting my big mayor's smile on my face, words ready to explain why I was ruining their moment.

Suddenly a tall, thin woman in a tight gold lamé dress stepped between me and my target. I realized, as I got closer, that it was Ann.

"Port?" She addressed him in the warm, familiar voice of a former lover. "Surprise seeing you here! What brings you to Duck?"

What is she doing? I looked around for Kevin but couldn't find him. *What is she thinking?*

Port seemed taken aback. He said something to Trudy and took her hand. "I think you've got the wrong man, miss."

Ann laughed, a cackle loud enough to make everyone notice. "I don't think so! I *know* you haven't forgotten dinner on the island and breakfast on your boat. Not to mention everything that went on—*in between*."

"I'm sorry, but I don't know you." Port's voice was calm and clear. "You and I have never done *anything* together."

"Maybe we should leave." Trudy started to get up.

"No. It's fine. Just a mistake." Port stared at Ann like he was finally starting to get angry. "We're staying."

"Oh, lover!" Ann threw her arm around his shoulder and leaned against him. "Ditch the little woman and we'll have some fun." She made kind of a loud squeaky sound, like a weird giggle. It wasn't a sound I'd ever expected to hear from her.

"Maybe you're right, Trudy. We should leave." Port shrugged Ann off and knocked over a glass of wine as he hastily got to his feet.

"Yes!" Ann grabbed him again.

Trying to get away from her, Port almost lost his balance. As he tried to regain his footing and get away from Ann, a man passed between the two of them. I saw his hand deftly slide into Port's pocket. He took something out and put it into his own pocket.

As he turned to blend back in with the interested crowd, Kevin winked at me.

The effort complete, Ann walked away from Port as though the whole thing had been a mistake. Port looked around like he couldn't believe it had happened. Trudy sat back down, like she'd suddenly deflated.

I couldn't believe it, but Ann had saved me from Trudy's wrath by intervening with her crazy stunt. Yet it was enough of a distraction for Kevin to get what I needed.

A waiter asked if I wanted to sit down. Knowing everything had been accomplished without making Trudy mad at me, I didn't take any chances. I said no and left the restaurant.

Kevin and Ann were outside on the boardwalk. It was dark at that corner behind the entrance to the restaurant. They hadn't seen me as yet.

"Good as ever!" Ann exclaimed, leaning against Kevin. "We are still a great pair, aren't we? We always worked so well together. Our relationship worked too, didn't it?"

He smoothed back a piece of her hair, ivory in the moonlight. "Yes, we were a good couple."

She took a step back from him. "I don't know why we're not a good couple now. I know I was sick. I know I let you down. But I'm back now. We can pick up where we left off. We can be better than we ever were. All you have to do is give it a chance."

"I can't do this work all the time anymore, Ann. I realized that when you got sick. I've built a new life here and I like it."

She laughed in a hard, brittle way. "Really? You like making soup and cleaning up after people? Come on, Kevin. You were made for so much more. Think of all the things we've done—of all the things we *could* do. You don't have to bury yourself in this little backwater."

"I like this little backwater. I wish you did too."

"That's not going to happen." She sighed. "I guess that makes you and Dae a good couple now."

Chapter 20

I didn't want them to know I'd been listening, so I walked out of the shadows right away. "That was amazing," I gushed to cover my embarrassment at eavesdropping on them. "Thank you for doing that, Ann. Now Trudy won't hate me for ruining her date."

"I hope it helps," she said. "Let's go somewhere and take a look at our plunder."

"I got his wallet," Kevin added. "That should be personal enough to know if he's part of all this."

I agreed, and we walked down to Missing Pieces. I hated to do it, but I had to leave the door closed and locked, not letting the potential customers inside. *Maybe another time*. I wasn't set up to do business anyway.

Besides, I needed quiet to hold the wallet and hoped to see Betsy. I sat on the burgundy brocade sofa. The shop was dark except for the boardwalk lights shining in on us.

Ann sat next to me—a sketchbook on her lap, pencil in hand.

It made me a little nervous, not because I was afraid of her but because I knew she was trying to see into my mind. The idea was a little disconcerting. What else would she see in there? I didn't have many secrets, but I kind of wanted the ones I had to stay secret.

Kevin stood near the door, looking out at the people on the boardwalk. The shadows of the people walking by passed him, like the shadows on the moon in the night sky.

It reminded me of another time when we were waiting for help after a mission that had gone bad. A killer had been stalking us, and we had to lie low until we knew who he was. Kevin was smoking his last cigarette—

No! Those aren't my memories.

"Is something wrong?" Ann noticed that I was restless.

"No. Just having trouble concentrating."

"Newbies," she scoffed.

Kevin looked my way, and I closed my eyes, trying to put my thoughts in order. I hoped the memories Ann had thrust on me would fade in time. Those were private things, events that were only supposed to be shared between Ann and Kevin. I didn't want to say anything to Kevin about those things, but it was hard.

Is Ann making notes about my (her) memories of Kevin as she sketches pictures from my brain?

I was holding the wallet, but nothing was happening. Usually it was immediate. I couldn't *stop* the images from coming. But not that night. I wasn't sure if it was because I was so busy trying to separate my memories from Ann's or because I was still so involved in what had happened, both in the restaurant and outside on the boardwalk.

I'd be lying if I said I didn't hope Ann would go back to

New York, or wherever was best for her, and decide to leave Kevin's life. He meant too much to me not to hope things could go back the way they were between us before she got here.

"I'm sorry." I opened my eyes. "I'm just not getting anything."

"Try harder," Ann snarled. "I don't want to sit here holding your hand all night."

I tried again. *Nothing.* Whatever caused my gift to work, wasn't working. "I don't see anything."

"Well then, maybe Kevin and I should go have some drinks and dinner while you keep trying," Ann said. "We'll come back later and maybe you'll have something."

"Don't pay any attention to her," Kevin said. "You must be hungry too. Let's go eat dinner and maybe you'll relax enough to get something from the wallet. You're probably just too wound up to concentrate properly."

Ouch!

Yes, I was a newbie, as Ann kept reminding me. Sometimes it was hard for me to know what to do. But Kevin's remark made me feel like a child. I definitely didn't need to go to dinner with them and feel like a third wheel too.

"No. Ann's right," I said finally. "I'll stay here and have some tea. Maybe that will help. You two go and enjoy yourselves. I'll call you if I see anything."

"I hate to leave you," Kevin replied. "We don't know what Port is up to. There may be some strong impressions on the wallet."

Ann stood up. "Oh for God's sake, we'll be just up the boardwalk, Kevin. Whatever she sees isn't going to kill her. Let's go and we'll come back."

She brushed by him as she went out the door. Kevin hung back until I reassured him that Ann was right. "Call me if you need me," he said.

I told him I would and locked the door behind him. It was the first time I was really able to draw a deep breath.

I was glad they were both gone. I didn't need all of those emotional issues pulling at my heart when I was supposed to be thinking about Betsy. I just couldn't seem to help myself when I was with them.

I shouldn't have listened to their conversation outside Wild Stallions. It had scrambled things between us. Just as my brain was convincing my heart not to get my hopes up, hearing Kevin and Ann discuss their past and future had made everything unsure again.

I needed to focus. Ann was right about that. I was never going to find Betsy with my heart racing and my hands shaking.

I took off the black velvet jacket I'd worn with the dress, kicked off my shoes and made some tea on the hot plate. I tried to focus on Betsy while ignoring Port's wallet, which seemed to mock me from the sofa. Why couldn't I see something from it? I should at least be able to see where it had been made and where he'd bought it. That wasn't so much to expect.

There was a knock on the door. *What now?*

I should have ignored it. I couldn't. I would have to get rid of whoever it was.

I peeked out the blind. It was Port.

I stumbled back from the door, not sure if he'd seen me. I shoved his wallet into a drawer behind the cash register. My heart was pounding. Had he guessed that I was involved in taking it and had come to confront me?

That was crazy. How could he know? I had to talk to him—send him on his way.

I went back to the door and looked out again. I didn't see Trudy. But there *was* someone with him. I recognized him right away. *Dillon Guthrie.*

With trembling hands, I unlocked the door and smiled at Port. "Hi there. Something I can do for you? We're not officially open. I just stopped in for a cup of tea. It's been a long day." I feigned a yawn.

Port smiled back at me, but he was clearly tense, not easy and open as he had been this afternoon. "Hi, Dae. I hope you don't mind, but when my buyer for the Flobert pistol heard about you having one of the silver bells, he was interested in seeing it."

I glanced at Guthrie. He smiled at me and stepped forward. "We haven't met, but my friend here tells me you have something very rare for sale. I'd like very much to take a look at it. My name is Dillon Guthrie."

I wanted to say no. Knowing he had killed Chuck and might decide to kill Betsy made me angry and scared at the same time. On the other hand, maybe this was an opportunity to learn something about him that would help in the investigation.

Feeling like I was inviting an evil vampire into the shop, I stood to one side and held the door open. "Please come in. Would you like some tea?"

As they stepped inside, I turned on the lights. I also left the door unlocked, slightly ajar. Probably neither one of those gestures would save my life if Guthrie decided to kill me and take the St. Augustine bell, but they made me feel better.

To my surprise, Guthrie wanted a cup of tea. Port declined. I made the two cups of tea and hoped no one would notice how badly my hands were shaking as I offered one of them to Guthrie.

He thanked me and continued his tour of Missing Pieces. He was much smaller in person than he'd been in my vision. He was shorter than Kevin and had a stockier build. His hair was brown with prominent streaks of gray. He didn't look like my idea of a smuggler, but that was probably because to me, smugglers should all look like pirates. This man was too well-dressed and polished to be a pirate.

"I'm sorry about this, Dae," Port quietly apologized. "I know Trudy is going to hate me, since I had to cut our evening short for this. Then I couldn't find my wallet and she had to pay. I shouldn't have told Dillon about the bell, I guess. Who knew he'd take such an interest? But he's a very good client—always pays in cash."

"That's okay. Don't worry about it. You did what you had to do."

I sipped my tea and tried to look like a calm shopkeeper who was just happy to have someone perusing her wares. I was anything but that—looks can be deceiving.

"I'd like to see the silver bell, please," Guthrie said finally. "You have many very fine pieces here, Dae. But the bell is what intrigues me."

I'd put the bell, away from the main floor, in the storage area after Port had looked at it earlier. I'd realized there was no point in tempting people to buy it when I wasn't ready to sell it. But I took it out for Guthrie and unwrapped the blue velvet that surrounded it.

"Unbelievable!"

I was careful not to touch him in the transfer. This wouldn't be a good time to fall on the floor and forget who I was while I tried to process whatever terrible visions might ensue.

"That's how I felt when I saw it," I admitted.

"When Port told me about this, I was stunned. I didn't know any of these bells had been found." He smiled at me. If I hadn't already been aware of the truth about him, I'd never have guessed he was a killer, and much more. "You know the legend?"

"Yes."

"Amazing!" He continued his thorough examination of the wonderful old silver work. "You never know where you're going to find the good stuff, right? That's what Port is always telling me."

"That's right," Port chimed in. "Like the pistol. I looked everywhere for it—Dae had a customer with one for sale. It all worked out."

Port was getting more agitated the longer they stayed in the shop. He knew who this man was and what he was capable of doing. He was afraid of Guthrie. Who wouldn't be? I was standing there trying to at least appear unafraid, but I was terrified.

"How much?" Guthrie put the bell back down in its bed of blue velvet, but his hand rested possessively on it.

"It's not for sale." I smiled when I said the words, but I could feel the corners of my lips trembling. I hadn't changed my mind about selling the bell. I was surprised Port had even mentioned it to Guthrie.

"Pardon?" Guthrie said as though he couldn't possibly have heard right.

"I'm sorry." I swallowed hard on the fear that threatened to overwhelm me. I knew he'd just as soon shoot me and take the bell. He didn't have to negotiate. "I thought Port had told you. The bell isn't for sale. I won't sell it until I find the other two."

Guthrie stared hard at me for what seemed like an hour. Then he burst out laughing. "This one is the find of a lifetime, Dae. What makes you think the other two will come to you?"

"I just know it," I answered honestly. "I can wait. They should be together as the monks wanted them to be. That's the least I can do, since they died to protect them."

"Are you for real?" Guthrie laughed again but without

any humor behind it. He turned to Port. “Is she for real? You’re my negotiator—negotiate.”

Port shrugged. “Dae, maybe you should reconsider. I know Mr. Guthrie would pay very well for the bell.”

“I told you how I feel. The bell isn’t for sale.”

Both men glared at me. I could tell Port was horrified that I wouldn’t give up the bell. Guthrie seemed like he couldn’t quite believe I wouldn’t sell to him.

If he only knew—and if I’d had the courage to speak out—I’d give him the bell in exchange for Betsy. But that would mean admitting I knew about Chuck. Maybe even signing Betsy’s death warrant if Guthrie learned she was still alive.

Finally, when it seemed the tense atmosphere of the room would explode, Guthrie dropped down into a chair and shook his head. “I admire your tenacity, Dae. And your integrity. I wish I knew other people like you. Normally, I don’t like to lose. I take it personally. But that’s okay. I’m sure we can work it out.”

It felt as though the storm had passed, but I wasn’t sure what would follow.

“I have a deal in mind.” He wrote a figure down on the back of a business card and passed it to Port, who gave it to me. “I’m a patient man when it comes to the things I want. If you’ll call me first when you have all three bells, that’s what I’ll pay you for them.”

It was an enormous sum—more money than I had made at Missing Pieces since I’d opened it. More money than most people saw in a lifetime. I gulped *and* swallowed hard.

Port made a face when he saw how much money was involved. “I’ll be glad to stay in contact with Dae, although I have to agree with you, the chances are she’ll never find the other bells.”

Guthrie didn't even flick a glance in Port's direction. Port seemed beneath his notice. "You're not involved with this. This is between me and Dae. And for the record, I believe the bells will come to her. Call me crazy, but I feel something here. Maybe Dae has finding mojo."

I tried not to panic. This was a *very bad* man. And his offer involved *a lot* of money. I wouldn't call him when that time came. The bells were worth that much and more on the open market. I'd done my research.

But I was willing to play along for now—anything to get him out of my shop. I knew I was lucky he hadn't decided to just take what he'd come for.

"All right. You've got yourself a deal," I agreed.

Guthrie got to his feet with a big, triumphant smile on his face. "Shake on it. That's the way I do business. I always tell everyone that works for me, *A handshake is my bond.* Your bond too, if we do business."

What was I supposed to do? I wasn't wearing gloves to protect myself from all the terrible things I might feel from him. I couldn't excuse myself and rush over to put on gloves. I was going to have to endure his touch.

I tried to prepare for it mentally. My mind was all over the place. No focus, as Ann would say. Maybe I'd be lucky and not feel anything. That was about the best I could hope for.

I had no choice. I put out my hand and shook the hand of the devil. It was warm and firm, holding mine as though it would never let go.

There was no defense. Colors burst into my mind. They surrounded and swallowed me. I opened my eyes and saw Chuck Guthrie and the blond woman from my previous vision.

"I'm just going to the coast for a few days," Dillon said as he pulled on a dark suit coat and straightened his tie.

"I'd like to come anyway." She smiled and straightened his tie again. "I just want to look around a little. I won't get in your way."

"I'm going to get your birthday present. That little pistol you wanted?"

"Thank you!" She kissed him hard on the mouth. "So I can come? I can take care of my business and you can give me the Flobert."

"Sure." He shrugged, wondering what was up, since she hated the coast. "Let's do it."

I drew in a deep breath.

Guthrie was still holding my hand, staring, wondering what was wrong.

"Are you all right? You look a little pale. Do you need to sit down?" he asked as I recovered from seeing Chuck's death again from another perspective.

"I'm fine." The words came out in a barely audible squeak. I had to repeat them because he couldn't hear me the first time. I searched for some excuse for my weirdness. "The money. It's a lot of money."

He understood *that*, and laughed at me. "Yes, it is. And worth every penny. Remember—call me. No middleman. I like you, Dae. Let's keep in touch in case something else turns up in your little shop."

He let go of my hand and gestured to Port, who followed him outside like a puppy. The shop door closed behind them, and I sank down on the sofa. My knees wouldn't hold me up any longer.

Chapter 21

I guess I fell asleep. I heard knocking on the shop door and looked at my watch. It was after midnight. The lights from the boardwalk had been turned off, and Kevin had come to see if I needed help.

"I was worried about you," he said when I opened the door. "Did you have trouble with the wallet?"

I was surprised to see him without Ann but didn't mention it. "I had a surprise visitor." I told him about Guthrie and Port coming to see the silver bell.

We sat together on the sofa while I explained the vision I'd had when I'd shaken hands with Guthrie. Kevin frowned.

"I don't like that he was here," he said, looking around the shop as though Guthrie had contaminated it in some way. "It's a little too convenient. Maybe while we've been finding out information about him, he's been learning about us. How likely is it that Port just brought him here to see a bell?"

I tried to make him understand the significance of the silver bell. His FBI mind kept seeing a smuggler and killer wandering around my shop for no good reason. He didn't understand.

"You'll have to trust me on this," I said. "I was wrong to leave the bell out. It's very valuable. But it's not something my average customer would appreciate or afford. I didn't think it would matter."

"So Port brought him here to see the bell—and *you* wouldn't sell it to him?" Kevin smiled. "That must've been a surprise for him. Men like Guthrie are used to getting what they want."

"I'm pretty good at saying no—especially when it comes to my treasures."

"Let me run you home. It's late. I think we'll have to go to the Sailor's Dream tomorrow. I'd like to make sure you get home safely. It might not be a bad idea to have Tim do a few extra checks on your shop for a while. Guthrie could change his mind."

I agreed, although I knew there was no way to stop Guthrie if he really wanted to take the bell. Kevin looked at the bell in its midnight blue velvet but didn't really understand what the fuss was all about.

I dropped Port's wallet into a protective velvet bag I usually used for jewelry. I didn't want to leave it here and thought I might try holding it again later at home. We closed the shop and walked down the quiet stairs from the boardwalk to the empty parking lot.

As I settled into the passenger seat of the blue golf cart, I said, "The thing that really bothers me about this—and I've experienced it enough times to be really bothered by it—I haven't actually seen Guthrie's face in the visions with Chuck. It's dark. A gunshot rings out and Chuck falls to the ground. I thought it might be that I wasn't sure what Guthrie looked like. Then after I saw him in the vision with his girlfriend, I thought it might be because I hadn't met him. But why would I see the vision with him and his girlfriend making plans to come here together? What did that have to do with anything?"

Kevin started the engine and headed out of the parking lot toward Duck Road. "I don't know. He didn't say anything about Chuck?"

"No. They talked about the pistol I had for him and that she wanted to come here with him. He was surprised because she normally didn't want to come."

"I don't know, Dae. Maybe it will come to you."

Duck Road was empty, making the short ride to my house even faster. Clouds had pressed in from the ocean, and the night had begun to feel like rain.

Kevin pulled into the driveway and turned off the golf cart. "Have you tried holding the wallet again?"

"I did. There wasn't anything." I pulled it out of the velvet pouch. "Let's do it again."

I closed my eyes and waited. Nothing happened.

"I don't get it. It's not like I've lost my gift. Guthrie came through loud and clear. Why can't I pick up anything from Port's wallet?"

"You know these things aren't made to order. Maybe you need a rest. Give yourself a break on this, Dae. You'll see more clearly if you let your mind relax."

"And Betsy gets to spend another night alone and scared. This just isn't working, Kevin. There has to be a better way."

"If there is, be sure to tell the FBI. They're not doing any better than we are. It's complicated—in a way, none of us is seeing what we need to right now. Later we'll all wonder why we didn't get it sooner."

I got out of the golf cart with the wallet and wished him

good night. "There has to be a break in this soon. I don't know how long Betsy can hold out. I don't know how long *I* can hold out."

Kevin got out and stood beside me. When he put his arms around me, I didn't pull away. I ignored the inner voice telling me that he belonged to someone else, that he and Ann needed time to make everything work out. I didn't care. We stood together for several long moments until the front door opened and Gramps called my name.

"Good night, Dae." Kevin's voice was husky.

"Good night. I'll call you if anything comes to me."

Gramps was waiting at the front door when I walked up, like he used to when I was a kid. "Is Kevin coming in?"

"I don't think so."

"You know, just because you two aren't dating doesn't mean I can't be friends with him." Gramps scratched the kitten's ear as it rubbed up against him. "How's it going with his old girlfriend anyway? The two of you looked kind of tight out there."

I didn't have the energy to complain about him spying on us. "I don't know how it's going right now, Gramps. I'm exhausted. I'll see you in the morning."

The black kitten followed me upstairs and jumped on my bed. I put Port's wallet on the bedside table, wondering how I was going to get it back to him without him thinking I took it from him. I ignored the kitten while I got undressed and put on a summer Duck T-shirt then curled up beside him. He purred and rubbed against me.

I spent the rest of the night with insubstantial arms wrapped around Betsy's trembling body. We lay together on the damp ground, and I promised that I'd find her.

But when morning came, I was no closer to the truth than I had been the night before.

Today, I was scheduled—no, *obligated*—to attend the

Duck Chamber of Commerce Barbecue. It had been held every year for as long as anyone could remember—a political event that attracted officials from as far away as Raleigh, sometimes even Washington, DC.

This year, as in years past, candidates would meet and greet over a slab of roasted pig, slaw, and sweet iced tea. The Duck Historical Society always provided desserts—pecan pie, banana pudding and my favorite, blackberry cobbler with homemade ice cream.

The event was usually held at Duck Municipal Park, but that area had been cordoned off since the last big storm because of damage. It probably wouldn't open again as the same park, since it wouldn't take long to get moving on the town hall plans now that the money was in place.

The official groundbreaking ceremony would happen quickly, probably in the next few weeks, but it would be a lot longer before the real work began on the project.

The Duck Presbyterian Church had offered their picnic grove as an alternate location. I'd have to write them a letter on my mayoral stationary, officially thanking them for their civic-mindedness.

The picnic grove was a parklike setting equipped with about thirty neatly arrayed picnic tables, a playground for children, and a large fire pit in the middle for campfires during the church summer camp. A podium had been added near the fire pit for anyone who wanted to make a speech or two. The venue would be a fine place to hold the barbecue.

I knew the pig had been roasting for several days already. It always took a few days to get the hickory chips just right. The president of the chamber, Bo Huneycutt, and the president of the Duck Business Association, John Poole, had been working on the event and the barbecue for weeks.

It was an important day in Duck that brought hundreds

of people out—rain or shine. It was a day for officials to get together and talk over the events of the past year with every Duck resident who chose to be there. It was a day for handshakes, for campaign promises—and for hats.

Everyone who came to the barbecue wore a hat—the bigger and crazier, the better. Men wore fishing hats, golf hats, top hats and every other kind of hat imaginable. Women wore pillbox hats with veils, large, poofy *Gone with the Wind* hats, and slinky city hats that rode on the sides of their heads like spiders. The hat tradition had been with the event since old Bunk Whitley wore the first top hat to the barbecue. Back then, the people of the town had expected he'd be the first mayor of Duck, but he'd been missing for years before the first mayor—*me*—was elected right after incorporation.

I'd attended the Chamber of Commerce Barbecue all my life. When I was a kid, Gramps would have me hand out flyers in support of his reelection as sheriff. In nonelection years, I'd go just so he could show me off, he always said. Now that I was mayor, my attendance was mandatory.

But this morning I wanted to skip the whole thing. It had been a ragged night followed by a worse dawn. My eyes were swollen from crying, and my heart just wasn't in it.

It didn't matter to Gramps. He was up and dressed in his finest—a gray morning suit, his matching top hat on the table, ready to go. I knew from past years that he would wear gloves as well and take a cane to complete the picture. Like everyone else, he went all out for the event.

I got up late and stumbled down to the kitchen with the black kitten at my heels. Every time I'd woken up during the night, the kitten had been there, licking my face. His rough little tongue was somehow soothing.

Gramps was whistling and stirring oatmeal with raisins.

He grinned at me when I sat down. "I was beginning to wonder if you were going to be late for the barbecue. You look tired. Bad night?"

The possibility that I wouldn't go to the barbecue had not even crossed his mind. My being late was the worst-case scenario he could think of. I so wished I could avoid what promised to be a long day of shaking hands and listening to people promise me their support for the election. I didn't want to talk about sidewalks or tell anyone that things would get better—if they voted for me. I wanted to go back to sleep. It was the only time I felt like I was able to help Betsy, when I could be with her, even if we were both dreaming.

"I'm not feeling very well, Gramps. I may not be able to go."

His face turned ten shades of red, contrasting starkly with his white hair and beard. "You *have* to go. No politician who misses the barbecue will ever get elected in Duck. You know that. Do you think Mad Dog will skip this opportunity? Hell, no. You've been going since you were a kid and I was running for office. You have to go if you want to be mayor again. I hear Senator Seeger is supposed to be there today. Good photo op!"

None of that motivated me. It just didn't mean anything. Added to that, I had no escort. Kevin had gone with me last year, wearing a dashing formal tux. No hat, but that hadn't mattered.

"If you're thinking you'll have to go alone, or with me, don't worry about it. I've got it all set up." The doorbell rang, as if on cue. Gramps put down his spoon and turned off the oatmeal. "And that should be your date. Run upstairs and get ready. You don't want him to turn around and run back out the door when he sees you looking like a zombie, do you?"

He waited—stubborn and unmoving—until I finally dragged myself out of the chair and up the stairs. I knew he was right. I wanted to be mayor again. It was just hard to feel inspired this morning.

I had a dress that had come into Missing Pieces a few months ago with a group of other formal wear. It was long and slinky, the color of the ocean on a sunny day. I'd found a hat for it that clung to the side of my head—all matching sequins and a shoulder-length veil. I'd planned to wear lots of eye makeup and dazzle my local audience.

But the more I looked at the outfit, the more I knew it would have to wait until next year. It was too cheerful, too filled with promise and important plans, for me to wear it today.

Instead, I wore a plain black pantsuit, and in keeping with the event's custom, I pinned on a black velvet hat that had belonged to my grandmother. With the veil stretched across my face, I thought I might be able to handle the event. The question was, who had Gramps found to escort me?

That question was quickly answered—Tim. I should have known.

He was wearing his usual brown suit and narrow, short tie. His cowboy hat rode easily on the back of his head. When he saw me coming down the stairs, he stood up and smiled. "Morning, Dae. You look great. Thanks for letting me take you to the barbecue."

I felt a little guilty at using him this way. But we went back forever, and he never seemed to mind—as long as he was between girlfriends.

He was already eating oatmeal. Gramps put out a bowl for me too. I sat down and made polite conversation with both of them while I forced myself to eat a few spoons of hot cereal.

"Thanks for taking me to the barbecue, Tim," I said, pushing the bowl away. "I know it was short notice."

"Don't worry about it. I kind of suspected this would happen when I heard you and Brickman broke up. Who else would want to go with you?"

He grinned at me and winked, as though that would take the sting from his words. My gloomy day got worse.

Gramps drove over to the church in his golf cart. Tim insisted on driving his police car, assuring me that it was worth the cost to the town because a police presence would deter any trouble. Besides, he said, it would look impressive.

Cars and golf carts occupied every parking spot around the church. Dozens of people were walking toward the picnic area. Most of them waved to us as we drove slowly by. It was going to be a good event—no rain in sight—the smell of barbecue floating through the air.

Senator Seeger was indeed present. He was shaking hands and making deals. I'd forgotten he was up for reelection this fall. Dare County Sheriff Tuck Riley was there as well, even though this wasn't an election year for him. He was wearing his dress officer's uniform with his flat brimmed hat as he made the rounds of politicians and Duck residents.

"Where do you want to start?" Tim asked as we surveyed the crowd.

"How about with a dark, shady picnic table, far from the biggest part of the group," I suggested.

He laughed. "I meant the barbecue or the dessert."

"We just finished eating."

"Since when did that ever stop me?"

We agreed to split up. Tim found a plate and loaded it up. I mixed and mingled, shaking dozens of hands and listening to hundreds of ways Duck could be improved. I walked slowly through the crowd, stopping occasionally to speak with Shayla and a few other friends.

La Donna Nelson, Chief Michaels's sister who was on the town council, shared a few words of wisdom on only wearing dresses to these political functions. August Grandin from the Duck General Store nodded to me and moved on without speaking. Apparently I'd done something or said something he hadn't agreed with.

I saw Chris Slayton trying to move a large trash can from beneath the trees to a more convenient location and offered to help him. "Shouldn't you be out there impressing the voters, Mayor?" he asked as I grabbed the other side of the can.

"You vote, don't you?"

He nodded and smiled. "Sure. But you already have my vote."

Even with the two of us, the trash can was almost too heavy to move. "Did someone fill this up instead of emptying it before the barbecue?" I asked.

"It's heavier than I expected," he replied. "Maybe I should empty it before we set it out. It's probably filled with water from the last rain."

We put the trash can down, and Chris took off the top. Both of us took a step back.

"Oh my God!" he muttered, his hand against his mouth.

Inside was Port Tymov.

Could the day get any worse?

Chapter 22

Port was dead. Someone had killed him and stuffed his body into the trash can. His wallet was still in my bedroom. I could already feel the weight of the questions Chief Michaels was going to ask bearing down on me.

Chris put the top back on the trash can. He cautioned me to stay with it and keep people from adding drink cups or paper plates while he went to get the sheriff. I stood there waiting and was joined moments later by several sheriff's deputies and Duck police officers, who formed a ring around me and the trash can.

Had Guthrie been so angry about my unwillingness to sell him the silver bell that he'd killed Port? It was a crazy idea. Surely he hadn't killed Port for that reason. But Port's death so soon after my meeting with Guthrie at Missing Pieces was too much of a coincidence to imagine anything else.

I was going to have a lot of explaining to do. Not only

was I involved in the pistol deal that had brought Port to Duck, but I might also be one of the last people to have seen him alive—*besides the killer.* My name and number were probably in his cell phone and on his calendar.

I considered that this terrible event *could* work in my favor. Maybe this would make the FBI admit that Guthrie was on some kind of personal killing spree. He might not usually do his own dirty work, according to them, but I was convinced he was doing it now. Maybe I could convince them too.

Again, I had no real proof. Not any more than I had that Guthrie had killed Chuck. Even if the FBI brought Guthrie in, it would be my word, my vision, against his.

Someone had finally found Chief Michaels, along with Sheriff Riley. The two of them broke through the perimeter line of deputies and police officers. I should've moved away before they arrived—my presence here was going to complicate my life to no end. But I didn't want to leave Port with no one to identify him, especially since I was the one who had his ID.

"Mayor." The chief tipped his hat to me.

"Mayor O'Donnell." Sheriff Riley shared his white-toothed smile. "You can leave now. We'll take it from here, ma'am."

Somehow Riley always managed to sound condescending even while he was smiling. Maybe he thought he was being solicitous, or at least appearing to be sympathetic. He needed to work on his people skills, as far as I was concerned.

I wished I *could* leave. I didn't want to be here, but someone had to answer questions about Port. "You may need my help identifying the man in the trash can," I said. "He's from out of town. I may be the only one here who knows him."

Except for Trudy. But there was no reason to involve her. She'd barely had any contact with him, thanks to me, Kevin and Guthrie. Maybe if Port had spent more time with Trudy, he'd still be alive.

"Don't worry about it, ma'am." Sheriff Riley's tone set my teeth on edge. "If we need your help, we know where to find you. You just run along now and let us do our job."

I started to argue with him, but he was too irritating. *Fine.* Let them call me when they couldn't figure it out. "Okay. I'll be at home. The chief has my cell phone number."

I thought that would also give me time to retrieve Port's wallet. Without it, they probably wouldn't believe me when I told them who he was anyway. I saw Tim in the ring of officers around me. He wouldn't be going anywhere for a while. I'd have to find Gramps to get home.

The barbecue was cancelled. Bo Huneycutt and Chris Slayton walked around, quietly explaining the situation to everyone. After hearing what had happened, people began to clear out quickly. The event would probably be rescheduled for some future date. It was too important to be canceled completely.

I saw Senator Seeger slip quietly into the backseat of his limo. He waved to me as his driver eased the big car out of the crowded parking lot. The exit had become a wild mix of cars and golf carts all trying to leave at the same time. The police were all too busy investigating the crime scene to direct traffic.

I noticed that Mad Dog had arrived just as everyone else was going home. He was still in the process of getting out of his golf cart, arms loaded with flyers and buttons to give away to the crowd.

"What happened?" he demanded when he met me and Gramps.

Gramps replied, "Dead man in a trash barrel. Doesn't look too good for the church."

"Dead man? *Another* one?" Mad Dog's bloodshot eyes narrowed. "That's two dead men in a very short time, Mayor—that's a lot—even for you and your administration."

I hadn't realized it, but Chris Slayton was right behind us. He'd put on an orange vest, probably to help out with the traffic.

"You don't know what you're talking about, Mr. Wilson. Mayor O'Donnell couldn't have known anything like this would happen. If you want to blame someone, blame the older people like yourself who have known for a hundred years that illegal smuggling was going on in Duck but didn't do anything to stop it."

It was a mouthful, especially for Chris, who was usually so quiet. Mad Dog fixed his eyes on the town manager and fired back. "Young man, you aren't even *from* Duck. Besides all that, you work for the town. Don't get high and mighty with me or you'll find yourself looking for work at one of the lighthouses. Do I make myself clear?"

I didn't want to jump in, but Chris was one of the best things that had happened to Duck in recent years. "He has a right to his opinion, Councilman. And we both know he's right about the smuggling. Just because our ancestors survived that way doesn't mean we should continue to condone it."

"I think you should stay out of this, Mayor," Mad Dog said. "You're in enough hot water for now. Don't drag him into the pot with you."

And with those words of wisdom, Mad Dog continued into the church park, probably to find out for himself what was going on. He was going to love it when he learned I was doing business with Port before he was killed.

"Sorry, Mayor," Chris said. "I shouldn't have gotten involved. It just burns me up when I hear him talk to you that way. Someone should teach him some respect."

I didn't reply. We shouldn't have been out here arguing in front of hundreds of pairs of interested eyes.

Chris nodded, as though he understood without me saying it, and walked down to Duck Road where he started trying to clear the intersection of the dozens of vehicles rushing to escape the parking lot. There was a lot of horn blowing and cursing at Chris, but eventually, everyone paid attention to him and began exiting safely.

"Don't worry about it, Dae," Gramps said as we walked to our golf cart, parked under the trees. "There wasn't anything you could do about this. Chris was right. And I think he might have a little crush on you. He was like a knight slaying Mad Dog's dragon, don't you think?"

I hadn't thought of it that way. Chris and I were friends who worked together to do what was best for Duck—nothing more.

"You don't know the whole story about Port yet," I admitted and then told him what had happened at Missing Pieces last night.

"Dae." He sighed and shook his head. "How do you get involved in these things? Never mind. I know it's your gift. Eleanore was the same way. Your grandmother was always into things that worried me. It was especially hard since I was sheriff at the time."

"I guess I should've sold the silver bell to Guthrie. It wasn't worth Port's life for me to keep it."

"Or you should've called the FBI after he was there. If they knew he was in town, they might've been able to prevent this. You can't do everything yourself."

"But they kicked me out of the investigation and acted like I was a crazy woman. Not to mention they wouldn't even *question* Guthrie about Chuck's murder. I didn't even think about calling them. I know you're right, though. I should've told someone. Maybe the chief. Maybe Port would still be alive."

"Do you still have the man's wallet?"

"Back at the house."

"Let's go get it. I'll take it in and tell them that I found it on the boardwalk yesterday. No one will question me about it, and you won't have to be involved."

I knew this was a huge concession for him. Normally, he would never consider such a thing. "You can't do that! I wouldn't ask it of you. You may not be sheriff anymore, but you have a reputation for doing what's right. And it won't work anyway. They'll know I'm involved with him and you're just covering up. I might as well take it in and explain everything."

"My plan is better. My career is over. You have your whole life ahead of you. You might be governor someday."

"Thanks, Gramps." I hugged him. "But you can't protect me forever. I'll handle this."

When we got home, I went upstairs and found the wallet where I'd left it on my bedside table. I stared at it for a while, wondering if Port's imminent death was the reason I'd been unable to sense anything from the wallet last night. That was a scary thought. Finding other people's lost treasures was one thing. Being able to predict who was going to die was quite another. I didn't plan on mentioning that fact to anyone. I didn't want to pursue it.

I snatched up the wallet and sat down on the bed, hoping my luck had changed now that Port was actually dead. I didn't want to experience a dead Port talking to me, like I had dead Chuck, but I thought perhaps I might be able to see Guthrie kill him. It'd be better than nothing.

But again, I had no reaction to the wallet. My mind was

a blank. The wallet wasn't going to help me catch Port's killer.

I knew my fingerprints were all over the wallet. I had to turn it in. Maybe the wallet wouldn't trigger a vision, but it wouldn't hurt to go through it and see if it held any useful information.

Port's California driver's license was in there, along with a one-hundred-dollar bill, a few credit cards and my business card. The police would love that. I could take it out now and save myself some grief. On the other hand, it didn't really matter, since I planned to tell them about our relationship anyway.

There was also a piece of paper, torn away from a larger sheet. Someone had written the words "Sailor's Dream" and the phone number for the bar, as well as my father's name.

That caused me to bite my lip. I took the paper out and put it to the side.

What good would it do to implicate my father in all of this? It would only add to the problem when they saw that he had a police record. He could be an easy scapegoat for everything that had happened in the last few days.

I knew Gramps would have a fit if he knew what I was thinking. And maybe I couldn't totally cover up for my father, but I could beat the police to it and talk to him first.

If not for last night's activities at Wild Stallions and then at Missing Pieces, I rationalized, I would've been at the bar looking for Derek Johnson before this had happened. As much as I disliked it, the bar was involved somehow.

Please don't let my father have had any part in what happened to Chuck, Port and Betsy.

I could hear Gramps telling me that he'd warned me about my father. He'd been in and out of jail his whole life. But that didn't make him guilty of anything now. It had taken a long time for Gramps to trust him. I hoped it hadn't been in vain.

I flew down the stairs and out the front door without a word of good-bye. It wasn't a long walk to the bar. If I went straight there, I could get answers quickly, before the police got involved.

Tim's patrol car pulled up in the driveway right in front of me. He leaned lazily out the window. "Chief wants to see you, Dae. It's about the dead man in the trash can. You said you know him, right?"

"I only know him because we worked together on an antique sale." I started skirting along the edge of the driveway to make my way to the road. What was I thinking? Tim would certainly follow me down Duck Road if he had to.

"Turns out the chief didn't need your help identifying him. He had fingerprints on file. He's wanted for burglary, making fake IDs. You name it. How'd you link up with him?"

"I don't mind answering those questions, Tim, but there's something really important I have to do right now. Could you pretend you couldn't find me for about an hour? I'll call you when I'm done and you can pick me up."

"That's kind of asking a lot, since you told the chief you were at home." He shrugged and glanced around as though he thought someone might be looking. "I'll really catch it from him if I'm not back in a few minutes."

"I understand. I appreciate the favor. Can you do it or not?"

"I guess. But you owe me."

"Dinner?"

"Dinner *and* a movie. And I don't mean a video at home. And it has to be just the two of us."

"You've got a deal."

"What are you up to anyway, Dae?"

"Nothing. I just need to talk to my dad." I tried not to look scared or nervous—not that I really thought he'd notice.

"Okay. But call me the minute you're done. I'll work on some excuse for being late." He nodded to me and smiled. "You know, I wouldn't do this for just anyone."

"I know. Thanks, Tim."

"You're welcome. What's this I hear about you dating Chris Slayton now? When did that happen?"

"I can't explain right now." I waved as I ran the rest of the way down the drive and into Duck Road. "Call you later."

"One day when all of this craziness is over, Dae O'Donnell, it will be you and me. You'll see!" he yelled back at me.

Incidents became rumors which became fact too easily in Duck, I thought. Normally I wouldn't explain something like this to Tim or anyone else. But since he was doing me such a huge favor, I knew I'd tell him what had happened that made people think Chris and I might be together.

The Sailor's Dream wasn't far from home, though I had to admit a ride in the police car would've been faster than walking. I didn't want anyone to see me and Tim together just then and ask the chief about it later.

I walked faster as I approached the Duck Shoppes but had made it only halfway past when Kevin's old red pickup pulled up beside me.

I took a deep breath and prayed for patience. Some days it didn't pay to know so many people who worried about me.

"I heard the news," Kevin said, pushing open the passenger-side door. "Get in."

"I'm going to talk to my dad," I replied with a trembling smile. "I'll call you when I'm done." *Add Kevin to the call list.*

"I told you I'd go with you."

"I need to do this alone, Kevin. I don't want you prejudging him before he's had a chance to defend himself."

When my dad had first come back into my life, Gramps and Kevin had frequently told me he'd be in trouble again. I didn't want that negative attitude creeping into the conversation I needed to have with him. He might not even realize that Guthrie and his gang hung out at the Sailor's Dream.

"I guess I was wrong," Kevin said. "I thought you were just going down there to see if Derek Johnson was around. There's more going on, isn't there? And it's made you suspect your father is involved."

I started walking again, ignoring him. He pulled the pickup into a parking space and got out.

"At least let me go with you. I won't come in if you don't want me to."

My hour's grace with the police was rapidly depleting; I did not have time to stand around and debate with him. I kept walking. He kept pace with me.

"Dae, I'm not going with you to turn your father over to the FBI. I'm going with you as your friend. If something else has happened, you can tell me. I think you know by now that you can trust me to keep my mouth shut."

"All right. But even one I-told-you-so puts you off my friend list. I hope you realize that." I told him about the scrap of paper in Port's wallet. "I'm going to tell the chief when I see him in about an hour. I just wanted to give my dad a heads-up about everything."

"Sure."

"You don't have to sound that way about it, Kevin. He only works at the Sailor's Dream, you know. The owner of the bar could be involved. Or it might just be a meeting place for Guthrie's men. I mean, if being a regular presence at a place is all it takes to implicate someone, people could say I'm involved in all of this too. I own Missing Pieces. Guthrie and Port were there last night."

"Technically, you *are* involved," he said.

"That doesn't make me guilty of a crime. The police don't suspect me of anything. But that's only because I haven't been in jail before. You know they'll think my dad is involved, just because of his past."

We had walked down the driveway toward the old, ramshackle bar that had been in business under one name or another for at least half a century. The parking lot was empty. Probably too early in the day for much bar traffic.

"I know he's your father, Dae," Kevin said. "I know you want to protect him. But you're walking a very fine line between being an observer who wants to help out and an accessory after the fact."

"You don't have to worry." I opened the side door to the bar, which I'd used many times since my dad had reentered my life. "My dad isn't involved in this."

The unmistakable sound of the cocking of a shotgun caught both of us by surprise. We looked down the sawed-off barrel as my dad yelled, "Get the hell out of here!"

Chapter 23

"It's me, Dad!"

"Dae?" He moved the shotgun and looked around it. "God, I don't know what I'm doing right now." His eyes were bloodshot, and he had several days' worth of stubble on his face. He looked terrible—as though he'd been waiting by the door for hours.

"I'm sorry." He stood back from the door. "Come on in. It's good to see you, Kevin." He locked and bolted the door after us.

"I know I'm a mess." He threw back a glass of whiskey. "I didn't mean to scare you. I was trying to surprise some very bad men who have been visiting me lately."

I arched a brow at Kevin. I wasn't above saying *I told you so*. "I know there's a problem," I said to my dad.

"You do?"

I explained about finding the matchbook cover that Derek Johnson had dropped and the paper scrap in Port's wallet. "Port Tymov is dead. We found him in a trash barrel this morning."

My father's face kind of crumpled in on itself. I'd never seen anyone that scared and desperate. "Oh no. Not Port *too*."

At first, Kevin didn't say anything. The look on his face was enough. His voice was calm when he finally spoke. "Start from the beginning, Danny. Tell us what happened. We might be able to help."

Kevin and I declined a drink, but Dad helped himself to another whiskey. "You know, it seemed like such a good idea at the time. It was going to be some fast, easy money. One nice score that would last the three of us for years to come. I was going to use my share to buy this place, Dae, and make you proud of me. I thought I could go the whole route—chamber of commerce, outstanding businessman. The works."

I don't want to hear any more.

I had no choice.

It all came pouring out of my father like whiskey from the nearly empty bottle.

Chuck had been working for Guthrie—smuggling a few paintings, some antiques, some illegal treasure salvage items into Duck and on to the network that was set up to receive them. He'd needed the extra money after he ruined his reputation in a scam and the area real estate market dried up.

"He thought he could use the money to hold on until people forgot what had happened with that old lady he'd tried to swindle," my father said. "But it was always just enough to keep him underwater with Guthrie. That's the way it works. Guthrie charges a fee to work for him. I tried to explain that to Chuck, but he wouldn't listen. You never come out ahead on something like that."

"What was the great plan?" I asked, feeling like an observer at a funeral. "You were going to swindle Guthrie?"

He nodded and drank some more. "He's got plenty, Dae. You should see how he lives. We're fleas compared to him."

But one afternoon, the story went, everything changed. Chuck and my dad took out Chuck's boat, which was about to be repossessed, for one last cruise. They were planning to explore one of the tiny barrier islands that clustered around the Outer Banks. Some of them were no bigger than an acre or two, but some were very large. Most of them were rarely, if ever, visited.

"It was low tide when we got out there," my dad said. "You know how some of the low tides are *really* low? It was like that. There was a large area of the sand exposed at the edge of the island. We found this skeleton of an old ship—you know, the bare wood ribs sticking out of the sand. It was falling apart. We got off Chuck's boat and started poking around. There was all this stuff. It was crusted over. A lot of it, you couldn't even tell what it was."

He took another drink, his eyes burning with the memory. "We found a wooden chest. It wasn't very big, but inside, we figured there was treasure. Salt water can't hurt gold, right?"

"Was there gold in it?" I asked.

"Not gold. But there was a necklace—an amber necklace—all crusted over. There were some other trinkets too. One of the rings had a ruby as big as your thumb. We looked around some more. It was like we were high. I wish you'd been there. We found a brass hatch cover and when we cleaned it off, we could read the inscription: *Andalusia*."

"The *Andalusia*?" I barely breathed the name, only wincing a little that their handling of the relics had probably destroyed their value. It was the first finding of any kind from the ship. "Are you sure?"

He nodded as he finished off the whiskey. "But that's all we found. We got stinking drunk, and then Chuck told me he knew a man who could verify that the stuff came from the *Andalusia*."

"Port," I added.

"Exactly. We were pretty sure that there wasn't anything else out there, but Chuck and I both knew how Guthrie feels about antiques. We thought we could show him one of the trinkets from the chest and then convince him to give us money to look for more treasure from the ship. Not that the ruby wasn't worthwhile. But we sold that before we said anything to Guthrie. We both needed some cash."

"What happened?" Kevin asked.

"It was a mistake." The words were painful and bitter. "We thought we could get the money from Guthrie and split it up. We'd go and make a show out of looking for treasure, but of course we'd never find any. Guthrie would think we'd done what he'd paid us to do, so he wouldn't get mad when we came up empty. It seemed like a brilliant idea."

In the vision I'd had of Chuck's death, Chuck said the items in the chest were real. Guthrie must have caught on right away, then killed Chuck for trying to cheat him. He searched his house, looking for treasure, only to find Betsy.

"That's why Chuck was killed," I said. "But what happened to the treasure you found?"

My dad shrugged. "There was no treasure besides the hatch cover, the ring and the amber necklace. The necklace and the hatch cover sold him. We figured we didn't have to find anything else.

"Why didn't you get out of town?" I asked the question over the lump that had formed in my throat. "You had to know you were in danger once Chuck was killed."

"I don't know. I've been a nervous wreck since Chuck

died. I heard Guthrie came down personally. I knew I *should* leave. I thought I could still make it right, you know? But if he killed Port too, I'm a dead man."

"I think Derek Johnson has been here watching you," I said. "Does Guthrie know you were directly involved with the treasure?"

"I don't know, Dae." He lit a cigarette with shaking hands. "I don't know what he thinks. Derek's disappeared from the bar. I've been trying to talk to Guthrie, to explain what happened, but he won't see me. I thought I could tell him that we tried but just couldn't find anything else. We spent the money he gave us but we really tried to find something. If he doesn't believe me, I'm dead. He's got a long reach. There isn't anyplace I can go that he won't find me."

"Do you have the money Guthrie gave the three of you to look for the treasure?" Kevin asked. "How much was it?"

"Two hundred thousand." My father smiled and took a big drink. "Port had it. He put it somewhere for safekeeping until we could split it. Bad idea, I guess."

I faced Kevin. "What do we do now?"

"He needs to turn this whole thing over to the FBI," was his response.

"No way. I'm not talking to them. They'll put me away even though I didn't really do anything—except try to earn a decent living. That's not a crime."

"That's debatable," Kevin said drily. "But they're the only ones I can think of who could protect you from Guthrie. Are you willing to go out on your own?"

"I don't know. I don't know what to do." Dad looked at me. "What do you think, Dae? I guess I *did* try to scam money from Guthrie. But he's a smuggler, a thief and a killer, right? They can't arrest me for swindling him. Maybe I could even make some kind of deal."

All of the angry words I'd thrown at Kevin and Gramps while I'd defended my father came back to haunt me. *Once a habitual criminal*, Kevin had said, *always a criminal.*

I couldn't think about my pride at that moment. Dad was in danger. We needed to get him out of there. The FBI seemed like the best idea to me.

"I think we should do what Kevin said," I told him. "I don't see any other option. Maybe if you tell them what you know, they can nail Guthrie and you'll be safe."

He put out his cigarette in a dirty ashtray. "Yeah. All right. I'll tell them everything."

There was one more thing. "Dad, do you know anything about Chuck's daughter? I think Guthrie took her when he searched their house. She's been missing since Chuck was killed. Do you have any idea where she could be?"

His face became a dark mask of anguish. "Honey, if Guthrie took Chuck's little girl, she's dead. There's no money for ransom. He wouldn't just keep her. I'm sorry. Her body will wash up somewhere—like Chuck's. Let me get my stuff and we'll go."

His words were like daggers in my soul. Betsy *had* to be alive. He had to be wrong. She had to be out there waiting for us to rescue her.

After my dad had disappeared into the back room, Kevin took my hand. "He doesn't know that for sure, Dae."

I moved away from him. "I guess you were right. I guess you were *all* right. Once a criminal—always a criminal." I couldn't hold back the tears. They spilled down my face, and I sobbed for the loss of the father I thought I'd come to know.

Kevin put his arms around me, and I didn't move away.

"I thought I could love him enough. That he'd want to have me around enough to be different," I cried.

"I know. I'm sorry."

"Maybe I'm just being stupid and naïve about Betsy. Maybe Ann was right to begin with. She's probably dead somewhere, and I'm imagining that I can see her and touch her. I'm a fool. I don't know what I'm doing."

We both heard a door slam closed. I lifted my head and stared at Kevin. "Was that—?"

"I'm a fool too," he snarled. He left me and ran into the back of the bar. When he came back alone, I knew my father was gone.

"It's probably for the best." I wiped my face and eyes on a bar napkin. "Guthrie probably would've killed him. This way, he's safe. At least *someone* is safe."

"Let's get out of here," Kevin suggested. "I don't want to find out if Danny's fears were justified."

I followed his lead toward the side door where we'd come in. "Thanks."

"For thinking we should run away?" He opened the door and glanced outside.

"For not saying *I told you so*."

"Come on. I think we both need some coffee and a chance to mull over everything your father just told us."

We walked down Duck Road in the deepening twilight, not talking. Ann called Kevin as we were getting close to the coffee shop. As they spoke, I remembered that the hour Tim had granted me was up a long time ago. I couldn't let him down.

"Ann's going to meet us at the coffee shop, and we can strategize what we should do next." Kevin put his cell phone in his pocket.

"I have to call Tim and go see Chief Michaels." I explained about our deal. "I'll call you later, when it's over."

"Ann and I could come too," he said.

"I think it's better if I go alone."

"What are you going to tell him?"

"I don't know yet. I'm still working on that."

"Dae, I—"

I smiled at him in the streetlight's glow. "Don't worry. I'll be fine. I just have a lot of explaining to get through with some people who won't mind saying *I told you so*."

We parted there. It was hard for me not to want to hold on to him. I thought he looked the same about me. Maybe that was wishful thinking too. I couldn't tell anymore.

I waited in the parking lot for Tim, dreading what was coming, despite my brave words to Kevin. I knew it was going to be bad. I wished I could avoid it all and just stay here with him. But I'd gone too far for that.

Tim had said he was on his way—complaining a little that it had taken me longer to get back to him than I'd said.

Ann ran across Duck Road and glanced at the coffee shop. "No coffee?" she asked. "Where's Kevin?"

"He's inside. I have to go down to the police station and talk to the chief. Or the FBI. Or both."

"You've been a bad girl, huh? Cheer up. It's not that bad. They only want to help. Sometimes they just don't know how."

"I get that."

She smiled and started toward the coffee shop.

"Ann?"

"Cold feet? It's not always easy being the hero, is it?"

"No. And I was just wondering—does it get any easier dealing with it?"

"I lost years of my life in hell for it," she snarled. "What do you think?"

"Sorry." *Why had I asked her*?

"Don't worry. You'll never experience the nightmares I have as long as you live here in this sugarplum world. Stay here, Dae. Don't try to follow Kevin and me when we leave. Stay safe."

I didn't reply. I would never understand her.

Tim pulled up a minute later. "About time. Where have you been?"

"Talking to my father," I said. "Like I told you. Let's go."

Chapter 24

I gave Port's wallet to Chief Michaels. The scrap of paper with my father's name on it wasn't in it. I was standing by my decision not to involve him.

I sat silently in front of the chief's desk and listened as he lectured me about honor, decency, my standing in the community and spending too much time with convicted felons.

"It's not like it was written on his forehead, Chief," I retorted, feeling like a limp rag. "It was a business deal. It happens all the time. I don't check out my contacts to see if they have prison records. Port was very highly recommended to me by several people I trust."

"Well maybe you'll rethink that policy in the future, Mayor." He tossed Port's large file on his desk. "He worked for Dillon Guthrie, Dae. That's probably what killed him. It could've killed you too. Horace would've killed me then died of grief himself if we'd found *you* in a trash barrel tomorrow."

He paused as though he was waiting for me to add something. I told him everything I knew—or thought I knew—about why Guthrie was in Duck, at least.

But I could tell he took it all in like a grain of sand.

Kowalski slammed into the chief's office during that brief silence. His face was red—anger or embarrassment—it was hard to say. But it was directed at me.

"So we find a dead man in a trash can and who's at the scene? Mayor Dae O'Donnell. We find that same man is a felon and who is he in town to see? Again, Mayor Dae O'Donnell. What's wrong with this picture, Your Honor?"

"I have a bad habit of being in the wrong place at the right time."

He slammed his fist on the chief's desk. "I could put you in a federal prison for obstruction and accessory."

"Not in *my* town," the chief said. "You're speaking to an elected official, Agent. Mind your manners."

"Fine." Kowalski turned a ladder-back chair to face me, then sat astride it. "I want to know what the connection is between the mayor, Dillon Guthrie and Port Tymov. I want to know how that plays into Sparks's death, his daughter's kidnapping and Tymov's death. We can just sit right here until I have those answers, Mayor. I wouldn't want you to think that I don't *respect* you."

So we spent the next few hours reviewing in minute detail everything I had said or done since I'd met Port Tymov. I kept my mouth shut about my father, however. Concealing that part of the story from Kowalski was the only thing that got me through his interrogation.

"Are you sure the last time you saw Tymov was at your shop?" Kowalski asked for the tenth time.

"Yes. He was with Dillon Guthrie. They were interested in buying something."

"And that's where Tymov lost his wallet?"

"Yes. I was going to give it back to him after the barbecue. But you know how that went."

"You just happened to walk over to that trash can and try to move it so people could put trash in it. Is that right?"

"No. I went to help our town manager move the trash can. We looked inside and found the body."

"What did Guthrie buy at your shop?" Kowalski fixed his stare on me as though by doing so he could force some case-breaking revelation out of me.

"He didn't buy anything. The only thing he wanted was something I wouldn't sell."

Kowalski laughed. It was a mean sound. "That doesn't make any sense. Why wouldn't you sell something to a wealthy collector? Oh, right. You knew he'd killed Sparks from your earlier visions, so you wouldn't do business with him."

"Not exactly. The fact that he'd killed Chuck obviously made me scared *not* to sell anything to him. But I couldn't sell what he wanted, no matter what. It's important for me to keep it. He understood that."

There were a few blessed moments of silence. Chief Michaels had stayed in the room with me. He was dozing in his chair. Too many late nights. He was used to Duck being quiet.

Kowalski shifted in his chair. "That was nice of him, huh? A high-powered smuggler came to your shop to buy something. You wouldn't give it to him, and he smiled and left. How *stupid* do you think I am?"

The chief made a snorting noise and tried to pretend he hadn't been sleeping.

"I don't think you're stupid at all," I told Kowalski. "Just a little too wrapped up in your version of how the world runs to be able to see what else is happening."

"Thanks for that opinion."

The moments ticked by on the big clock above the chief's head.

"Is that about all, Agent?" Chief Michaels woke up and looked around.

"I guess it'll have to do for now." Kowalski frowned. "Don't go anywhere, Your Honor. I know we'll talk again. I hope you have some better answers for everyone's sake. Time is running out for that little girl, you know.

Chief Michaels nodded toward the door, and I got out of there as quickly as I could.

Tim had waited for me, even though his shift was long over. "I'll take you home."

"Thanks." I dropped into the police car with a grateful sigh.

"Is there something I can do?" he asked as he started the car.

"Not that I can think of. But thanks."

I was supposed to call Kevin. I just couldn't. The idea of talking to anyone else about everything that had gone on the last few hours was too much. I felt overloaded.

Instead, I spent most of the night on the widow's walk at the top of the house. I looked out over the lights in Duck and watched the patterns made by the lighthouse beacons as they swept across the sky. I had known them all of my life. Currituck. Hatteras. Bodie. Oak Island. Cape Lookout. Ocracoke.

Toward dawn, a heavy mist rolled in from the sea and covered everything, including me, with fine water droplets.

I wasn't tired, though. The night had quelled my urge to feel sorry for myself about losing my only living parent. I'd always suspected the relationship with my father would be short-lived. I would probably have to get through the rest of my life without him. I'd cried my tears and made peace with reality.

I needed to focus on Betsy. I wanted her mother to see her again. I knew I'd have given anything to see my mother again.

Betsy needed rescuing as badly as a baby turtle trying to return to the sea. I wouldn't give up until I found her. *One way or another.*

The night had renewed me, filled me with strength and faith again. I could do this. I could find Betsy. Maybe no one else could. I still didn't know how, or what I needed to do differently, but I was determined to fulfill my promise to her.

I took a long, hot shower until the chill of morning air left my body and my fingers pruned up. Then I got ready for the day.

It was going to be a long one, starting out with the groundbreaking ceremony for the new town hall at noon—Nancy had texted me last night that they had pulled everyone together for that event. It would end with a specially called town meeting at which Mad Dog was going to push to have me removed from office and Chris fired from his position as town manager. I didn't plan to let either of those things happen.

I dressed accordingly, in several layers. I wore a short, light jacket over my black dress. The pale orange jacket was a perfect foil for my sun-lightened hair and year-round tan.

I looked into my determined (slightly bloodshot) eyes in the mirror and wrote Betsy's name in the steam left from the shower. I put my feet in my good tennis shoes—too much walking in dirty sand for sandals, even though the groundbreaking was symbolic. The official groundbreaking had to take place when everyone from the town council could be there. The real work would begin later when contracts were awarded.

Gramps was barely awake for a change, stumbling around in the dark kitchen making coffee.

"I'm going down to Duck's Donuts to get us some breakfast," I announced, leaving him with a quick kiss on the cheek. "Drink some coffee. I'll be back in a flash."

"Don't forget your umbrella." He yawned. "It might rain later."

"I've got nothing from my storm knee. Maybe light rain, but not too bad. Are you coming to the groundbreaking at noon?"

"I wouldn't miss it. Are you going to get those donuts or what?"

I hugged him and skipped out the door. Every bush, every streetlight was covered in tiny droplets of mist. They made a glistening net across town that seemed to glow as the sun started to rise in the troubled sky.

White caps rippled on the Currituck Sound as I walked past the Duck Shoppes. Maybe Gramps was right about the rain. I hoped it would hold off until after the groundbreaking. The area that was set up for the event would turn into sand soup without too much help.

A young man who looked vaguely familiar to me was behind the counter at Duck Donuts. He introduced himself as the owner's son, Walter Perry Jr. We joked about him coming home from college. He told me that he planned to stay in Duck and start his own construction business. Good news, since many of Duck's young people left for college and never came back.

He was very sweet too, giving me the thirteenth donut to make a baker's dozen. I thanked him, asked him to vote for me, then went back outside with breakfast.

A burgundy Lincoln was waiting at the bottom of the steps. It seemed like a bad dream as I watched the two front doors open and Derek Johnson get out of the driver's side.

Chapter 25

I thought Guthrie might get out of the passenger side. I was surprised when the woman I knew as Guthrie's girlfriend—the sexy blond from my vision—stepped out instead.

She smiled at me. "You're Mayor Dae O'Donnell," she said. "I've been looking for you."

Her strong jaw kept her from being truly beautiful, I realized, but she was very striking and dressed expensively—the kind of woman I'd expect to be with a rich smuggler.

"That's right!" I came down the remaining stairs, pasted on my bright mayor's smile and shifted the donut bag to free up my hand so I could shake hers.

I wished I could lie about who I was, but I'd already introduced myself to Derek at Old Man Sweeney's house when he came to get the medallion Chuck had dropped. My only recourse now was to feign ignorance of Derek and the woman's connection to Guthrie and his illegal activities.

The donut bag dropped to the ground at my feet. I just left it, hoping she wouldn't think anything of it. It might provide some evidence that I didn't leave here a happy camper. Gramps was bound to come and look for me when I didn't come back with the donuts.

"Oops! I guess I won't be eating that high-carb breakfast. What can I do for you?"

She shook my hand. Immediately, I saw Guthrie with her as they arrived in Duck. I saw her talking to Betsy, though I couldn't tell where they were. I saw her handling an antique necklace made of amber beads.

"My name is Jackie Vagts. You don't know me. I'm a visitor to Duck. I was wondering if you could do me a favor."

I smiled again. "Of course. We *love* our tourists."

Jackie took the tiny Flobert pistol from her jacket pocket and pointed it at me. "Get in the car."

Looking at the tiny but lethal pistol made me think the old caveat *buyer beware* should also extend to *seller beware*. This was instant karma.

Derek kind of snickered, but I ignored him and moved to the back door of the Lincoln. When I touched the handle, after Jackie prodded me with the gun, I saw poor, dead Chuck looking at me through the window.

"Where are we going? If you want to rob me, you're going to be disappointed. I used all my money to buy those donuts. I'm afraid I don't have any cash with me."

"You don't need cash." She opened the back door for me as I faltered at the sight of dead Chuck. "All you need are the right answers, and our business will be over very quickly."

I had no choice but to get in. There were no cars, not even a passing bicycle on Duck Road. No one to see what had happened to me. That was the worst. I knew Gramps would be sick with worry.

I tried to convey my fear and uncertainty to Walt Jr. as he looked out at me from the donut shop window. I hoped he'd noticed the gun and that I was definitely in distress. I didn't dare try to get him to come out—we would both be in the same spot then.

Walt. Jr. smiled and waved at me, then turned around to go back to his counter, no doubt. So much for trying to convey my problem with a look. I wasn't telepathic like Ann.

I had to step over poor dead Chuck to get into the car. I didn't look around as Jackie closed the door. I sat rigidly still as Chuck dissipated, or whatever ghosts did. At least he was gone, leaving me with the killers. It would have been nice if he'd offered to help me out, since I was trying to save his daughter.

Jackie sat beside me and told Derek to drive toward Corolla.

"Duck is a very progressive community to have a woman mayor," she remarked, her blue sapphire earrings sparking in the sunlight. She held the gun steadily on me. "It's a nice little town."

Despite my own best interests, I opened my mouth and the words just came out. "Thanks. We usually have a very low crime rate too. Sometimes things happen—like Chuck Sparks's death and his daughter being kidnapped. You wouldn't know anything about that, would you?"

She laughed. She was more attractive close up, probably in her midthirties, her long blond hair thick and lustrous, like models have on TV. She was curvy rather than stick thin like Ann, and her clothes were expensive, probably made for her. I envied her pretty, green heels that matched her green dress.

"I'm just a visitor. May I call you Dae?"

"Sure." I watched as the car picked up speed on the empty

highway between Duck and Sanderling. Large sand dunes shielded the houses on either side of the road from traffic. No one would see us passing this way. I wasn't sure how I could let anyone know where I was. The Outer Banks was only a hundred miles long, but locating a missing person in that space was a near impossible task. I knew that from trying to find Betsy.

"Like I said, I have a few questions for you. Well, one really. Where is Danny Evans?"

"I don't know."

"Don't think I won't kill you and dump your body out here in the dunes," she threatened. "I know you're his daughter. He talks about you all the time."

"That's true. I am his daughter. But your guess is as good as mine about where he is." I told her how he had run out on me last night. "He could be anywhere. Like he was for the last thirty-six years of my life. He didn't even know he had a daughter until recently."

Jackie's blond brows knit together. "That's not the answer I was looking for, Dae. You see, your father has something that belongs to me. I'm not leaving Duck without it."

"Have you looked in the back room at the bar where he lived?"

"Yes. We tore apart the bar. It wasn't there." She studied me like a cat studies a mouse. "Maybe he left it with you."

"As far as I know, he didn't leave anything behind. But tell me what you're looking for and I'll tell you if I have it."

"I'm looking for a big pile of money that he and his friends, Port and Chuck, stole from me. I took care of those other jokers. I meant to take care of Danny too. He got away faster than I expected."

"I have a lot of things in my shop," I said. "But not a big pile of money."

"That's right." She glanced at the pistol. "You helped

Port get this for me, didn't you? Dillon was at your shop with him, trying to buy some other antique piece of crap to put in one of his houses somewhere. Maybe we're headed in the wrong direction. You have the money at your little shop, don't you?"

If I said no, I'd end up somewhere in the sand where no one would find me for a long time. If I said yes, she'd have to turn around and head back to Duck. Sometimes a lie is the best bet.

"I don't know about a large pile of cash," I replied, inventing as I went along. "But my father has a key to my shop. I found him in there not too long ago. There are a thousand places at Missing Pieces to hide money."

It sounded plausible to me. The Lincoln was quickly eating up the miles. We were passing the Corolla library and the historic village around the Currituck Beach Lighthouse. Soon, we'd reach the end of the highway and a big stretch of water.

If we made it that far, Jackie would surely view the lonely spot as an open invitation to get rid of me.

"I suppose we'll have to go back and search your shop then." She sighed and signaled Derek to pull the car over. The tires made that strange crunchy sound as they rolled to a stop on the sand.

"I'll be happy to show you around." I looked out the window and saw nothing but sand, water and plant life. I wondered if this was the last I'd see of the ocean rolling in, the sky, my home.

"I appreciate the offer, but I think we can do this without you. Still, you've been a big help. Maybe you don't know where Danny is. I understand he has a way of disappearing. But you've probably sent us in the right direction. I think we should let her live, don't you, Derek?"

Derek grinned and shrugged. "Up to you, sweetie."

"What about the girl?" I threw out the question like a person shoving extra baggage off a sinking boat—hoping to gain more buoyancy. "You have her, don't you?"

Jackie frowned, and the Flobert faltered a little from its target on my chest. "Sparks's daughter? I have her. She's fine. As soon as all this is over, I'll let her go. Nothing is going to happen to her."

Was it my imagination or was Jackie defensive about kidnapping Betsy?

"I'll trade you a valuable treasure I have at the shop for her freedom," I said quickly, hoping to play on that momentary weakness. I explained about the silver bell. "It's worth a lot of money. You can ask Guthrie. He wanted to buy it from me."

"And you didn't sell it? A woman with integrity! You're astounding." She lifted the pistol back into place. "I'm not really interested in anything Dillon wants, but I'll take a look at it while I find the money your father owes me. Thanks."

"And you'll let Betsy go."

"She was never in any danger from me. And you're starting to sound like my mother. Nag. Nag. Nag. Just when I was beginning to like you."

I didn't respond. She was going to do what she wanted anyway.

"I'm doing everything to get this money back. Then I'll be free of Dillon and I can live the way I want to. I never planned to hurt the girl. She'll be safe. I promise. I just had to finish up my business here before I set her free, you know? I couldn't have her telling everyone about her father and us."

"And me?" My heart pounded as I went back to that subject.

"You'll be safe too—after a while. I need a little time

without you running to the police. Tie her up, Derek. Leave her somewhere. I don't want her showing up at an inconvenient moment."

As Derek got out of the car, I turned all my attention toward him and away from Jackie, since she didn't seem to be a threat.

My mistake.

Out of my peripheral vision, I barely caught the movement of her arm before she hit me hard on the side of the head with the pistol. For a few minutes, I saw stars. The pistol might look like a toy, but it certainly worked like the real thing.

Derek dragged me out of the car. I couldn't coordinate my arms and legs to fight back. My poor scrambled brain couldn't decide on a game plan. He laughed at me and kept walking through the sand, pulling me behind him.

He tied me with some rope and left me in the shadow of a large sand dune. No one would be able to see me from the road or the beach access where people flew their kites and started their treks looking for the wild horses.

I heard the Lincoln drive off, and my heart sank.

During the height of the tourist season, thousands of people came through this area every day. It was a pilgrimage of sorts after driving down the road through the middle of the island.

But at this time of year, only the occasional fisherman or dedicated horse watcher came through here. Otherwise, the area was deserted. It might be days before anyone found me.

My head hurt—probably a knot where Jackie had hit me. She was as vicious as she was rude. She and Guthrie deserved each other.

But at least I understood why I'd kept seeing her in the visions. She had Betsy. It struck me that Guthrie might not even know what his lady friend was doing. It looked as though the FBI knew what they were talking about after all.

I understood suddenly that the blood I'd seen on Guthrie's tie in the vision couldn't have come from Chuck. Jackie had killed him, not Guthrie. They must have offered the treasure to her. Port was probably too afraid to ask Guthrie about the scheme. I'd seen how scared Port was of him. She was trying to increase her stash to get away from Guthrie. When there was no return, she came looking for them and her money. It had cost Chuck and Port their lives.

I hoped my father wouldn't be next.

I prayed for Betsy not to give up.

And I started worrying about myself.

After a while, I could control my arms and legs again. Not that it mattered. I was trussed up from behind, a sour smelling rag in my mouth to keep me quiet. With my face shoved in the sand, I couldn't see anything. I couldn't tell if I'd be affected by high tide, when it came in. If so, the number of days it might take to find me was irrelevant. I'd be dead—drowned—long before.

The rain Gramps had predicted started falling. My clothes were soaked in no time. I tried to use the moisture to my advantage, wiggling my hands in the rope to find a little extra space. The coarse rope chafed my skin, but I kept pushing against it, hoping to get free.

I was finally able to force the rag out of my mouth with my tongue, and I started yelling. The sound of the waves crashing was very loud. I wasn't sure anyone would hear me unless they were close by. After a few minutes, I decided to keep quiet so I wouldn't lose my voice for when I needed it.

All I had to do was wait until I heard someone on the beach.

I tried to get my feet free, but that didn't work out so

well either. The way Derek had tied me up, the more I pulled, the tighter the ropes got. I was covered in sand from rolling around on the dunes.

I won't give up, I told myself as I rested my face in the wet sand. The rain continued to pelt me, and I could feel something crawling across my neck and legs.

People are looking for you, I reminded myself. Gramps would call the donut shop when I didn't answer my cell phone. Walt Jr. would notice the bag of donuts on the ground. He'd remember seeing me outside with Jackie and Derek. He'd know something had happened. From there it would go to Chief Michaels. Someone would find me. It was just a matter of *when*.

The rain finally stopped and the sun came out. I could hear gulls playing in the surf but no human sounds. I must've slept for a while—courtesy of my headache. When I woke up, my mouth was full of sand. I spit out what I could, but my voice was hoarse and dry from it. There were tiny crabs scuttling across me.

What else can I do?

I thought back to all the TV shows I'd watched and books I'd read where clever heroines managed to escape from much more dire consequences than these. A man had come to the fire department last year and taught a course in protecting yourself from an enemy. I couldn't recall his name, but I remembered thinking that he'd had great advice. Too bad none of it pertained to my situation.

I didn't know how long I'd been lying there. It felt like days. My mind was bursting with fears about myself, Betsy and Missing Pieces. The shop would be totally trashed, no doubt. But if I survived, I could clean it up and start again.

I wished I'd had a chance to say good-bye to Kevin and Gramps. I was sorry I would never find the other two silver bells that the monks had hidden. I hated that I would never see the new town hall.

I heard a snorting sound and realized that one of the wild horses must have found me. They roamed freely across this end of the island. Left behind by various shipwrecks, their ancestors had made the Outer Banks their home, adapting and reproducing through the centuries. The wild horses were protected now, although their fate, like mine, was uncertain. Tourists enjoyed visiting them, but population growth—human and horse—on the island might still destroy them.

This horse, a little chestnut, pushed at me with his nose. He snorted again, and I heard him paw at the ground. I wished there was some way to communicate with him. I wished I had a carrot or something to bring him closer. Maybe I could reach up and hold on to him. He'd drag me away from the dunes and into the open. Or he might be able to bite at my ropes and break them.

I closed my eyes on those fantasies. I had to have a concussion to be thinking such strange thoughts.

Maybe now would be a good time to start yelling again.

Chapter 26

"Well, what have we got here?" A deep, male voice startled me. "Looks like you were having a little too much fun on vacation, ma'am."

"Kidnapped!" I rasped, trying to get my mouth out of the sand. "Not on vacation!"

Gloved hands flipped me over. "Kidnapped, huh? You look all trussed up like a Thanksgiving turkey."

"I'm waiting to be rescued," I croaked, not caring that he'd just called me a turkey. "You look like Prince Charming to me."

"Prince Charming, huh?" He chuckled as he felt around for the knots to untie me. "I don't think anyone's ever called me that. I'm Jake Burleson, since we seem to be getting personal. And you are?"

"Mayor Dae O'Donnell from Duck." I briefly told him what had happened.

He made appropriate "hmms" and "ohhs" as he wrestled with the knots. But I knew he was listening and the tale would be retold. He was undoubtedly a Banker.

Finally I was free. He helped me to my feet and brushed the sand and my wayward hair out of my face with a gentle hand.

He was a good-looking man, in a cowboy-type fashion. He had longish blond hair and bright blue eyes with dark lashes fringing them. His skin was deeply tanned. He wore a dark T-shirt and tight, low-slung jeans that seemed barely held together by a thread. And he had a very nice smile.

My legs weren't too steady, and I was grateful for his hands on my arms. "Thank you. Thank you so much, Jake. I-I wasn't sure if I was going to be found."

"I'm sure you have friends already out searching for you, Miss Dae. Just relax now. Everything is gonna be fine."

"I have to get back to Duck right away." I hated to ask but it was important. I didn't even know how long I'd been out there. "Can you help me?"

"Course you do. I'm sure you're a busy lady. I've been working on my old truck all morning. I don't think she'll get you there. Maybe you could call the police and they could come and get you."

I searched my pockets, but my cell phone was gone. "They must have taken my phone. Do you have one I could use?"

He looked contrite. "I'm sorry, Miss Dae, but I don't have a phone. Some rescuer I turned out to be, huh? Do you ride?"

As we walked toward his home, Jake explained that he had taken in three wild horses several years back when it looked as though all of the animals might be kicked off the island. A few newcomers had complained about them getting into places they didn't belong—yards and gardens. That was why the state had moved to protect them. I had hoped they'd never be threatened again.

Jake's home was a one-room cabin set off in the woods, surrounded by fences and horses cropping grass. When we got there, the hunky cowboy looked me over and asked me how much I weighed.

"About a hundred and twenty," I said. "Why do you need to know?"

"Penelope can get you to Duck fastest, but she won't tolerate inexperienced hands on the reins. I'd have to go with you. She shouldn't have any problem with our weights together—as long as you're telling the truth."

His sky bright eyes searched mine as though he could see into my soul. "That's what I weighed this morning," I said in my most sincere tone.

He grinned. "All right. Then we should be good to go. Let me get a blanket. Penelope doesn't like saddles."

A few minutes later, I was on the back of one of the wild horses. My escort sat in front of me, and I was holding on for dear life, hoping not to fall as we galloped down the side of the highway.

I'd never ridden a horse before, wild or not. It was a lot worse than a motorcycle. I hoped I'd be able to walk once we got back to Duck.

Jake clearly lived off the grid. He was one of those strong, silent types. He hardly said two words to me as he spurred the brown and white along. I kept hoping we'd pass someone who was looking for me and willing to give me a ride. But I wasn't that lucky.

It had been hours since Derek and Jackie had dropped me off—I'd checked a clock at Jake's cabin before we left. Anything could've happened during that time. It was more than enough time to search Missing Pieces.

Jake and I, astride the sure-footed mare, were nearing Sanderling. My legs and feet were numb. I was also barefoot since I'd been unable to find my shoes on the beach. My suit was wet, sandy, and torn in a few places. There were rope burns on my wrists and ankles.

I was a mess.

All I needed was long hair streaming down, blowing in the salty air, and I'd look like one of my Banker ancestors. I was glad my hair was short. I was also grateful to be alive.

"Okay back there?" Jake called out as we went around a sharp curve in the road.

"Fine. Thanks." I clenched my teeth and held on tight. I hoped he didn't think I was groping him. It was more that I was terrified by all the up-and-down, back-and-forth motion. But my hands were still all over him. He *was* very lean and muscled.

I couldn't believe we hadn't seen a car all that way. I knew it was off-season, but still, wasn't anyone out looking for me? Surely they would've come in this direction. It seemed to me we should've passed someone going from Corolla to Duck or back again. Where was everyone?

"So you're the mayor of Duck."

I nodded, then realized he couldn't see me. "Yes. I'm up for reelection."

"I'm not much on politics," he said. "But if all mayors looked like you, I could be persuaded."

"Thanks." He'd meant it as a compliment and I smiled. He was very sincere. "It was wonderful for you to take those horses. I hoped someone would at the time. I didn't want all of them to go to people off the island."

"They belong here," he said. "They're part of our heritage, like the sea and the wind."

A cowboy poet, I mused, as we reached the police/fire station.

"Do you want to stop here?" he asked.

There were no police cars in the parking lot. One FBI agent in a dark suit was getting into his plain black car. He stared at us with narrowed eyes as we slowed our frantic pace.

"Would you mind taking me farther into town?"

"No problem."

I didn't stop to ask for help from the FBI agent. No doubt it would have taken me an hour to explain who I was and what had happened. I didn't have that kind of time.

We finally galloped into Duck, past the big blue water tower. I wanted desperately to go home and change clothes—but what if I didn't stop Derek and Jackie at Missing Pieces? They would get away with what they'd done to me as well as the two murders. Without their help, we might never find Betsy.

I knew I'd have to go on to the shop. If people saw me looking like a wild creature, there was a good story that went with it. I was prepared to tell it as many times as I had to. It would take a while for people to discuss and understand what had happened. But if I could catch Derek and Jackie red-handed, it would all be worth it.

I asked Jake to let me off in the Duck Shoppes parking lot. He slowed the obedient horse, jumped down and put his hands on my waist to help me slide to the pavement. I had a moment when I wasn't sure if my legs would hold me, but Jake kind of smiled and stood there as though he understood.

"Where is everyone?" He looked around at the cars packed into the parking lot but no one to be seen.

The groundbreaking! Of course! I forgot. "They're at the groundbreaking for the new town hall." I didn't want to seem ungrateful, but I needed to get to Missing Pieces. "Thanks for your help."

"If these people are as bad as you say they are, I'll come with you. This isn't something you should try to do alone."

I didn't have the time or the energy to debate him. "Come on!"

Every part of my body was screaming in pain as I forced myself to run up the stairs to the boardwalk. I stopped at town hall. No one was there. Nancy was at the groundbreaking and reception for the new town hall with everyone else. I regretted that I had to miss it, especially since Mad Dog wouldn't hesitate to step into my shoes and take over. But I had bigger fish to fry.

I ran to Missing Pieces, not sure what I'd do when I got there. Jake was big and looked like he could handle himself, but Jackie had the little pistol, and I felt sure Derek had something bigger. I didn't want Jake to get hurt trying to help me.

I thought if I could catch them at the shop, I could keep them there and call for help. There was bound to be at least one part-time police officer on duty that day.

But I was too late.

The door to the shop was wide open. They'd plowed through everything on the shelves and in the aisles like wild animals. I wasn't sure if there was a single piece of china or glass that wasn't broken. They'd split the cushions on my sofa and knocked over the cash register. The glass case in front was smashed.

I sat down on the wounded sofa anyway and choked back tears. All my beautiful things that I'd collected, cleaned and cherished while I waited for their rightful owners were destroyed. I hadn't checked on the St. Augustine monks' bell in the storage room. I didn't have the heart to look.

And I'd let everyone down. Dead Chuck, Betsy and Port. Without Derek and Jackie, there would be no justice. They were gone. It was over.

"Guess they beat you here," Jake acknowledged. "Are the police at the groundbreaking too?"

"Probably.

"Let's head over there," he said in a brisk tone. "No good feeling sorry for yourself right now. You might still be able to catch the culprits. Come on!"

He took my hand, and we ran back down the boardwalk. He put me up on the horse first this time, then climbed up behind me. "Which way?" he asked after he'd wrapped his arms around me to hold the reins.

"That way," I sniffled, pointing toward Duck Municipal Park. "Thanks."

"My pleasure, ma'am."

The horse moved quickly along the side of the road. As we rounded the curve, I could see the large crowd at the site of the new town hall and hear people speaking at the make-shift podium.

"Sounds like this must be it," Jake said as we reached the spot. "Plenty of police cars."

I agreed. "I can get off here. Thanks for your help. I don't have any money to offer you for your time, but I'd be glad to cook you a meal at my house whenever you can make it."

He jumped down first and lowered me to the ground. "I'll be sure to take you up on that. It shouldn't be too hard to find the mayor of Duck."

People had started to notice me and Jake and Penelope. Mad Dog's voice faltered as he spoke into the microphone.

"I'd love that. Thanks again, Jake."

"Any time, Dae O'Donnell." He smiled, lowered his head and kissed me lightly on the cheek. "You take care now."

I knew I had things to do, but I hated to see him go. He'd saved my life. He'd brought me back home. It was all I could do not to start crying again.

He jumped back on the wild horse and started back down the road toward Corolla.

I turned, faced my family, friends and neighbors, and walked resolutely to my place at the podium. I knew I was a mess, but I was past caring about that either. Without considering my actions for once, I bumped Mad Dog out of the way and gave the speech that I'd prepared for this day.

When I'd finished, there was complete silence.

A moment later, thunderous applause broke out. I smiled at everyone and thanked them. It was great to be mayor of Duck. I loved this town.

Bypassing the people who surrounded me at the podium, I made my way quickly to where Chief Michaels stood at the edge of the crowd. I told him my story, and he got on his radio.

"Are you okay?" he asked once he'd gotten the word out about Jackie and Derek.

"I will be," I promised.

He started to speak, must have thought better of it, nodded and walked toward Tim. The two of them got in a police car and headed away from the groundbreaking.

Paramedics were on the scene because of the large gathering. One looked at the cut over my eye to see if it needed stitches, then gave me a bottle of water and examined my badly bruised wrist.

"What the hell happened to you?" Kevin demanded when he'd reached me. The crowd was breaking up, but they were buzzing with plenty of fodder for the grapevine. "Are you okay? Why didn't you call me? Who was the cowboy?"

I answered in my rasping voice, giving him the simple version. Gramps came up while I was speaking, so I didn't have to repeat it.

"It doesn't matter now. They're already gone." I looked up at Kevin. "Didn't anyone know that I'd been kidnapped?"

"No. I don't think anyone realized. Did they make some kind of ransom demand for you?" Kevin pulled out his cell phone to call Ann.

I was amazed that no one had picked up on the clues. Gramps had called my cell phone a few times but said that I never answered my phone regularly anyway, so he thought I'd forgotten about the donuts.

Apparently Walt Jr. hadn't even noticed the dropped bag of donuts. Gramps and Kevin had only begun to suspect something was wrong when I wasn't at the groundbreaking.

I declined going to the hospital for tests. I was sore and upset, but my injuries were nothing that a hot shower and fresh clothes wouldn't help. No amount of badgering from Kevin or Gramps would make me change my mind. The paramedics wrapped my wrist and put a butterfly bandage on my forehead. They advised me to drink as much fluid as I could so as not to get dehydrated.

"What were they looking for?" Gramps asked.

"Money. A lot of money. I told Jackie it might be at the shop. That's the only reason she didn't kill me. She said she has Betsy hidden somewhere on the island. She told me she'd let her go after she finds the money."

"And you're sure the money *isn't* at Missing Pieces?"

I told Gramps about my and Kevin's meeting with Danny; I figured it was safe to do so since the chief was long gone. "I guess she thought it was possible he could've left it in the shop. She said he talked about me all the time."

"I think we should reconvene at the police station after Dae has a chance to get cleaned up," Kevin said. "Agent Kowalski needs to hear about this."

Gramps agreed. "After she's had a chance to rest. Good speech, though, honey. And nice entrance! Who was that cowboy?"

I explained as we headed for home in the golf cart.

Kevin came with us. When we got back to the house, Gramps immediately put on a pot of coffee and started rummaging around for food to go with it. Kevin sat down in the kitchen with him. I ignored them both and went upstairs.

I knew I was a wreck (who wouldn't be after the day I'd had?), but I hadn't realized just how bad a wreck until I looked in the mirror. The kitten raised his head but didn't move when he saw it was me. He was curled up on the pillow, flexing his claws into the blanket.

"No wonder everyone was staring at me like I was crazy," I told him as I stripped off the ruined suit I'd put on that morning. "This day seemed to have a mind of its own. Maybe I shouldn't make any more plans for it."

I'd done what I thought was best. I'd survived, even though I wasn't sure about my shop or, more important, Betsy. I'd tried to protect everyone and had at least managed to make it back home.

I stood in the shower until all the hot water was gone. When I'd done that as a kid, Gramps had come down on me like a thunderstorm, telling me that using up all the hot water was rude and inconsiderate.

Of course, that had been when my mother was still alive. There were more of us to be considerate of back then. We hadn't had a discussion like that in a long time.

I cleaned off the steamy mirror with a towel and looked at the cut on the side of my head. It hurt a lot for being so small. I tried to bear in mind that Jackie could've shot me with the Flobert. It could have been the last antique gun I ever handled.

I wasn't sure I would ever get all of the sand off me. It was worse than a day at the beach. Even after all that water pouring over my head, I still found some in my hair.

Why did they leave me alive?

I looked at my face and realized that I might never know.

Maybe it was the same reason Jackie hadn't killed Betsy. She certainly hadn't had any qualms about killing Chuck and Port.

But *they* had stolen from her. She seemed more than angry about that—she was afraid. She was desperate to get that money back. Maybe she was afraid of Guthrie. She'd made it clear that the whole thing had happened because she wanted to finance her freedom from him. She would've killed my father too if she'd found him. I had no doubt about that. He was right to be nervous. Did he get away with the chest they'd found from the *Andalusia* and all the money they'd cleverly tried to steal?

I might never know.

One thing Jackie gave me, besides a knot on the head, was the truth about Betsy. I firmly believed Betsy was alive somewhere out there. At this point, all I could hope was that Jackie would live up to her word about setting her free.

But if she didn't find the money at my shop, which I'm sure she didn't, was it over for Betsy?

Though I liked going barefoot, my feet were a little raw from my adventure. I put some lotion on them and found some soft old sandals that I'd thrown into the back of the closet. I planned to walk as little as possible for the rest of the day. I could always change before the town meeting tonight.

I went downstairs, stopping midway when I saw Gramps and Kevin in the living room talking with Chief Michaels and Agent Kowalski. They all looked up at me. There was no time to run and hide in the bedroom.

Chapter 27

"Gentlemen." I decided on a smooth political entrance since there was no way out. "Thank you for coming. As you can imagine, I'm not really feeling up to a trip to the station."

Of course, even Kowalski had to be apologetic and ask after my welfare. They couldn't ignore my bruises and cuts. At that point, I was glad to look like I'd had a rough morning.

We all sat down around the old wood kitchen table. Gramps poured coffee and brought out fresh donuts. He must've sent Kevin out for them while I was showering. Better him than me. I might never buy donuts again.

Maybe this was supposed to be some kind of debriefing. I wasn't sure what to expect. All four men seemed subdued.

I remembered how, as a kid, I'd wanted so much to be part of the group of police, and sometimes fire department members, sitting around this table with Gramps. At the time, I didn't understand half of what they were talking about, but it all sounded exciting. My mother always told me there was nothing exciting about it. I didn't believe her—until I grew up.

"Is this the woman who kidnapped you, Mayor?" Agent Kowalski got right to the point, holding up a small photo. He had already put a powdered-sugar donut on his plate, however. Nice to know he was actually human under that suit.

"Yes." Jackie stared back at me from the picture. "I think she's Guthrie's girlfriend."

"You're right." He put down the picture. "And she was with the same man the police picked up for attempting to buy Chuck Sparks's medallion. Is that correct?"

"Yes. I think he was working for her. I think he was trying to get the medallion to cover up what they'd done. But he sounded very intimate with her. They might be lovers."

Kowalski wrote everything down in his notebook. "That doesn't make any sense. We know Derek works for Guthrie. I don't see him being brave enough to sleep with the boss's girlfriend."

I didn't feel up to arguing with him. Not about that anyway. "Jackie told me Betsy is still alive. She said she'd let her go. I think she'll live up to her part. I'm just not sure when."

Kowalski laughed derisively and sat back from the table. "According to you, Jackie and Derek killed Tymov and Sparks. She almost killed *you.* I wouldn't put too much faith in her."

"She didn't kill me. She could have. But she didn't. I think that deserves a little faith."

"I know you've had a rough day, Mayor, and I'm sure you're glad to have lived through all of it. I think that may be coloring your judgment of Jackie. But this woman probably wouldn't know the truth if it bit her in the butt. I think we can assume that Sparks's daughter might be collateral damage."

"Betsy," I reminded him. "And why bother lying to me at all? She had nothing to gain."

"She could hold it over your head later. Use it as a bargaining chip if we catch up with her. If she's desperate enough to do all these other acts, what's one more?"

From his perspective, I supposed he thought he had a good point. But from mine, he was dead wrong, and I wasn't backing down again.

"Look, I've got everyone out here looking for this burgundy Lincoln. If it's still on the island, we'll find it. If she makes it off the island—" He shrugged. "Do you think the girl could be in the trunk?"

I thought about the sand and dripping water. "I don't think so."

Chief Michaels asked me about my ordeal. He was particularly interested in how I'd gotten away and how I'd ended up on the wild horse.

I explained, keeping Jake's name out of it. He'd done me a favor. I didn't want to repay him by putting him on the grid he wanted so badly to stay off of.

It seemed there was nothing more to say. Kowalski and the chief promised to keep in touch. We all knew the chance that we'd find Betsy alive was fading. If Jackie and Derek got away, there might be no chance at all.

When everyone else had left, Gramps and I looked at each other over the kitchen table, now covered in dirty coffee cups and donut crumbs.

"What happens now?" he asked.

"I don't know. I don't know what to do next. I can't identify the place in my visions."

"Maybe you should try something else. When I was

chief, if something was totally baffling, I walked away from it. I tried to see it in a different light."

"You went fishing." I grinned at him as we both got up to clear the table. "I remember Mom complaining about it. She didn't understand the whole walking-away-from-it thing."

"That's right. Your mother was like a water buffalo sometimes. All she could see was where she needed to be, and she kept her head down, kept going, until she got there. Your grandmother, rest her soul, was the same way. Like you, I guess."

"I guess."

"Sometimes that's a good thing. But sometimes, you need to clear your mind. The answers are there. We can't always see them for the clutter."

"That makes sense. I just don't know if I have time to go fishing."

"And speaking of the clutter, don't you try and clean up all that stuff at Missing Pieces by yourself. I know you have the meeting tonight. We'll go to that together, and tomorrow I'll help you with the cleanup. Deal?"

"Sure, Gramps. Thanks. Hey, did Tim drop off the mother cat?"

"She's around here somewhere. Tim brought her over this morning." He looked around the floor as though he expected to see her standing there. "I think she needs some time to adjust. She's in and out. Don't worry."

"I'm not worried—except maybe about you. Taking in two stray cats isn't like you. All that sun while you've been fishing might not be good for you."

"You've got that sassy mouth like your mother and grandmother before you too. Go on upstairs and change for the meeting. I'll tidy up down here."

"Okay. Don't eat all those leftover donuts. You know they're not good for you."

He waved me on with his big, callused hand. I smiled as I went back upstairs. Maybe Gramps was right. Maybe I needed to look in another direction.

In less than an hour, Gramps and I were on our way to the town hall meeting room. I knew there would be a crowd. Everyone knew what was going on. Supporters on my side, and on Mad Dog's side, were bound to drag in everyone they could.

I was surprised to find there wasn't even room to park the golf cart in the Duck Shoppes' lot. Cars and carts were everywhere, parked without any regard for the lines striped on the blacktop.

"Wish we could get this many people out to vote," Gramps grumbled. He finally parked the cart on the side of Duck Road. "What do they think is going to happen tonight?"

"If Mad Dog gets his way, he'll be mayor after the meeting," I said.

"You know he's not going to get the council to do that. He might as well go fishing for a whale. The whole thing burns my butt."

I smiled and hugged him. "Don't worry. I can take care of myself. Don't forget I have a sassy mouth and the disposition of a water buffalo. I think I can handle it."

He hugged me back. "I know. I just can't believe the man would stoop this low. The job doesn't even pay. You'd think this was New York City politics."

We walked into the crowded meeting room. Residents were spilling out into the main office and onto the boardwalk. The people on the boardwalk were the lucky ones—they got free ice cream courtesy of Andy's Ice Cream. Andy gave me a thumbs-up sign as I walked by him. It seemed I had at least two friendly faces in the crowd.

Gramps and I separated. He patted my back and nodded at the crowd. I knew that was his way of telling me to go get them on my side. I'd seen it many times before. It was his pep talk.

I watched him join a group of his friends—firemen, ex-police officers, fishermen and others. They all waved to me from their corner. Alternately, they glared at Mad Dog, who was at the other end of the council table.

Chris Slayton came up to me right away. "How are you, Mayor? I heard what happened. Should you be here tonight? I think after the trauma you've been through today, a postponed meeting could be in order. This is nothing but a witch hunt after all."

"I think it's important for me to be here. I appreciate the sentiment, though. I'm fine. Just a little sore. What does the agenda look like? I haven't had a chance to review it."

"Basically, you call the meeting to order and Councilman Wilson accuses both of us of gross negligence. Then he asks for both of us to resign."

"And someone has to second that motion for the council to vote on it."

He nodded at Mad Dog's sidekick on the council. "Councilman Wilson will make the motion. Councilman Efird will second. Then there will be a discussion and you call for the vote."

"Do I get to say anything?"

"Of course. You can be part of the discussion," he said. "It's your right to defend yourself."

"That's what I'll do then. You can defend yourself at the same time if you want to."

He smiled in his usual bashful way. "That's okay. I don't think it would do much good at this point. I'm an employee of the town. You're an elected official. I think no matter how it goes for you, I'm out of here."

I felt so bad for dragging him into all of this. "You've been such a good friend, Chris. I'm so sorry I involved you. I was wrong. But trust me, I won't be the only person on the council who doesn't want to see you go. I think Mad Dog will fall short on a vote to get rid of you."

"Don't worry about me, Mayor. I can get another job. I'm glad you have friends on the council too. Frankly, if you leave, I don't want to be here anyway."

That really broke my heart, since he'd done so much good for the town. We had been blessed to have him on staff. Duck wouldn't be the same place without his clever ideas and ability to pull off daily miracles.

This couldn't be the end for Chris as town manager, or for me as mayor. I stared out at the crowd of friendly and not-so-friendly faces. I took my place at the head of the council table. Despite making a scene this afternoon at the groundbreaking, I believed most people would be willing to forgive and forget. They probably had a million questions for me—not only about the groundbreaking but also about the body at the barbecue and the continued presence of the FBI in Duck, not to mention my and Chris's ill-conceived inspections of local basements. There had to be a way to make people understand what had been going on the last few days.

I hit my gavel on the table at exactly seven P.M. The room came to order. There were as many people standing in the room as there were sitting down, roughly about a hundred. Those peeking in the door from the office and waiting on the boardwalk made probably another fifty or so.

"I want to thank everyone for coming out tonight for this specially called meeting," I said. "We'll start with the Pledge of Allegiance and then go on to the matter at hand."

Everyone stood, faced the American flag and put their hands over their hearts. Collectively, the citizens of Duck repeated the same words of national loyalty they had so many times before.

We sat down again and before I could introduce the agenda, Councilman Wilson lumbered to his feet. His jacket lapels were covered in his campaign buttons.

"I'd just like to say that what we are proposing here tonight is radical. We've never seen the like of it in Duck before. I pray we never see it again. But we owe it to the citizens of our town to make sure that our elected officials are not using town resources to their own benefit."

"Thank you, Councilman Wilson," I cut in. "I believe we'll need to introduce the facts before we make a motion and discuss the problem."

"Of course, Madam Mayor." He bowed his head to me and took his seat.

"We have two items on the agenda for tonight," I continued as though he hadn't spoken.

"That's right." Councilman Efird took up where Mad Dog had left off. "The problem we have is that our mayor decided to use three town employees, being paid by our taxes, for personal matters. Not only is this illegal, but it is also immoral. I would like to make a motion that we ask for Mayor Dae O'Donnell's resignation. I'd like to further motion that we ask for the resignation of the town manager, Chris Slayton. The other town personnel were under duress and had no idea that what they were doing was not part of town business. They should be excused."

I almost laughed out loud. Apparently, Councilman Efird hadn't received the memo about his place in the grand scheme of things. I was especially amused to see the look on Mad Dog's face as his friend stole his thunder.

"All right," I said with as calm a demeanor as I could. "We have two motions on the floor. Do we have a second before discussion?"

Mad Dog frowned but seconded Efird's motions.

"Thank you, Councilman Wilson." I acknowledged him carefully. "I believe now we can discuss the matter."

Before I could add my part, Councilwoman La Donna Nelson slowly rose to her feet. "I have something I want to say." She turned to Mad Dog. "Shame on you, Councilman Wilson. This is only our second election in Duck, and you've tainted it by attempting to oust Mayor O'Donnell before the two of you have even heard from the voters. I'm ashamed to be part of this tribunal."

"Thank you, Councilwoman Nelson." I smiled at her as she sat down.

"I want to speak as well." Councilman Rick Treyburn got to his feet. Rick was a retired investment banker who'd moved here a few years back and immediately become involved in town matters. I'd expected him to run for mayor this year. He'd seemed ambitious. Maybe he was happy as a councilperson.

"Go ahead, Councilman Treyburn." I wasn't sure where he'd stand on the resignation issue. I didn't really know him well enough to say.

"I want to commend Mayor O'Donnell for the job she's done as mayor. She and Chris Slayton have worked hard the last few years to bring so many improvements to Duck. She's part of the younger generation who is willing to share her time and abilities to make this a better place to live. I can say right now that I won't vote to ask for her resignation."

A smattering of applause went up across the room. Of course, I had to use my gavel and ask for silence. I appreciated the support, but this wasn't the appropriate response in the council chamber.

"I'd say that makes us tied," Mad Dog said. "That would make the mayor the tiebreaker. In this case, I make a motion the mayor recuse herself from the vote since it involves her personally."

"First of all, we have two previous motions on the table," I told him. "Unless Councilman Efird is willing to withdraw his motions, we have to vote on them first."

Councilman Efird looked pointedly at Mad Dog as though to ask what he should do. That raised a few giggles from the audience. *No doubt where his loyalties lie.*

Mad Dog finally shook his head, and Councilman Efird said he wouldn't withdraw his motions.

I got to my feet and looked out at the people in the crowd. Many of them I'd known since childhood. Many of them had known my family since before I was born. I knew I owed all of them an explanation.

"I would like to take a few minutes and explain what's been going on in Duck the last few days." I told them about Chuck Sparks and Port Tymov. Then I told them about Betsy.

"I understand that a lot of you have questions about what happened this afternoon at the groundbreaking and about why I asked for help from the public works crew and Chris Slayton. It's really pretty simple. There is a six-year-old girl out there somewhere tonight who hasn't been home in several days. She's cold, hungry and terrified. The FBI can't find her. I haven't had much luck at it either, and as most of you know, I'm unusually good at finding missing things."

The audience smiled and nodded.

"That's why I enlisted Chris and the public works crew to help me. But if it wasn't town business to search for this little girl, then I don't know what town business is. In my mind, pulling together in a time of crisis is what being a community is all about. I apologize for not asking permission first. I take full responsibility for Chris Slayton being out there with me. But as long as I'm your mayor, I'll always put the people of Duck first. And I can tell you now, I won't resign. You'll have to tell me to go."

Chapter 28

People applauded like crazy—except for the few who sat still and frowned up at me. I thought I'd sounded all right, especially since I hadn't planned out what I'd say. I spoke from my heart, and that was the best I could do. I hadn't realized until I was speaking that I wouldn't resign. That had just come out, but I knew it was true.

I called the room to order, then took the vote. Mad Dog and Councilman Efird voted to ask for my and Chris's resignation. A chorus of boos followed. I used my gavel to bring quiet to the room again.

La Donna and Councilman Treyburn voted to keep both of us on. That left me with the deciding vote. Normally, as mayor, I had no vote. It was only in instances of a tie that I had a say. That didn't happen very often.

What now?

I looked at La Donna for assistance. She shrugged and

started organizing her papers. She didn't know what to do either.

"If I could weigh in on this matter, Mayor." Chris stood up at his desk at the side of the council table. "There is precedence that would allow the mayor to recuse herself from casting the tie-breaking vote and allow the Duck citizens present at this forum tonight to vote on the matter. The vote would be final."

He nodded and took his seat again.

"Thanks, Mr. Slayton. I think that sounds fair." I turned to the council. Of course, Mad Dog and Councilman Efird loved the idea. I tended to agree with them. It hardly seemed fair that I'd get to cast the deciding vote that would allow me to keep my job.

La Donna wasn't sure. "Perhaps we should table the vote and research this legal precedent. I'm not sure how this will reflect on the council. Shouldn't it be up to *all* the people of Duck?"

Treyburn agreed with Mad Dog, to my surprise. "I think this is the way to go. I trust Mr. Slayton's judgment. He hasn't steered us wrong before."

So the vote was three to one to allow the hundred-plus people at the meeting to decide my and Chris's fate, in two separate votes.

As Nancy handed out slips of paper to everyone, I wondered who had the most friends in the crowd—that's what it would come down to. I knew Mad Dog must think he did, but there was no sure way to know until the vote was taken.

It took about fifteen minutes for everyone to write yes or no on their impromptu ballots. The council took a recess during that time. Mad Dog used his time to speak to his friends in the audience.

I stayed where I was. I'd be glad when the whole thing

was over, one way or another. I agreed with La Donna that Mad Dog's call for my resignation was a political ploy to get me out of the way. If that happened, Mad Dog wouldn't have to face anyone in the election. It was too late for any other candidates to file. But my continued position as mayor had become a hot-button issue, preventing the council from doing the important town business. It had to be dealt with.

Nancy picked up all the ballots. She had to count them alone, since Chris's position could be compromised if we won the vote. She stacked all the yes and no papers for Chris first, putting the ballots into separate envelopes and labeling them. Then she counted yes and no ballots for me and did the same thing again. At least there would be no question of the integrity of the vote count. *Smart Nancy!*

Everyone waited quietly—if a little impatiently—for the answer. The only sound in the room was the occasional shifting in chairs and Mad Dog's fingers drumming on the table.

Nancy looked up at eight forty-five. "I have tallied the votes, Madam Mayor. There are twenty yes ballots, indicating the mayor should resign. There are one ninety ballots indicating the mayor should stay."

There was a lot of booing and angry remarks both from council and the audience. I used my gavel to quiet things down and took a deep breath. I hadn't realized how much this meant to me until that moment.

Chris was next. "There are one-hundred and ten no ballots, indicating that Mr. Slayton should stay on as town manager," Nancy announced with a smile on her face. "Only ten yes ballots, indicating that Mr. Slayton should leave."

There was applause and good wishes. A few of Chris's friends came up and slapped him on the back, then shook his hand. I brought the room to order again. Everyone took their seats. Mad Dog wanted to speak, and I acknowledged him.

"I think we made a mistake with this poll. We should reconsider and table this matter for a later date."

Treyburn laughed. "You consider it for a later date, Wilson. I'm going home knowing that the best woman won tonight, and hopefully next November too."

"I insist we take a vote," Mad Dog said.

"What good will that do?" La Donna asked. "The two of you will vote to table. Rick and I will vote to proceed. Then either Dae will break the tie in her favor, or we'll ask our citizens here to vote again. We could be here all night."

Finally Mad Dog conceded. "I still think each citizen should remember what happened here tonight and vote accordingly in the election. I will *never* show up for a town event looking like I'd spent the night on the beach. And I will *never* ask town workers to help me look for a missing child."

The room got very quiet when he'd made his final statement. Then Andy Martin yelled out, "Then you're not *my* mayor!"

The room erupted again. I brought down the gavel, but since it was just to adjourn the meeting, I didn't follow through by demanding quiet.

"You won!" La Donna said with a smile. "Smart move, not casting the tiebreaker. That's why you're such a good mayor."

A long line of people had formed, stretching from the council table to the back of the room. Cathi Connor was closest. "We all want to help find Betsy," she said. "There are a lot of us, Dae. Put us to work."

Tears welled in my eyes. This was *my* town and *my* people. "Leave your names and phone numbers with Nancy. As soon as we have some idea where to look, I'll give you a call. Thank you all for volunteering."

Chris came up and shook my hand. "I knew you'd win if the people had their way."

"I don't know. It was close."

"Only because Councilman Wilson had his friends packed in here. Wait until the election. He won't stand a chance."

"Thanks, Chris."

"Hey, you want to go and get a celebratory drink at Curbside?"

I saw Kevin walking through the departing crowd toward me. "Maybe another time. But thanks for your help."

"Sure. You kind of had that deer-in-the-headlights look when there was a tie. I just wanted to help you out. See you around." He nodded to Kevin as he left.

"Looks like you won," Kevin said as he reached me. "Congratulations. I hope the election goes the same way."

"Thanks." I picked up my pocketbook and the folder I always brought to the meetings.

"I'm sorry about what happened with the chief and Kowalski at your house."

"I didn't expect it to go any different."

"I guess we'll have to hope they can catch Derek and Jackie before Guthrie does."

"I hope my dad got away. It was good he left when he did."

"I don't know if I'd say good, but he might be safe if he doesn't come back here for a while. Or make the mistake of crossing Guthrie again."

"I guess so. But that still doesn't solve my problem. Jackie and Derek admitted to killing Chuck and Port, but now that they've left town, how do we find Betsy?"

"I don't know." He looked around the empty meeting

room. "Would you like to go and talk about it? We could get a drink or something."

"I don't think so. Thanks. Not tonight. I need to go home and get some sleep. We'll start again tomorrow, okay?"

He looked disappointed, but he smiled anyway. "Just give me a call. I'll talk to you later."

But going home wasn't really on my agenda. I was exhausted, but I knew I wouldn't be able to sleep without dreaming. And my dreaming about being with Betsy wasn't doing her any good—nothing in the dreams had enabled me to determine where she was.

I needed that fresh look Gramps had talked about. I just wasn't sure where to find it.

But there was something useful I could do. I walked from town hall to Missing Pieces. The boardwalk was empty, all the lights turned off for the night. The lights from towns around us—Sanderling, Kill Devil Hills, Manteo—shone on the still, dark surface of the sound. I stood at the rail and looked at the water for a long time before going inside.

The shop was a disaster, but I had to start somewhere. I put on some old clothes I kept in the back for emergencies. The kettle started whistling on the hot plate a few minutes later. I brought in the big trash can that usually went in back for trash collection day and began cleaning up the debris.

It wasn't long before Gramps joined me. "I knew this would happen. Didn't I tell you to wait until morning and I'd help you? You never listen to me. You always have to go your own way."

I shrugged. "Yeah. That's the way water buffalo are."

He laughed. "All right. If it has to be tonight, where do you want me?"

We worked in companionable silence for a long time. After an hour or so, I could actually see the floor again. "I'll have to take the sofa over to the upholstery place and see if he can mend it."

"I'm sure it'll be fine," he said encouragingly before taking a long sip from a can of Coke. "Are you going to claim this on your insurance? That's what it's there for, you know."

"Probably. At least some of it. You're supposed to have all of your inventory listed. I don't think all of this made it to the list."

"Well, claim what you can. Regardless of what you told those two criminals, this was still a break-in."

We continued cleaning what amounted to mostly rubble. I found the silver bell where I'd left it in the storage room, still wrapped in the blue velvet. "I guess they just wanted the cash. Too bad it wasn't here."

"Do you think Danny took it with him?"

"I don't know, Gramps. I made up the whole story about Danny having visited the shop recently—I was hoping they'd bring me back to help look for the money. As for Danny, he left in such a hurry, who knows? But he said he didn't have it."

"He said a lot of things. I wanted to believe him for your sake." He picked up a shovel full of glass that had once been the front counter. "I guess the old axiom still applies."

"Once a criminal—"

"I'm sorry, Dae. It's hard to get out of that life—always chasing the next big score. This one was too big for Danny, I guess. Maybe he'll straighten up now."

"But you don't really believe that, do you?"

"No, honey. I'm afraid not."

A lot of the destruction had come not from Jackie and Derek's search of the shop but from their desire to be vindictive. They knew there was no money hidden in my old tea sets, but they smashed them anyway. A hundred-year-old mirror lay in pieces, for no reason. Pillows were shredded, and candles were snapped in half.

Most of my treasures were a total loss. I'd have to find other items to take their place on my shelves and in my heart. It was hard to say what this would cost me, both financially and emotionally. There were so many items that I hadn't priced, hundreds of pieces that would never have good homes.

I sat down on the sofa for a few minutes as Gramps started sweeping up some smaller slivers of glass. My tea was cold, but I drank it anyway. As I looked at the floor, I saw something odd—something that didn't belong there.

It was an earring. The back must have come off of the post, and the earring had slipped out of the wearer's ear. If I didn't know every piece in the shop, I might've thought it was part of my collection. But I knew this piece of jewelry didn't belong here.

I remembered that when Jackie had been waving the pistol around, threatening me mostly, the light from the window had caught on a blue earring in her right ear. Momentarily distracted by it, I had speculated on whether or not it was a sapphire and where she'd found it. The earring looked like an antique. Then I'd gone back to wondering if she'd really kill me.

The light from the ceiling caught on the blue earring now and fractures of color swept through it. It was a round sapphire surrounded by several smaller stones cut to resemble flower petals. At the same time that I knew the stones were real, I also knew Jackie had lost it here when she was searching for the cash.

My heart started to pound. It would be risky to pick it up without gloves. There was no telling what I'd see besides her time with Guthrie and the deaths of Chuck and Port. But I had to take that risk—Betsy might be there too.

"What did you find?" Gramps came and leaned over the earring.

"It belongs to Jackie. I'm going to pick it up. If I drop on the floor, just leave me there. I'll come around soon enough."

"How in the world can you tell? Shouldn't you do something to protect yourself?"

"I'm doing all I can by trying to be prepared for it. If I wear gloves, I won't be able to learn anything from it." I smiled at him, hoping to be reassuring. "It'll be fine. I've picked up things that had much worse histories. Just don't panic."

I carefully lifted the earring out of the trash around it and held it in my hand. Immediately, the fractures of light and color I'd seen in it became the hands that took the sapphire out of the ground in Afghanistan, the man who cleaned and cut it, and the broker who sold it to Dillon Guthrie.

I saw Guthrie put the earrings on Jackie. She smiled and gave him a passionate kiss. But even then, she was plotting how she would escape from him. I saw them together as she wore the earrings to please and placate him through the years, in many provocative ways.

She was wearing the earrings when she met Port for the first time. They became lovers soon after. She believed he could help her get away from Guthrie. It was later that he came to her with the story of the treasure of the *Andalusia*. He tried to get her to put on the amber necklace from the treasure chest, after it had been cleaned. She refused. But she agreed to give him $200,000 to find the rest of the treasure.

Danny had been wrong about where the money had come from. Guthrie had never even known about the treasure.

She and Derek had killed Chuck in the Harris Teeter parking lot. They'd ransacked his house, looking for the treasure Jackie had been promised. They'd found Betsy instead.

I heard Port begging Jackie not to kill him. She was more ruthless with him than she had been with Chuck because she'd thought he loved her. He hadn't been dead when Derek had put him in that garbage barrel.

I heard her talking to Betsy in a sweet and gentle way that surprised me. I understood that Jackie, for all her ruthlessness and desperation, had a soft spot for children. She couldn't have any of her own. It was that loss that had made her want to leave Guthrie, and it was the reason she'd spared Betsy's life—and mine.

It was really weird seeing myself through her eyes. If I hadn't challenged her, demanding to know where Betsy was, she would've had Derek kill me.

I came back to myself with Gramps hovering anxiously over me. "It's about time," he said. "I don't like this new stuff, Dae. Why couldn't you just be happy holding someone's hand and finding their wallet?"

"It wasn't like I had much choice. It just happened." I forced myself up and off the sofa. "I've seen something new. I have to find Ann."

"Okay then. I'll finish up here. You just be careful."

I gave him a big hug. "You don't have to stay. We can work on it tomorrow."

"No, that's fine. I need something to do, besides worry. I'll see you later."

"All right. Just don't throw anything away that isn't broken."

He smiled. "I'm surprised you can bear to throw this stuff away even if it *is* broken!"

I didn't comment on that. He understood how I felt, even if he didn't share my sentiments. I loved him for it.

I ran through the dark streets, my feet complaining and

my lungs burning. I'd never been much of a runner, but I had to reach Ann as soon as possible. The vision hadn't revealed much additional detail about the place where they were holding Betsy, but even a sliver of information might make a difference.

And I'd kept the sapphire earring in my pocket, in case Ann could learn something else from it.

Kevin answered the door, looking wonderfully disheveled. His hair was sleep mussed, and his shirt was wrinkled. I almost forgot why I was there. The cramp in my side reminded me.

"I have to talk to Ann," I told him, barely able to catch my breath. "It's about Betsy."

"Come on in." He held the door open for me. "Did you run all the way here?"

"Yes. I wish I could've been here sooner. I've seen something else, Kevin. I'm hoping it's enough that Ann and I together can put an end to this."

"Midnight tryst?" Ann came down the long stairs.

I smiled, knowing Kevin's bedroom was on the main floor. This wasn't a good time to be petty. I couldn't help it.

I explained to Ann and showed her the earring, holding it carefully with a tissue that was also in my pocket. "I need your help. Don't ask me why—I think this may be it."

Chapter 29

"Beautiful rocks," she said, coming the rest of the way down the stairs. "Belong to anyone you know?"

"I found it in the shop after Jackie and Derek trashed it."

"Of course you did."

I had hoped she wouldn't be difficult just this one time. I tried again. "I saw Betsy again, but this time from Jackie's perspective. There was something a little different than before. I thought you might be able to take that and turn it into a sketch."

She stared at me as though I were speaking a language she couldn't understand. My heart sank. I was so sure this was going to do it. I wished I didn't need her help, but I couldn't seem to do it on my own. There had to be some way to reach her.

"I know you've been through a lot. I know I can't really understand all of the terrible things you've seen. But if you could help me get through this, maybe we could both have a happy ending this time."

She stopped staring at me and started back upstairs. "You don't know anything."

"Maybe not. But I know you're scared. That's why you gave up so soon. That's why you won't reach out. You're afraid she'll be dead and your heart can't bear it. I may not know a lot, but I know that much."

She turned back to me. I tried not to flinch. I really expected her to fly down the stairs at me. Picturing that wasn't pleasant.

But instead, she came calmly back down. "I'll see what I can do—so long as you lay off the psycho babble. I've had enough of that to last me the rest of my life."

It was as if we all let out a collective sigh of relief.

"I'll make some tea," Kevin said. "I think there are still some lemon muffins left over from dinner too."

"Better make it coffee," Ann warned. "I need it straight, strong and hot. And don't ever try to impress me with left-overs again."

"You got it."

When he'd gone into the kitchen, Ann and I sat at the round table in the bar area. It had just been polished and smelled like lemon oil.

Ann took the earring from me and played with it for a few minutes. "I'm not getting anything from this."

"Maybe if we hold hands," I suggested. "Let me find some paper for you." I rummaged through a drawer where I knew Kevin kept crayons and coloring pages for kids who stayed at the inn.

"I'm leaving in the morning," Ann said. "I thought you'd like to know."

My heart beat a little faster. She'd said *I*. "I know you don't like it here."

She nodded and tucked her feet up under her on the chair. "It's not just that. It's a nice enough place. I just can't learn to be who I am now, here. You understand?"

I stood, looking at the crayons I held. Inside, I was jumping up and down and dancing. I would have Kevin back. Ann would be out of the picture.

Unfortunately, I couldn't just leave it at that. The images she'd shared with me—her and Kevin—I knew they'd loved each other. She'd come to find him because she still loved him. I was sure she couldn't imagine the rest of her life without him.

Time had moved on without her while she'd been locked away. It was unfair. I wanted to cry for her loss even though it meant my gain.

"Are you sure?" I asked.

"I am. But you're brave asking me. What if I reconsidered? You and Kevin would have no future together while I'm here. He'd do the honorable thing and marry me. That's the way he is."

"I'm guessing since you know that, it's not what you want."

"No. I want my life back the way it was before—before I lost it and Kevin found you. If I had a fairy godmother, that's what I'd ask for and the hell with you, Dae O'Donnell. I wouldn't feel sorry for *you*, believe me."

She drew a deep breath and almost smiled. "But don't worry. I've always had a habit of landing on my feet. Kevin's changed, you know. He's lost his edge. I guess that's what comes of cooking for people and cleaning up their messes. He's not the man I loved. I'm sure I'm not the woman he loved either. It's better for both of us if we start over apart."

Kevin came into that awkward silence that follows when the person you've just been talking about enters the room. He had dressed and combed his hair. He glanced at both of us, then set the tray of cups and goodies on the table. "I can leave again, if that will help."

Ann smiled at him. "Not unless I run out of coffee. Do you want Kevin to leave, Dae?"

It was a double-edged question. I answered it as evasively as I could. "I'm comfortable with him staying if you are."

"Then let's get going on this."

I sat beside Ann after she finished her coffee. She ignored the lemon muffins, as she'd promised. I wondered if she'd told Kevin she was leaving. I wasn't brave enough to ask either of them that question. Still, I had to chase the thought from my mind so I could concentrate on what I'd seen from Jackie's earring.

Touching Ann was electrifying. It sent bolts of energy—like prolonged, powerful static shock—through me. We both closed our eyes.

I saw so much of her. She had to open up to me in order to see those details about Betsy. I saw her as a child with her father who was in the military. I saw her growing up, daydreaming at the beach, in love for the first time when she was barely sixteen.

I saw her again with Kevin, the two of them working together, in love with one another. I saw what she saw during the good cases where they found children still alive. And the nightmares of the children they'd found dead.

Far worse was taking in her breakdown and the horrible years she'd spent locked away from the world. Thinking of Kevin was what had kept her going, what had eventually healed her and brought her back to reality, to the here and now.

I knew she saw everything about me too. It was the only way this would work. My life was like a fairy tale compared to hers. I could only guess what she would make of it.

Suddenly, the connection between us was broken. Ann gave a little screech and grabbed for the paper and crayons. "I see it! I see what you mean, but I don't know what it is."

Her nimble fingers flew across the paper, sketching what she saw almost faster than my eyes could keep pace. On the back of a coloring page illustrated with a teddy bear carrying flowers, she drew a vague shape, but quickly the lines began to look familiar. In seconds, I knew what it was, though when I'd seen it in my own mind it had been obscured somehow.

"It's a boat! I think it's the old wrecked boat that's been out in the woods near the Sailor's Dream for as long as I can remember. The town council tried to make the owner clean it up last year. Nothing ever came of it. Let's go!"

I waited impatiently with Kevin as Ann went to get sandals—she was already dressed in shorts and a T-shirt—and then the three of us ran out into the rain. None of us had noticed the hard rain that had begun falling after I'd arrived. The drops were enormous on the truck windshield as we crammed in.

"Drive fast," Ann urged Kevin. "None of that old-lady driving you usually do."

"Shut up. I've got it," he said with a careless familiarity.

I didn't say anything. I was glad I was on the outside with Ann in the middle. For once I wasn't jealous. I was too caught up by the notion that we might have found Betsy.

Kevin didn't drive like an old lady. I never knew his old pickup could go that fast. It was enough to catch the attention of the Duck police officer pulling traffic duty. I wasn't sure which officer it was, but when the police cruiser's blue light flickered on and its siren cried out, I took out my cell phone and called Chief Michaels. If we were wrong about Betsy being held in the abandoned boat—then we'd be wrong.

I explained the situation in the barest of terms, but it was enough to still the siren, though the car with the blue lights continued to follow us down Duck Road.

Kevin spun the truck around on the Sailor's Dream driveway, gravel flying up around us. He had barely stopped when Ann and I jumped out. There was a streetlight near the Sailor's Dream itself, but the wooded area around it was pitch black.

"All I have is a flashlight on my cell phone," Kevin said, the rain pushing his hair into his face. "We have to have a light or we won't be able to find the boat."

"I know about where it is," I told him. But I wasn't sure I could find it. In the daytime, it was clearly visible through the underbrush, but at night, it wouldn't be so easy to see.

I knew from my childhood explorations of the small sailboat that it had once been painted pale blue. It was already dilapidated back when I was a kid. No one had touched it in years. Most of the paint had flaked off and the sides were caving in. I remembered that its sail was missing, probably stolen years before, but the broken mast was still attached.

"I have a spotlight, Mayor," announced Officer Scott Randall as he approached us, a large flashlight in hand; it was his cruiser that had tailed us to the bar. "What are we looking for?"

"That old boat that's been falling apart out here for years," I explained, starting into the dark woods. Ann was already wading into the blackness ahead of me. "You know the one I mean, Scott."

"I know what you mean," he agreed. "Let me get in front. We can see better with the light guiding the way. I've seen that old boat plenty of times. But I couldn't tell you right now exactly where it is. I'll call for more help."

I stepped back behind him. Kevin was next to me. We couldn't even see Ann anymore. I hoped she didn't hurt herself on the fallen trees and other debris. The town hadn't always offered waste removal service back in the days before incorporation. People often dumped large, expensive-to-dispose-of trash like old refrigerators in places where they thought no one would notice.

I wanted to run into the dark with Ann, but I knew we were better off being a little cautious. After being in Ann's mind, I knew how desperately she wanted to find Betsy alive. In some ways, it was even more important to her than it was to me.

"Ann?" Kevin yelled out when we heard a yelp from the darkness.

"It's okay," she yelled back. "I think I just stepped on a nail. Keep going. I can see your light."

"Why don't you come back with us?" I asked loudly.

"I'm better alone. I'm heading left from where you are. You go right. Doesn't Duck have any construction lights or something more powerful than a big flashlight?"

"We do, ma'am," Scott said. "We just don't bring them out in the middle of the night on two minutes' notice. Sorry."

Ann didn't respond. We all continued shuffling through the woods, wary of what lay beneath our feet. It seemed stupidly impossible that we hadn't located the boat by now. I knew it was half buried in sand and covered with undergrowth, but surely we could find it.

"This is ridiculous. We could be at it all night." Kevin stopped walking and looked at me. "You're the best at finding lost things, Dae. Let's take a minute and have you find this boat."

My mind was whirling with hundreds of images—of Betsy, the boat, Jackie and Derek, Ann and Kevin. My heart was pounding. The one thing I couldn't do was concentrate.

"I would've found it already if I could," I fired back at him. "Don't you think I want this to be over?"

"I know you do." Kevin put his hands on my arms. "You want it *too* much. You have to clear your mind. Forget everything else but finding that boat. You can do this, Dae. Take us to it. Let's save the girl."

I took a deep breath, ready to yell back at him. What he said made sense; I just wasn't as confident in myself, in my gift, as he was.

Finally, I nodded, swallowed my angry words and closed my eyes.

How many times had I explored that old boat on the way home from school or the museum? It had always looked like a child's toy—not more than ten feet long. Much smaller than the *Eleanore*, Gramps's boat. I dreamed of fixing it up and sailing away to foreign lands where there were bright and beautiful things.

The last time I'd visited the boat, I noticed there was an elder tree right next to it. It had grown up through the side of the boat and blossomed over the top of it. There were white flowers everywhere. It looked like it had snowed on the deck.

"I've got it!" I opened my eyes and started walking in the same direction that Ann had gone. "I haven't been out here for so long—but I know exactly where it is."

Scott scratched his head but kept up with me. Branches and other debris cracked under my feet. I heard more cars arrive in the parking lot behind us. Someone had brought dogs too. They began barking and baying as they let them out of the vehicles.

"Ann?" I called out into the darkness. "Can you feel her?"

"No. I wish I could. Can you?"

"No. But I think I know where the boat is."

"Let me see."

I felt her presence in my mind and tried to form the

image of the old boat and the area around it. "That's where she is. Can you see it?"

"Not yet. I see your light coming my way. Are you sure it's this direction?"

"Yes. Absolutely."

We kept going. Scott answered a call on his radio and explained what was going on, where we were. He had the new searchers spread out in the direction we hadn't taken. "Sorry, Mayor. Just making sure. Not that I doubt you."

"That's okay. Let's just find her."

We pushed through an area littered with an old stove and what was left of someone's living room furniture. Kevin stumbled but regained his footing without falling. Scott's light wavered as he stepped into a hole in the sand.

For just a minute, it was like I was a girl again. It was late spring, just before school let out for the summer. The weather was warm, and I was walking home, goofing around like usual. I stopped to look at the old boat. The sunlight was golden on it, slanting through the trees that had grown up around it.

And when I opened my eyes, there it was.

"I found it!" I yelled. "Let's get her out!"

Kevin and Scott came up beside me. Ann ran through the brush as though angels guided her feet.

The boat was small. There was no reason to climb on it and risk collapsing the structure further. We located the hatch where Derek had dropped food to her. I leaned over and opened it. "Betsy?" I called into that damp, dark place.

"Hello?" she called back. "Please help me. Please get me out of here."

The rain started falling even harder. Scott held the light steady. My heart was pounding, breath coming faster as I prepared to lift her out of her prison.

Before I could move, Ann made a calculated leap into

the hole in the boat. Like a snake, she slipped inside and disappeared—emerging a minute later with Betsy in her arms.

Scott shone the light on them. Everyone was crying. Or maybe it was just the rain.

Kevin took Betsy from Ann so she could get out. Scott and I helped Ann make the more difficult leap out of what was left of the boat, then Scott called for an ambulance. Betsy clung so tightly to Kevin that there was no way to separate them. He walked back to the parking lot with her in his arms.

Still in the dark area of the woods, Ann and I trailed behind Scott and Kevin. Just as we reached the clearing and light of the parking lot, we fell against each other and sobbed.

"She's *alive*," Ann gulped and tried to talk. "You were right. She's alive."

"She is."

"You don't know. No one will *ever* know how much I needed her to be alive."

We stared into each other's eyes, having shared an intimate bond most people would never understand. "I know," I sobbed. "I know."

We all rode to the hospital, Kevin, Ann and I in the ambulance with Betsy, and the rest following behind. We had a full police escort all the way, lights flashing and sirens blaring. People who saw us pass must have thought the president or some other dignitary was on their way out of town.

When we arrived at the emergency room, hospital officials were waiting for us. So was Melinda. They all ran out to the ambulance. Ann and I stepped out before they moved Betsy.

Melinda took one look at her daughter's face and collapsed on the pavement. The hospital staff were so focused on the little girl, they didn't notice. Ann and I helped Melinda up and held her between us as we walked into the hospital. Melinda was sobbing so hard she could hardly breathe. "Oh my God!" she cried out. "Betsy! My baby is still alive!"

We sat her down on the bench near the door. There was nothing more we could do but wait as the medical team began examining Betsy. But no one wanted to go home. We were exhausted, drained—and jubilant.

The waiting-lounge coffeepot emptied quickly as we poured paper cup after paper cup of the strong, dark brew. It was awful, but at least it was warm.

Surprisingly, someone had thought to call the media. It was even more of a surprise when a reporter from the TV station in Virginia Beach showed up. Despite my flattened hair and sandy clothes (perhaps this was a new public look for me), Chief Michaels and Agent Kowalski thought I should be the one to talk to them.

It was a little strange—the reporter stood in front of the camera to describe the scene, then went behind it. He was wearing a tie and sports shirt with khaki shorts. No one could see the shorts.

"How are you feeling at this moment, Mayor O'Donnell?"

"I guess I'm feeling lucky and blessed to have found Betsy Sparks. Everyone in Duck has been helpful in looking for her the past few days."

"And she's unharmed?"

"We don't know yet. I rode with her to the hospital. She seemed in good spirits, and she was happy to be going home."

"What about her kidnappers? Is there any word on who did this?"

I suddenly had bookends. Chief Michaels pressed in close on my left, Agent Kowalski on my right. I didn't realize until after we were done talking that Sheriff Riley had sneaked up behind me to get in on the shot too.

"We believe we will have the kidnappers in custody by the morning," Agent Kowalski said. "We've had a good working relationship with the Duck PD and the county throughout the entire experience."

The reporter nodded and turned off the camera. "Thanks. Anyone know if there's coffee inside?"

"Good job, Mayor." Chief Michaels shook my hand as though he was expecting someone to take our picture.

The reporter was already inside, so I assumed his praise was genuine.

"It wasn't only me. You should congratulate Ann Porter too. We couldn't have found Betsy without working together."

The chief, Agent Kowalski and I—Sheriff Riley had left pouting after he wasn't allowed to speak on camera—went inside to look for Ann. It was obvious to me that she wasn't in the large crowd still waiting in the lobby for word of Betsy's condition.

I saw Kevin and left the chief and Kowalski by the door. "Have you seen Ann?"

"She's gone. I think she went out another exit. She said she was taking a car back to the inn."

"I wish I'd gone with her. I don't think she'll be able to find a taxi this time of night."

He smiled. "I don't think she meant a taxi when she told me she was taking a car. She has a skill set that makes finding a taxi irrelevant."

"I see."

"She was so happy to find Betsy," he said. "For a few minutes, she was like she used to be. I hope she can find what she's looking for."

I searched his face. He knew she was leaving. "I'm sorry, Kevin. I know you wanted it to work out."

"We weren't the same people anymore, Dae. That time and those people are gone forever. Going to New York won't change that."

"She said pretty much the same thing."

"I'm amazed that she talked to you about it. I think you two bonded there at the end."

"It's what happens when you get into someone else's mind, I guess. It was like I was thinking what she was thinking. I've never experienced anything like it."

"And never want to again?"

"I think it would be great between the right two people. It's very intimate."

I didn't look at him as we spoke. I didn't want to discuss what was going to happen in the future. Tonight was for Betsy. That was all that mattered. Everything else could wait till tomorrow.

The attending physician came out of the exam room and told us that, except for some dehydration, Betsy seemed to be fine. After that announcement, a celebration erupted. All the Duck rescue people began cheering, and another round of hugging and backslapping went on.

Kevin hugged me tight, and I let myself relax into it, closing my eyes, enjoying the smell and feel of him against me. I wondered if our relationship would ever go back to the way it had been before Ann came. I had no hard feelings about what had happened. Kevin had done what was necessary and honorable, as I knew he would.

Once the level of excitement died down, the crowd quickly began to thin out. There was a wreck on Duck Road that required the EMS workers and ambulance. Chief Michaels nodded to me and asked if I needed a ride home since I'd come in the ambulance.

I glanced at Kevin but didn't want to go into that yet. "Sure, Chief. That would be great. Thanks."

We left right away. I had to listen to Kowalski and the chief argue all the way back to Duck. Each of them had different ideas on whether the search for the culprits should continue.

"We don't have either of the two suspects in custody," Kowalski raged. "How will that look on the record?"

"We got the girl back. We know who killed Sparks and Tymov," the chief argued. "If those two are still in Duck, we'll find them. If not, either you or the sheriff will."

"And you're satisfied with that? Your resident psychic tells you what happened. There aren't even any arrests. You can live with that?"

"I'm not as worried about my record as you are, Agent. The whole thing will come out in the wash. Always does. As for my resident psychic, you were plenty willing to let that Porter woman use her gifts to help you out." The chief smiled at me in the rearview mirror. "Our mayor is a gem. I'll take her help any day—especially when I can't figure out what's going on by myself."

I smiled, but I knew this was only talk that came from a brief success. The next time something came up that I thought the chief could use my help on, we'd be right back to square one. Still, I was surprised and pleased that he'd made those flattering comments about me to Agent Kowalski. Maybe he really was starting to acknowledge my gifts.

Chapter 30

After Betsy's rescue, life in Duck resumed its leisurely pace. There was still cleanup to be done from the tail end of Hurricane Kelly, but most of it was small stuff. Duck was shaping up nicely for the Jazz Festival at the end of November, a few weeks away. The whole town seemed eager to put the kidnapping and related murders behind them and look forward to this annual event.

I couldn't help thinking about Jackie and Derek as I volunteered to assist with food, musical groups and decorations for the festival. The FBI had packed up and abandoned the police station—to the satisfaction of Duck's finest. They'd left no word as to whether they'd found Jackie and Derek or made an arrest for the murders of Chuck and Port.

It was unnerving, thinking Jackie and Derek could still be skulking around out there. But life had to go on, and what better way than a festival?

The Jazz Festival was a big deal, Duck's last hurrah before the long winter lull. In the days and weeks that followed it, many shops and restaurants would close, and people would migrate to Florida and other sunny areas. Those who stayed would spend the chilly months watching a lot of TV and doing a lot of home cooking until spring.

There were about a hundred festival committees I could've signed up for, but I decided to limit my responsibilities this year. I still had my election to think about. The Chamber of Commerce Barbecue had been rescheduled. The event was too important to cancel completely. Then there were flyers to put up and supporters to impress. As Gramps said, campaigns couldn't run on hot air alone.

I'd had no more visions of dead Chuck. He was finally laid to rest in his hometown of Galax, Virginia. Betsy was out of the hospital and flew back with her mother for the funeral. She'd survived her ordeal in remarkably good health and spirits, according to the doctor who'd treated her.

Betsy had given me and Gramps the black kitten. We called him Treasure because of what I'd told Gramps was in the box the night I'd brought the kitten home. Melinda and Betsy had taken the mother cat to their new home.

I smiled when her mother called me a week later, wondering if Betsy and I could meet. At least Jackie had been truthful with me, it seemed, about not wanting to hurt the girl. Jackie was a self-confessed killer and a thief, but she'd spared me and Chuck's daughter. She couldn't be all bad.

Melinda had come back from Virginia after the funeral to collect Betsy's clothes and toys and sign the papers to sell Chuck's house. They would be in Duck for only one night. "Betsy would really like to meet you in person. I hope you don't mind."

"Not at all. I'm at Missing Pieces on the boardwalk, and

I even have some tea and homemade peanut butter cookies. Come on over."

Melinda said they were on their way. I looked around the shop, glad it was presentable again. Of course, so many of my treasured pieces were missing. Insurance could compensate me for their monetary value—though I could only guess at that. But I'd never be able to truly replace what had been destroyed, since so many of the items were one of a kind.

I tried not to dwell on it. I was the one who'd made up the story about my father possibly hiding Jackie's money here. I was the one who'd sent the couple back to pillage my belongings. But in doing so, I'd managed to save my life—and buy us the time we needed to find Betsy.

It was worth the loss, I told myself during the good moments. The rest of the time I tortured myself by considering all the other, possibly smarter, things I could have said to Jackie and Derek.

After putting on the tea and arranging the cookies on a pretty, flowered plate, I sat down on the repaired burgundy brocade sofa and stared out at the gray sky over the sound.

I hadn't heard from my father since his hasty departure. I thought if he was still alive that he might try to let me know. Yes, he'd left abruptly—but only because he feared for his life. I couldn't fault him for that.

That he'd reverted to his past way of life was a disappointment. Still, I hoped he'd survived and we'd have a chance to meet again. There was an invisible bond between us that I didn't want to lose. I felt it in my heart where my memories of my mother lived. Danny belonged there too.

I hadn't seen Betsy since the night Ann and I had freed her. She was like a ray of sunshine when she walked into the shop, clean and wearing a pretty pink sweater and jeans.

She was carrying the doll she'd dropped at her house the night she was kidnapped. Her cheeks were rosy from the brisk November wind.

"I know you don't really remember Miss O'Donnell," Melinda began with an apologetic smile for me. "She's one of the people who helped bring you home."

Betsy took one good look at me. "I know you!" Then rushed to throw herself against me. "I knew who you were right away. I thought you were an angel when you came to visit me in that place. I thought God was protecting me from all of those terrible people who killed my daddy."

"I'm not an angel," I said hoarsely. Tears clogged my throat even as they spilled from my eyes. "I was just someone who was trying to find you."

"How could I see you?" she asked.

"You couldn't really see her, honey," her mother answered. "You were just dreaming."

"No." Betsy pulled back from me and stared. "I'll never forget you. You were there with me. You protected me. Tell her."

"Betsy!" Melinda looked embarrassed. "She's having a little trouble right now. I plan to get her some counseling."

"It's okay," I said. "Would you mind if I have a minute alone with her?"

"I-I guess that would be all right. I'll just step back here and look at some of your pretty things." She seemed uncomfortable with the idea. I didn't blame her, considering what she'd gone through.

Betsy and I sat side by side on the sofa, eating cookies. "You know how sometimes you can see people in your dreams?" I asked her. "Maybe you've even seen your daddy."

"I have," she admitted. "But I knew I was dreaming. I wasn't dreaming when I saw you."

"It was something like a dream." I tried to explain it in a

way that would be understandable but not frightening for her. "It looks just like real."

"It looked real to me. Did it look real to you too?"

"Yes. It looked real. I knew who you were right away too."

Betsy glanced back at her mother. "She doesn't understand. She thinks I'm dramatized."

I had to smile at that. "You probably have been—traumatized—but this is something else. It's something special that most people don't understand. You have to let her figure it out for herself."

"But it really happened, right?"

"Yes it did. I won't ever forget either."

She looked at me with big, solemn eyes. "Not ever."

I hugged her as I saw Melinda coming toward us with an I'm-ready-to-go expression on her face. "We'll see each other again sometime."

"Really? Because we're moving away, you know. Mommy doesn't want to live in daddy's house."

"It doesn't matter. We'll see each other again."

Melinda came and stood beside us until we both got to our feet. "I don't know how to thank you for everything that you did. I don't know how you did it, but I'm very grateful that you did. Thank you for saving my daughter."

"You're very welcome. Have a good trip to Richmond. Be safe." I waved and smiled at the door until they had disappeared down the boardwalk.

I knew, after looking into her eyes, that Betsy and I would always share a unique bond. It was much like the bond I now had with Ann. It was an odd sensation, knowing I had shared something so personal with two strangers, like nothing I had ever felt before.

Even now, I could still feel little bits and pieces of Ann in my brain. I knew that she was in New York, that she was still confused and unhappy. She hadn't wanted to leave Kevin behind, but they were just too different now to be compatible.

I wondered what I was going to do about Kevin. I'd seen him around, even talked to him a few times. But it was like talking to an acquaintance. He wouldn't look me in the eye and had avoided any time alone with me, though we were both on the food committee.

I'd been waiting for him to say something about wanting us to get back together now that Ann was gone. I half thought he might come over right away. But that hadn't happened.

Maybe he wasn't ready yet. Maybe he was still upset about Ann leaving. It was awkward and I hated it, but I wasn't sure how to handle the situation. Later that afternoon, on a break from the shop, I talked to Trudy about it while she tried a new nail polish remover on me. It was supposed to be gentler than the old variety.

"Just go see him," she said. "Give him a big kiss. He'll get the message."

"What if he's grieving or doesn't want to get back together with me? What if he realized how different I am than Ann and he doesn't feel the same way anymore?"

"That's stupid. Just do like I said, Dae. You're just moping around without him. Don't make me go and talk to him for you."

We both laughed about that. She'd talked to Ricky Allen for me when we were in seventh grade. She'd ended up going to the year-end dance with him.

"Okay. You don't have to threaten me."

"Good. I met a nice sales rep who's taking me out for dinner tomorrow night. That's why I need to try all of his products before then. I don't want to order from him just because he's cute."

I was glad she'd gotten over Port so quickly. Of course, they'd only known each other briefly before he was killed. Still, hurts like that can linger if you're not careful. I decided she was right. I didn't want this problem between me and Kevin lingering. I needed to take care of it.

At five o'clock, I closed the shop and headed for home. The sun had just about set, so it was already pretty dark on the boardwalk. I almost bumped into Cody Baucum, who apologized as he raced by me. It seemed Wild Stallions had run out of onions, and he was on his way to Harris Teeter in a big hurry.

Nancy was in the parking lot, unlocking her car. I was glad to see her going home early for a change. Chris Slayton was standing in the lighted doorway of the Coffee House and Bookstore talking to Phil's sister, Jamie. Everyone had noticed *that* rapidly budding romance.

I walked down the stairs, thinking about seeing Kevin that night at the food committee meeting for the Jazz Festival. The whole committee—Walt Perry, Martha Segall, Betty Vasquez, Kevin and I—were meeting at the Blue Whale. We were supposed to try several types of cheesecake and make a decision on which one we liked.

If I got there early, I plotted, I might have a few minutes to talk with Kevin alone. If he needed more time to get over Ann, we could discuss it. Or if he'd decided he didn't want to be with me anymore—well, either way it was better to know where I stood.

I was thinking about what to wear, perhaps something nice instead of my usual jeans and Duck T-shirt, as I passed an election poster of myself. Gramps had paid a group of high school kids to put them up all over town. I looked a little *too* happy about wanting to be mayor again, at least to my critical eye. *Vote for Dae O'Donnell. She knows how to get things done.*

Gramps had become my unofficial campaign manager. I wasn't sure what all he had up his sleeve, but he certainly knew how to run for elected office—he'd done it several times himself as sheriff. I just hoped that whatever he had in mind wasn't too embarrassing.

Mad Dog had hired an expensive outsider to run his campaign. He'd ended up in the middle of Duck Road yesterday asking drivers for donations. He'd started a new charity whose mission was to help any Duck children who were kidnapped. Since Betsy was the first—and hopefully the last—it seemed noticeably desperate to me.

I was rounding the corner from the parking lot when a long black limo pulled up next to me on the street. "Get in," a husky voice said.

The last time something like this had happened, Jackie and Derek had forced me into their car. I wasn't about to go through that again.

I glanced around in what I hoped was a nonchalant manner. How many times had Tim been waiting out here after I'd closed up? Usually he just wanted to talk. Why wasn't he out here now demanding that I take him out for dinner and a movie like I'd promised him? How often did someone I know jog by me as I headed home from the shop? Where was everyone when I needed them?

I kept walking, at least for a few paces. Maybe if I played it cool—"Thanks," I said, acting as though they were just offering me a ride. "I want to walk."

I couldn't see into the shadowy interior of the car, but before I took another step, a pair of strong arms reached out and dragged me inside.

The door closed behind me. It took a few seconds for my eyes to adjust to the dim light. When I could make out the faces around me, I saw that one of them was Dillon Guthrie. I recognized one of the other men as well—he'd been in my dream about Guthrie and Jackie. That was when I'd still thought Guthrie had killed Chuck.

"Good evening, Mayor." Guthrie was wearing a tuxedo with a white silk scarf around his neck. His dark hair was slicked back from his face. He might not be the devil, but he looked like him. "Could I offer you some champagne?"

"No, thanks. What's this all about?"

"I'm celebrating. Since you were instrumental in helping me reach an important goal, I thought I'd like to have you along for the ride."

I could see the scenery flying by as the limo went quickly down the road—again toward Corolla. Was this some kind of payback for something I'd done when I was younger? Was I doomed to be kidnapped and driven to the edge of the island yet again, my fate hanging in the balance?

"What are we celebrating?"

"A large sum of money was stolen from me. I believe the person who took it meant to give it back. It was awkward, to say the least. But now, I have it back again and the culprit has paid a penalty. I believe you call that justice."

I held my breath. As far as I knew, my father had probably taken Jackie's money with him, if he'd found it before he'd left. Had the money actually been Guthrie's and Jackie had stolen it from him? Was my father at the bottom of the ocean? Or had Guthrie killed Jackie?

"I'm glad for you. I'm not sure what I did to help you, but if you're sincere about appreciating whatever it was, you'll let me out here."

He smiled. "You don't have to be uncomfortable around me. I don't mean you any harm. Quite the contrary. You're the one who's going to find the third monk's bell from St. Augustine. I want you to be alive and well so you can sell me the set and become a very wealthy woman."

"You'll understand if I'm less than enthusiastic about

once again being driven off to who knows where against my will."

"I know Jackie gave you a hard time, and I'm sorry for that. Believe me, she won't give anyone else a problem again. If it makes you feel any better, neither will Derek. Jackie was such a sweetheart. I don't know what happened to her. People get greedy sometimes, you know?"

Jackie *was* such a sweetheart. *No*, I thought. I didn't want to hear any more about that. I wanted to ask about my father, but I was afraid the question would put him on Guthrie's radar.

Obviously, Jackie and Derek had met with an unpleasant end. Had they found my father and taken the money from him just in time for Guthrie to catch up with them?

"You see, Mayor, I've been doing some research about you. I heard how you helped find that little girl, Chuck's daughter. I asked around, and you have quite the knack for finding things. I'm wondering if you might consider taking Port's place. I could use someone like you to guide my collection."

I knew this could be a life-or-death decision. But if I agreed to work with him, I'd become like Port, scared to look the wrong way. I didn't want to live like that, although I had hoped to live a lot longer than this night.

If I came right out and told him there was no way I'd ever work for him, I might find myself in worse condition than Derek and Jackie had left me on the beach. I was walking a very fine line.

"You don't have to answer right now," Guthrie said. "You can think about it. Get back to me. That Flobert was a very nice acquisition. I'd bought it for Jackie. It was her birthday gift. I guess I'll keep it now."

"Thanks. I'm not always that lucky. I wear many different hats, professionally speaking. I couldn't devote myself full-time to locating items for your collection." That sounded like a reasonable excuse, and it seemed as though I was safe—at least for now. I might as well throw a few obstacles in the way while I still could.

"I know. You're up for reelection, right? I've got a contribution I want to make to your political campaign." He nodded to the man sitting beside me, who withdrew an envelope from his inside pocket and handed it to me. "My personal cell number is in there too. Don't be shy about calling me if you need more."

I didn't dignify the offer by looking at what was in the envelope and instead, put it on the seat. "Thank you, Mr. Guthrie. I'm surprised you want to involve yourself in small-town politics."

He leaned toward me, close enough that I could smell his aftershave mingled with the scent of tobacco smoke. "I want to be involved in *everything* you're involved in, Mayor. You and I can be great partners. I know it's a lot to take in right now. Think about it. Give me a call. That's all I ask."

I was so tense that I hadn't even noticed that the limo had stopped. We were outside the Blue Whale. Warm, welcoming light poured out from the windows. Safety and friends were just inside. All I had to do was get out of the car and reach them.

"I'll think about it." I raised my chin and held my shoulders back as I faced Guthrie. I didn't want him to know how scared I was. He'd use it against me. "No guarantees."

He smiled again. "Of course. That's fine. But as a gesture of good faith, I have something for you."

"I think you've given me enough already."

"But not like this. You and I appreciate this far more than

cash." He again nodded to the man beside me, who handed me a large box. "Open it," Guthrie said. "You won't be disappointed."

I knew I wouldn't be able to leave until I opened the box. Inside was the second silver bell, wrapped in red velvet. Together, the two bells were worth a fortune, even if I never found the third.

"Why?" I asked him.

"You're a very special lady. I trust you. And I know you're going to find the other bell. When you do, the world will change for both of us. Have a nice time with your innkeeper friend. You know he used to be with the FBI, right? Just wanting to make the playing field level, in case you didn't."

"I know. Thanks. I guess we're partners after all—at least as far as the bells are concerned. Good night, Mr. Guthrie."

The man sitting next to me got out of the limo and held the door for me. I tried not to rush out into the night air. I didn't want him to see that my legs were shaking. I gripped the heavy box holding the bell tightly to my chest.

As soon as I got out of the car, it sped off into the night. I stood there for a minute with my eyes closed, grateful to still be breathing. Attracting the attention of a man—a criminal—like Guthrie was unbelievable. Who knew that doing that deal with poor Port would end up this way?

"Nice wheels," Kevin said from the darkness of the veranda. "New friend?"

"You might say that. Dillon Guthrie offered me a ride. He also made a contribution to my campaign fund. I didn't take it, though."

"I didn't know you had one. Put me down for something."

This wasn't how I'd envisioned my few minutes alone

with Kevin. He sounded suspicious, like he actually thought I was interested in doing business with Guthrie.

"What's in the box? I thought you didn't take his contribution?"

"I didn't. It's the second bell, like the one I showed you at the shop?"

"Oh."

"Is all the cheesecake gone?" I was trying to break the ice that seemed to have grown between us. I wished I could see his face. It might give me a clue about what he was thinking.

"We waited for you to get started," he said. "Any idea where you're going with all this?"

"I'm not sure. I was hoping we could come to some kind of mutual agreement on what comes next."

He walked down from the veranda and put his arms around me. "I've missed you."

"You've seen me almost every day," I reminded him.

"You know what I mean. I'm sorry about what happened with Ann. I didn't know what else to do. I felt like I owed her another chance."

"I understand. But now that she's made her choice, where does that leave us?"

"Here." He kissed me gently. "And inside, tasting cheesecake. Does that sound okay with you?"

"Throw in some coffee and you've got yourself a deal."

But before we could walk inside, a horse trotted up from the street to stand near the old hitching post, possibly for the first time in fifty years. "Miss Dae."

"Jake! It's good to see you!"

He got down from the wild horse. "I hope things have been going better for you."

"They have been. Thanks." I introduced him to Kevin.

"The cowboy." Kevin shook his hand.

"And you must be the boyfriend." Jake grinned.

"We were about to go in and have coffee," I said. "Come in with us. You can try some cheesecake too."

"I believe I will. Thank you. But I came for that dinner you said you'd fix."

"Dinner?" Kevin asked.

"Dinner," I agreed. "I know Gramps was making some of his famous stew earlier. We'll go home and eat when I'm done here, if that's okay."

Jake nodded, glancing at Kevin. "Sounds just fine to me."

Chapter 31

One year later, two weeks before the election.

Stan the UPS guy was waiting for me at Missing Pieces. The sun was breaking through the morning fog that had gathered across the island. It was early for him to be in Duck delivering packages.

"I wanted to get a good start on the day," he said. "I hope you don't mind. Lots to do."

"No. That's fine." I signed for the packages he was picking up and the two he was delivering. "How is your daughter doing in preschool?"

"She's doing great!" He took his signature pad. "Thanks, Dae. Have a good one."

I waved to him as he hurried down the boardwalk. I looked at the packages he'd left. One was for Vergie Smith from her daughter in St. Louis. Vergie's birthday was coming up, and her daughter always sent something nice. Nothing would've been as nice as Vergie's daughter actually coming for a visit, but she was busy with her kids and her job. It had been at least five years since she and her mother had seen each other face-to-face.

I called her to let her know the package was in. She said she'd stop by later.

I looked at the name on the second package, humming a little tune because everything seemed so right in the world.

It was for me from a post office box in Chicago. My fingers tingled as I opened the plain brown paper. I knew then that it was from my father.

Inside was an old wood case—no doubt the case he, Chuck and Port had found from the *Andalusia*. There was a brief note: *I wanted you to have this, Dae. I know I left in a hurry, but I'll be back when I can. Take care, Danny.*

The case had once been a thing of beauty with intricate carvings and inlaid gold and jewels. It had obviously been made for someone of wealth and standing. That it had survived the shipwreck at all was a miracle. It was a dull gray now with pieces broken off.

I put on my gloves to open it. I was expecting a customer at any moment and didn't have time for a three-hundred-year-old flashback.

Inside the case was the beautiful amber necklace my father had spoken of. I could see why it had convinced Jackie to lay out some money to find the rest of the treasure.

I picked up the necklace very gently, hoping it wouldn't fall apart in my hands. Immediately, I felt a jolt from it—like an electric shock—even with my gloves on.

"You didn't come from the *Andalusia* at all, did you?" I could feel the power and legacy of the necklace.

In Richmond, three hundred miles away, Betsy Sparks started crying and asked to be excused from her classroom.

She ran to the office and called her mother. She had to go back to Duck right away.

And in New York, more than eight hundred miles away, Ann Porter sat up in bed after a long, restless night and said, "Put it down, Dae. Just put it down."

Truth can be deadlier than fiction . . .

ELLERY ADAMS

The Last Word

A BOOKS BY THE BAY MYSTERY

Olivia Limoges and the Bayside Book Writers are excited about Oyster Bay's newest resident: bestselling novelist Nick Plumley, who's come to work on his next book. But when Olivia stops by Plumley's rental she finds that he's been strangled to death. Her instincts tell her that something from the past came back to haunt him, but she never expects that the investigation could spell doom for one of her dearest friends . . .

"Visit Oyster Bay and you'll long to return again and again."
—Lorna Barrett, *New York Times* bestselling author

facebook.com/TheCrimeSceneBooks
penguin.com

M1049T0212